# GEEK
## FANTASY NOVEL

# FANTASY NOVEL

### BY E. ARCHER

SCHOLASTIC PRESS

Library of Congress Cataloging-in-Publication Data Available

ISBN 978-0-545-16040-7

10 9 8 7 6 5 4 3 2 1                    11 12 13 14 15 16

Printed in the U.S.A.    23
First edition, April 2011

The text type was set in Centaur MT.
Book design by Phil Falco

FOR THE GEEKS,
AND EVERYTHING THEY BECOME

Mary & Steve Stevens

Gert & Gideon Battersby

Ralph

Cecil & Daphne

# A GEEK FAMILY TREE

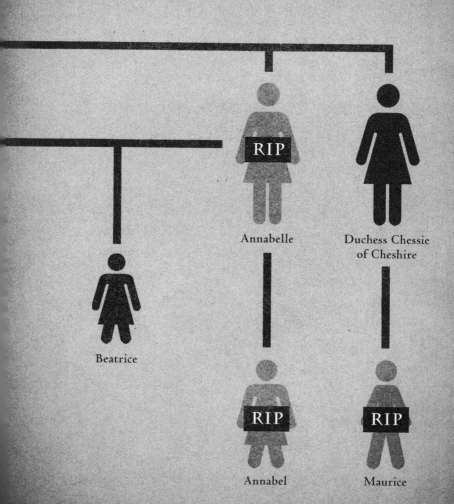

Beatrice

Annabelle

Duchess Chessie
of Cheshire

Annabel

Maurice

BOOK I:
# BORING
(BUT IMPORTANT)

# CHAPTER I

Wishes are dangerous.

Or at least that's what Ralph's parents had always told him. After all, why should a random fairy grant a child power out of nowhere, because, say, the child had wastefully tossed a coin into a fountain? Childhood, Ralph's parents informed him, was all about learning your limits, not learning your limits only to break them in one spectacular moment for all the wrong reasons.

Ralph believed his parents. But he remained curious.

His parents kept the family tree hidden under their bed, wedged so far behind the dusty holiday decorations that Ralph had to be careful not to set off the dancing Santa when he sneaked it out. He'd creep back to his bedroom, secret himself under his superhero comforter, and tremulously unfold the parchment. It was a lengthy and complicated thing, as trees go, with many wild touches. Branches ended abruptly, marked with skulls and crossbones and labeled with cryptic phrases like NASTY CAULDRON INCIDENT or WHOOPS — DANGLING MODIFIER or WHUMP BY DRAGONTAIL? All until it got to the most recent century, where the deaths were labeled with words that still sounded magical but were actually commonplace, like ANEURYSM and METASTASIS.

Steve and Mary Stevens were not the sort of parents to make a lot of rules. They didn't need to, because their son wasn't the sort of boy to need them. Ralph had always been a peaceful child. Some might even have called him happy. But had anyone sat him down and asked him whether such a thing were true (which, incidentally, no one ever had), that person would have discovered that he was an awfully serious boy. He would have replied that he'd always felt directionless — that even the most clever of minds couldn't piece his life together in such a way as to produce meaning.

And Ralph certainly didn't have the most clever of minds, much as he may have believed otherwise. In a boy of average looks and below average athletic ability, cleverness was simply the one attribute relatives could find to compliment him on. So his self-esteem grew a little out of whack. Seven years old: He challenged the Ukrainian kid in his class to a lunchtime game of chess, dared Becky Phister to finish the Belgian Bears books before he did, and argued passionately with his teacher that Portland was the capital of Oregon. Ralph failed in all these things: The Ukrainian kid trotted out a textbook four-move checkmate, Becky Phister finished *The Last Strudel* while Ralph was still on *Boofer Makes a Bungle*, and his teacher made him look up the capital of Oregon. Which was, in fact, Salem.

Despite such defeats, Ralph had something many of his classmates did not have: permission to make mistakes. Ralph's mother and father never punished him when his so-called cleverness led him astray — as when, for example, vapors from his homemade chem lab eroded the floorboards and caused the dining room to tumble into the basement. They were, in fact, endlessly tolerant — except when it came to their one ironclad rule:

Ralph must never, ever, make a wish. Not under any circumstances whatsoever.

As a result, for the first nine years of his life, Ralph was blissfully unaware of what his peers were doing whenever they spied the first star of the night or caught an eyelash or ripped apart a turkey's Y-shaped furcula.

Once fifth grade came around, though, the school calendar finally shook out in the right way that he could celebrate his birthday on the very first day of class. His parents sent him to school with two dozen chocolate-frosted cupcakes, along with a sealed note to his teacher informing her that while the Stevenses were happy to provide treats for Ralph's birthday celebration, he was to sit out in the hallway for the whole thing. The risk of someone's adding a candle and peer-pressuring him into making a wish was too great.

The first day of school is an ordeal for anyone, but it was especially hard for Ralph, who had to wait in the hall staring at a SCHOOL IS COOL poster (a bespectacled worm emerging from an apple) while everyone inside ate his cupcakes. His humiliation only grew when he found out that, while he was outside, Johnny Keenes had gotten into the secret pocket of Ralph's backpack and pilfered the portrait of a level-eight paladin, whom Ralph had spent a great amount of time sketching in case he ever came across anyone willing to play a role-playing game with him. The character's life story was written on the back, and was soon lampooned in Bic graffiti and pasted on the wall of the classroom, where a stream of cupcake-eating cretins shuffled past and made fun of the missing birthday boy's hero. Sir Laurelbow was of a forgotten order of Lamp Knights responsible for journeying the realm and spreading their light, both ideologically and literally (*ha ha!*), following a lonely quest until the day the Lamp Knights would rise again, aided by the Priestesses of Julanisthra (*Julanisthra! Geek!*), should they ever be awakened from their slumber by the suitable sequence of magical runes (*Magical runes! Woot, woot!*).

When Ralph returned and saw his hero smeared with marker and spit-balls and chocolate icing, he ran from the room, seeking refuge in the nurse's office. Through the glass cylinder of tongue depressors he could spy a corner of the infirmary door's chicken-wire window, at which Johnny Keenes regularly found reason to peer, sneer, and leer "Sir Laurelbow!" before bolting away. *Laurelbow*, Ralph thought angrily. *Why couldn't I have named him Sir Commando? Sir HeartofSteel?*

Once he got home, Ralph typed out a spreadsheet of arguments he could draw from to convince his parents how very cruel they had been. Foremost among them, of course: If they'd let him make a stupid wish, he'd have been saved massive humiliation and pain.

The Stevenses read the spreadsheet, listened politely to their son's accompanying rant, served him a pair of chocolate-frosted cupcakes Mary had placed in the bread box that morning precisely in case Ralph had felt left out at school, then gave him the Talk.

The real reasons for his parents' wish prohibition was far more gruesome than anything Ralph had anticipated. Wishes, they told him, had destroyed many of his ancestors. Those who hadn't been destroyed were maimed, crippled, hobbled, enfeebled, deranged, or made to disappear. The examples they used to make their case were certainly graphic. Margaret Battersby (b. 1750, d. 1761) had wished for money and wound up with a coin-shaped tunnel through her body after a gold piece was shot at her from a cannon. Xavier Battersby (b. 1752, d. 1761) had wished for his sister back, wound up with Evelyn's rotting backside affixed to his own, and died of infection. Amy Qualin (b. 1819, d. 1841) had wished for children and wound up financially ruined when she was deeded an orphanage built over a sinkhole. Rupert Battersby (b. 1830, d. 1894) had wished for peace in Europe, and caused Prussia to disappear entirely. Sigmund Seinhold (b. 1899, d. 1917) had wished to be better at rugby and kicked a ball so hard at his next game that it disemboweled three teammates. Bethany Heald (b. 1940, d. 1949) had wished for magic ponies, gone on a long quest to find them, and finally wound up squashed beneath magic ponies.

The ends of most wishes, the Stevenses finished sadly, were less dramatic but equally tragic. The child never returned, forever lost on a quest to obtain his or her heart's desire.

Thoroughly swayed by his parents' parade of gruesome examples, Ralph gave up on wishes and settled on hard drives instead. He played as many computer games as he could, tinkering with them and developing his own mods and maps and dungeons. He even, unbeknownst to anyone else, applied to the holy grail of jobs, the only job that he'd ever really, really wanted: video game designer.

Not a programmer, mind you, but a *designer*: the guy who dreams it up and puts it all together, then sees his vision fulfilled by millions of kids mashing buttons at his command. And not at just any company — at MonoMyth, the one with all the coolest licenses and long-running franchises, designed simultaneously for all platforms. MonoMyth had famously employed a teenager to develop the bestselling Goddess of Misery line of console games, and Ralph was sure that someday he could best even that.

Yes, Ralph was only fourteen. But he had a programming portfolio to dream of, a sheaf full of game concepts inked into bent spiral notebooks, and a flash drive's worth of code. What had the ad in the back of *Computer Gamer* said?

> *MonoMyth seeking designer with intimate knowledge of the electronic gaming industry, 3–4 years programming experience, and employment history reflective of capacity to helm high-profile projects.*

Check, check, check. Surely the genius of Ralph's ideas would make up for his lack of any employment history beyond mowing lawns! He assembled all his samples (they filled a shoebox that he wrapped in brown paper and banded twice over in packing tape) and mailed them off well before the deadline.

The MonoMyth rejection letter, a fuzzy photocopied slip of paper addressed to "applicant," suggested he reapply as an entry-level software coder. At the bottom of the letter was a scrawled blue consolation:

> Appreciate the breadth of your work, but find that your otherwise adequate preparation would be assisted by more life experience. Attending high school, for example. Suggest you steer your efforts in less derivative directions.

Derivative! Who could find the *Green Wizards of Cartesia* derivative, or the subtle group dynamics of *The Elementalists*? Could anyone read his description of the final boss fight in *The Chosen Four* and not realize that gamers having to hit Lord Lavish's *thighs* in order to kill him was the most unexpected development in gaming history?

Derivative, indeed! More life experience, indeed!

Ralph was about to wish some very bad things upon the men and women of MonoMyth, but stopped himself just in time.

No wishes.

And no job.

A murky, geeky despair filled his soul.

# CHAPTER II

Luckily (or not so luckily, depending on whom you ask), another letter arrived the day after the horribly thin envelope from MonoMyth. It was a card from the long-lost British side of Ralph's family. He'd never received a card before! He raced back from the mailbox, put his backpack down on the kitchen table, and read the card over ramen noodles and Cocoa Puffs.

Ralph,

I hear from my Cecil, who happened to do a web search on you and found your "blog" (sp?), that not only are you alive and well (we never hear a peep from your parents — are they scared of us?), but that you're applying to design your own games! You must feel so very proud of yourself, to have developed so interestingly despite such murderously dull parents. . . . I do hope that you don't mind that I wrote that. One never knows quite how to phrase things in such situations. I know it's been a long time since you've seen us, but in any case we have a request. We've moved back into our remote old castle (little Daphne calls it a "chateau," as if she's ever really seen one, can you imagine?), and the walls are crumbly and the electricity's bad, but nonetheless we're intrepidly trying to get a wireless network set up! Do you smell a challenge? We need someone to come and be our "tech guy" for the summer — sound like anything you'd be interested in? I imagine you have to set your charming games in castles all the time — you could call it research. We'd pay, of course, your travel expenses and beyond. I've purchased you an open-date ticket (redemption info enclosed).

I know we could get someone nearby to do it. But honestly — can you imagine a local bloke being any good at this stuff? I can't, either. And my own children live in the clouds.

All best,

Your Aunt(ie),

Gert Battersby

Had Ralph allowed himself to believe in fantastic fulfillments of fate, he might have seen the timely receipt of the card as evidence of some higher power. But as it stood, he saw Gert's card as a lucky break.

He emailed immediately and accepted her offer.

Then he wondered how (or if) he was going to tell his parents. . . .

# CHAPTER III

After confirming his departure time with the airline and making sure he had enough allergy medication for the trip, Ralph went to face his parents. The Stevenses lived in an imposing but slipshod mansion of recent construction, purchased not through their public school teachers' pensions (no, no), but with funds skimmed off the extensive coffers of Mary's extended family, a family that included the aforementioned British aristocracy.

As retired schoolteacher parents so often do, Mary and Steve had settled in the front room to read: Steve his paper, Mary a novel about a young woman who challenges conventions but realizes in the end that family is the most important thing. Mary's book was from the library; the cellophane covering the call number had partially peeled away, and she slid it between her fingers as she read, rubbing away flakes of old glue.

Yawn.

I'm not trying to slight Mr. and Mrs. Steven Stevens, understand. But remark on this — I've given them boring names (I couldn't go with their true names — they never sent back a release form to be included in this book). They're boring people. Don't get too attached to them, because our tale will be rid of them at the first opportunity.

I've been improper. I promise not to butt in ever, ever again.

When Ralph came in, Mary was more than ready to put her book down and engage in some reassuringly dull family conversation. She balanced the novel on the slipcover of the armrest and greeted her only son.

"Greetings, Mom. Greetings, Dad," Ralph said.

Steve grunted and maintained his focus on his paper. It was his most reliable trick, to seem to ignore conversation while following it intently, so that when he finally said something it would emerge pre-written, as if spoken with semicolons.

"So what's going on?" Ralph asked.

We'll skip forward in the conversation — even the most well-spoken person is ninety percent dull, unless he's appearing in a book. Ralph and his family are only somewhat well-spoken, barely averagely so, so I'm obliged to excise whole chunks.

Ralph stood in the hallway and said a few sentences, to which his mother responded with smiles and mute wisdom. Ralph said something more, switching his weight from one leg to another. (*When will he be comfortable enough with himself to stand up straight?* wondered Mary.) Steve's pages flipped with more and more velocity until finally he cleared his throat to coin his aphorism — but that's when Mary shouted and he discovered that Ralph had carried home meat scraps from the grocery store to feed his cats and the plastic bag was dripping something vile and red onto the carpet. Ralph put his hand over his mouth and nodded — yes, it was blood, or at least meat juice — and now everyone was scurrying, Ralph to get the carpet cleaner from the garage and Mary to pour ice from her diet soda onto the beige pile, Steve using the energy that he had been building for his declamation to bounce to his feet and swat the spreading stain with his newspaper, dancing a frantic little jig.

Then Ralph was back and running the carpet cleaner over the splotch, now made darker with newsprint and soda, taking pains to avoid bumping his parents' feet. This was tricky, as they were pacing. Once he was finished, Ralph prudently excused himself to feed the cats.

When he was younger, when imagination seemed safe, Ralph thought that his cats were lions. It was easier back then, when they had that post-kitten leanness and instinctual aggression that hadn't yet been deadened by a mouseless life. But he still refused to feed them cat food — it was one of the few fancies he allowed himself. He imagined being fed bran flakes for three meals a day, even for snacks and late night desserts, and couldn't wish that on his charges. So they got meat. When he dropped the slick scraps into their bowl, the cats beelined for the feast and then conspicuously ignored it, as cats will do.

As he returned to his parents, Ralph wondered if he would be like the old cat lady across the street, if he were old and a lady.

Mary had prepared Meat Dish for dinner. As they sat down to eat, Ralph pushed his glasses up his nose and asked them what they thought about the card from Gert. He had left it on the kitchen table, knowing full well it would be read and processed and placed next to the paperclip holder by the time dinner was served.

"It doesn't take mail at all long to get here from England, does it?" Steve observed.

"No, not anymore. Isn't that fascinating?" Mary said between chews.

"I looked at the postmark. It only took three days."

"Amazing," Mary said.

"How do you think they got it here?" Steve asked Ralph.

"By airplane. There are no land routes and a boat would have taken longer," Ralph said automatically, eager to be done with his father's side of the questioning as soon as possible.

"Good, good. So's the casserole." This line came out like music.

"Thank you!" Mary said.

"So what do you *think* about it?" Ralph asked.

Steve Stevens regarded him quizzically. "Absolutely not!" he said.

"But I want to go." Ralph's voice caught.

"Nope. And I won't tolerate any more curiosity about the matter."

Ralph was seated in a prime position to watch the multi-paragraphed look that passed between his parents. They both knew their son felt abandoned by his peers and had turned sullen. His dream to be a video game designer had been squashed. They knew he had a polyester-focused sense of fashion, and a sense of humor that tended to irritate all but the most devout nerds. Any change was bound to do him good. He hadn't expressed wanting anything in months, and they knew this was a development that was to be encouraged.

All this was weighed, of course, against the fact that they would be sending their only son into the lair of a killer sorceress.

And wanting — well, wanting could easily lead to wishing, and wishing had to be prevented at all cost.

Ralph's parents had always considered it safer not to tell him any details of the British family situation, so his curiosity wouldn't draw him over there. And now they couldn't start giving him information without firing his inquisitiveness all the more for the length of time it had been withheld.

"Honey," Mary Stevens said, "the answer is simply no."

# CHAPTER IV

Once Ralph slammed into his room, Steve Stevens's words were far less mild.

"What are we going to do?" he asked Mary, banging his hand down on the table so hard he caused her to squirt ketchup all over her plate.

"We said he couldn't go, dear," Mary said. "So he won't. He's a very moderate boy, and so unlikely to go getting himself into trouble."

"We've worked so hard to keep him unspoiled by all this nonsense. And it hasn't been easy. I don't need to remind you, I trust, about the TV incident?"

Mary nodded and nervously held her fingers against her cheek the way she would have held a cigarette, back before she had learned better. How could she *not* remember? A year earlier she had woken up late at night and crept downstairs to tend to the last bite of an éclair she had been saving in the back of the fridge. On the way, she spied her son up way past his bedtime, sitting in his boxers before the glowing TV, watching a program he most certainly should not have been watching.

It wasn't anything involving bad language — that would have been alarming but nothing on the order of true horror — but rather an infomercial featuring a tabloid British duchess demonstrating the proper way to use a $19.95 electric device to tone one's buttocks. She was the same tacky, forbiddingly attractive sister Mary remembered from her childhood, only now with hair extensions and a plumpness that gave her fishnetted body an extra, witchy seductiveness.

Paralyzed, éclair halfway to her mouth, Mary had no idea what to do. The family resemblance was definitely there — the overpronounced jaw, the still-lovely eyes set within a puddle of blue-black eye shadow, the whiff of the otherworldy. And if Ralph realized that the duchess-turned-spokeswoman on the television was his mother's other sister (besides Gert), how would Mary explain herself?

She decided the best plan was to hope her son wouldn't notice. There was a very good chance of it; he was criminally unobservant. Though he was aware every time the price of RAM dropped in the Korean wholesale market, he obliviously trundled past his parents' birthdays (not to mention his own, except for that terrible fifth-grade year), and had once taken a full half-hour shower without realizing that he'd forgotten to turn the water on. She finished her éclair, went back to bed, and informed her husband of the situation. They'd wondered ever since if their son now suspected that the arresting pitchwoman he'd seen on television was the real reason for the wish prohibition.

"We simply aren't allowing it," Steve said now, sucking in his breath and tucking his hands under his arms.

Mary picked up her novel and opened it to the bookmark, trying, as she balanced the spine on the rim of her plate, to determine whether she had stopped on the left-hand or right-hand page.

She knew, more than her husband did, that her son may have been a geek, but he was a geek with a sense of adventure.

And, as we all know, there's no way of stopping a geek with a sense of adventure.

# CHAPTER V

By the time Steve thumped up to his son's room to remind him that he was by no means allowed to go to England, Ralph had already boarded a flight and turned his cell phone off.

He checked his email from the airport and discovered a message from Gert instructing him to take the train from Heathrow to Durbanshire upon arriving, connecting in Paddington. These three names displaced him — Heathrow sounded like an elderly man's complaint, Durbanshire a land of sheiks, and Paddington a bear. He made each connection anxiously, surprised each time a location turned out to be an ordinary area of the world, not a fantastic realm shaped by its outlandish moniker.

As Ralph had made an earlier train connection than Gert had thought him able to, he anticipated a long wait to be picked up. He lined up his belongings with care on the tartar-colored stone steps in front of the Durbanshire station and wondered what the Battersby car would look like; he pictured a pert motorcar with goggles draped on the windshield and, in place of a side-view mirror, one of those horns that sends out cheery blasts that send geese flapping up from ponds.

He was surprised, therefore, to be picked up by a talent search contestant in a hatchback. The boy who peered out of the car had that arrogant charm, that leer, that said he was certain you would love him all the more for the frankness of his self-love. The neckbands of at least four different T-shirts crowded the V of his partially zipped sweatshirt. His face was a slick riot of red and white.

The boy — no more than fifteen — careened to the curb, opened the driver's side door, placed an arm on the roof, and removed his aviator sunglasses. "You're Ralph?" he asked.

"I am."

"Figures. Get in."

Once Ralph did, they shot out of the parking lot and down a sleepy town street. The boy played his reggae loudly enough to exert an almost physical presence, and between that and the car's breakneck speed, Ralph was too distracted to make conversation. The boy was focused on the road, periodically tweaking his cool expression into new variations, as if reacting to cues from a music video director.

"You're Cecil?" Ralph finally prompted.

"Yup. Mother and Father were busy, and I'm the only one of the kids allowed to drive. Well, I don't actually have a license, but they don't worry about stuff like that. They'll pay the fine or whatever if I get caught. I've *got* to have the car because I work at a clothing shop in town — I don't think we should be out of touch with the laboring people, you know? Mother was all intent on having us secluded for the summer — she's big into 'family' — but I talked her into letting me have a car. She didn't even bother to ask about the license part. She's totally daft."

"I'm Ralph," Ralph said after a pause, before remembering this was already traveled ground.

"Mmm-hmm."

"What's this castle like?"

Cecil shrugged. "It's a castle. I dunno. We're not heading there, anyway."

"We're not?"

This reaction was surprising enough for Cecil to lower his sunglasses. "You don't know? Why did you fly in today, then?"

"I don't know. Why did I?"

"We're going to a funeral. I wondered why you were wearing trainers."

Ralph nodded knowledgably.

"Those," Cecil explained, pointing to Ralph's feet.

"Oh. Sneakers."

"Have it your way."

Ralph had never been to any funeral before, especially not a British one. He knew little of what to expect, and had no idea whatsoever who had died. Funerals didn't seem like something one could ask curious questions about, though. So instead he stared out the window and let the blasts of reggae water his eyes.

"What do you do at the clothes store?" Ralph finally yelled.

"I work there. I'm an em-ploy-ee."

"Yep. Just wondering what that involved."

"Oh. I do stock. I put in lightbulbs, change the mannequins' outfits, all that."

"No way. That must be kinda fun."

"It's the *working life*. It's not supposed to be *fun*."

"Okay."

Then: "So back-to-school season is starting, right? And I'm in charge of getting the mannequins ready for it. I've got this stack of just-shipped clothes, and I'm heading to the front of the store. There are these round windows, and the mall is so crowded because it's back-to-school, and I have to undress the mannequins in front of everyone."

"Huh. Weird."

"That's not the end. I've got to get right behind this girl and unbutton her blouse from behind, button by button —"

"This is on a mannequin, right?"

"Yes, on a mannequin, are you following me?"

"Totally."

"And so then I have to wedge the jeans off her hips. All the kids from school and their mums are watching from outside. So now I've got this naked plastic woman in front of me, in this crowded little window, and I have to dress her somehow." Cecil shook his head ruefully and bopped his fingers on the steering wheel.

"You got it done?" Ralph prompted.

"Yeah. It was so embarrassing."

"Well, it can't have been too embarrassing, if you're telling me and I just met you."

Cecil grunted and pulled up short at a red light that, judging by all prior evidence, he would generally have run. "Who *are* you?"

"I'm your cousin. We met before. A long time ago. I was seven."

"And you're what, hanging out with us for the summer?"

"Yeah. I'm helping set up your network." Ralph laughed through a clenched silence. "Just helping set up the network." He paused, waiting for Cecil to say something. "It's not too hard, really —"

"It's a little weird, don't you think, to say I'm lying about my story being embarrassing."

"Oh! Sorry."

"No, it's totally fine — but it's weird, too. It's like, someone's really putting himself out there when he tells you something, you know? You have to respect that."

"Okay. It's different in America, maybe."

"No, it's cool. We're going to be friends no matter what."

With that, Cecil pulled into a damp cemetery. He placed a finger over his lips, though he did nothing to quiet his music. They bumped along a muddy willow-hemmed road until they arrived at a somber crowd surrounding a casket. Cecil parked at the end of a line of cars, respectfully removed his two baseball caps, placed them over his heart, and opened the car door.

A bass-studded measure of *rump, rump, iza gonna thump ya rump* blasted over the gathered mourners. They turned to glare and took in not Cecil, who was protected from view by the vehicle, but Ralph, jet-lagged and puffy, jabbing at the radio in alarm as he simultaneously placed one ragged trainer/sneaker and then the other onto the wet grass.

He beamed an apology to the indignant funeralgoers and then joined Cecil in crossing the lawn to assemble behind the rest of their huddled family. Gert — so serene as to be almost motionless, silver hair piled high — reached a hand out and pressed Ralph's shoulder in much the same way one tests whether a roast beef has gone cold. The touch was soon over, and when he smiled at her, Ralph saw Gert pat her powdery hair with a liver-spotted hand. He nodded solemnly, stared at the shining casket, and wished he had a tie around his neck and a comb in his back pocket.

If any event calls for silent reflection, a funeral surely does. Ralph did his best to think tragic thoughts.

It appeared that the corpse was a close friend of the Battersbys, since they lingered while the other attendees shot their regards and rushed back to their cars. Eventually Ralph; Gert; a man he assumed to be her husband, Gideon; and their three children were the only mourners left. Once the last guest's car door slammed shut, Gert dropped all decorum and rested her arms on Ralph's shoulders.

"Welcome. Sorry about the funeral. Terrible timing. We're so glad to have you. Everybody, this is Ralph. We all remember Ralph. His parents are Mary and Steve Stevens, who weren't invited."

Everyone murmured a greeting except Cecil and the taller daughter, who kept her dark liquid gaze fixed on the shovelfuls of black earth being tossed on the coffin.

The smaller daughter, a frilly little girl whose role in life was evidently to counter her older sister's gloom, took Ralph's hand and patted it as she bent into a mini-curtsy.

"Hello, Daphne," Ralph said. "We've never met, but your mother told me about you. I'm your cousin, Ralph. Have you heard of me?"

"I'm Daphne!" she said, quite as if he hadn't spoken. "Pleased to meet you. The sad girl is my sister, Beatrice. You drove in with Cecil. Those are Daddy and Mummy. I'm seven." Daphne leaned closer and sparkled. "Some lady Daddy used to know *died*. And that dead lady, she's Beatrice's *real mummy*."

Gert's husband inserted himself between them. "I'm Gideon Battersby. Remember me?"

"Your parents are Americans, aren't they?" Daphne asked, peering at Ralph from around her father and pronouncing "Americans" like "Martians."

"Uncle Gideon. It's been some time," Ralph said. He tried to dredge up a memory of this stuffed eagle of a man, but came up short.

"I swear," Gideon said. "You were only a boy when I last saw you, and now look! I'm sorry I haven't been over to the States very regularly. I tend to travel to the Far East when I go anywhere. Have you ever been, I wonder?" It sounded like the beginning of a speech, and sure enough, the rest of the family inched away, leaving Ralph alone when he politely answered that he hadn't.

Gert lifted six silver inches of stiletto heel from the muddy grass, only to see it stab back into the earth when she lowered her foot. "Ooh!" she exclaimed with a twitch, effectively shutting down Gideon's blooming oration on Indonesian politics. "Let's go home and warm up. We'll have some hot chocolate."

"Yay!" Daphne squealed, taking her father's hand and clapping it.

The family processed toward the two remaining cars.

Gert and Gideon managed to fold themselves into their vehicle without ever disengaging from Daphne, who hung from them like an oversize pendant. Her dress, Ralph noted as the ruffled seams disappeared within, was all pink crinoline: a Valentine's cookie.

"Love your sister's funeral outfit," Ralph said as he slid into the passenger seat. Cecil was already inside, and the reggae had started pounding its rump poetry again. Beatrice took the back, her chin cradled on her palm as she stared out the window. Her torso was fully in the seat, but her face was pressed against the door, as though she were split by equally strong urges to exist fully in the car and to dash herself on the road. In her mind, she was writing rhyming verse full of gray adjectives and deep feeling, in which every crow is called a raven.

"That princess costume?" Cecil asked. "She bought it from British Home Stores. At first Mother refused to allow it in the house, but Daphne wants to be a princess, and, well, that means Daphne gets to be a princess. She's got a chip on her shoulder because a lot of her friends actually *are* princesses. It was all Mother and Father could do to rip her scepter away for the funeral."

The tides of conversation would have called for Beatrice to speak next. But when Ralph glanced back, he caught her staring at the dingy shopping centers outside the window, her plain face impassive, her marble eyes shining and impenetrable under the sheaves of hair that almost covered her face. Perhaps she was trying to think of a word to rhyme with "anguish."

"So she wears pink frilly stuff all the time?" Ralph asked distractedly.

"Sleeps in it, too, except when Mother puts her foot down."

"Well, that's good," Ralph said.

Beatrice snorted, her first social interaction for the day.

"Dad had a special room constructed for Beatrice in her wing," Cecil continued mutedly, after swerving around a loping tractor. "It's got all her books. She's big into trilogies with yellowed pages. She's a total dork. Aren't you, Ugs?" Cecil glanced at her and turned up the music. "I think she really wants to *be* the characters she reads about."

"Well, I guess that's the point of it all," Ralph said, out of dork solidarity.

Beatrice nodded, glared at her brother, and snorted a second time.

"Yeah, I guess so," Cecil said, moving quickly from wounded sniff to impassioned rant as the little car chugged up a rise. "But I'm like, there are bigger issues out there, you know? Sure, yeah, she's just seven" — Ralph surmised they were back to Daphne now — "but should we really be encouraging her to be all fake? There are real people suffering out there, who aren't princesses worrying about snagging princes but working mums trying to buy formula for their sickly infants, and because we have money we can afford not to think about these things. It makes me so mad. She's in a *princess costume*, and there are kids in, like, Bangladesh who don't have any costumes! Don't have any clothes at all, for that matter! I'm just trying to say that — oh, this is our vale, by the way."

Their vale. The car finally crested the top of a sunny hill and began to putter across a bumpy bridge, which crossed a river into a radiant bowl of trees. Cecil sped up and zipped along the lane as it threaded between the trunks. The uneven road threw the car's occupants against the doors and, on especially big bumps, the roof.

"I take it 'our vale' is home?" Ralph asked.

"Yeah. It's an island of sorts." Cecil turned off the radio.

The lane bent to follow a shelf of rock, and from this new vantage point Ralph could see a skyscraper of a tree at the center, throwing its great leafy umbrella over the glade. To one side of its circumference, a castle had been offhandedly placed. The castle would have been monumental in any other context; next to the tree it was a mere cake decoration.

The titan's leaves permitted little sunlight, so Cecil had to turn on his headlights as they approached the center of the vale. The old car grumbled through the dim quiet, the only sound of their passage the squeaks the car's tires made on the gravel, the pawfalls of small fleeing mammals, and periodic sniffles that might have been produced either by the radiator or by Beatrice.

"You live *here?*" Ralph asked.

It was on Beatrice's third snort of the day that they pulled into the driveway before the huge, crumbling castle. Cecil wedged his car between two matching Mercedes. Beatrice threw herself out of the hatchback, then Cecil and Ralph eased over the gearshift and followed her. By the time Ralph got to his feet, Beatrice and Cecil were almost at the front door. "Hey!" Ralph called. "Wait a sec. I need to get my bag."

Cecil looked back, startled. "I'm sure there's a footman on duty, or something."

"That's okay. I want to get it," Ralph said.

Cecil stood paralyzed until Beatrice plucked his keys from his hand and hurled them at Ralph. They landed on the gravel a few paces away. "You're staying in the gatehouse. Silver key," Cecil called. The last Ralph saw of him was a large finger silhouetted in a hallway window, pointing in the direction of the giant tree.

"Thanks!" Ralph yelled.

Ralph re-opened the hatchback. The tidy wheeze of the pneumatics was so like that of his parents' little car that he suddenly missed them. But once he heaved his old duffel out of the back and heard it hit the pure white gravel of the driveway, once the movement of slinging it over his back made him look up and take in the oddly-shaped manor and the monumental tree and the vale around it, Ralph was charged by the adventure of his new situation. What was this side of the family about? Where did his own room lie? He would make this a grand adventure better than any MonoMyth had ever conceived.

Ralph's duffel was heavy and unevenly stuffed; when he moved toward the tree, he staggered. His building was a stone-walled affair, only modestly immodest compared to the stained-glass excesses of the castle. Though it was a separate structure, with two stories and painted wooden shutters, he couldn't determine why it would be called the gatehouse, as that would seem to imply it protected a boundary — but there was no gate or fence. The only thing the gatehouse could possibly defend the castle from was the tree itself.

The silver key slid in and the door swung open under Ralph's hand. The interior was sparely furnished, sporting only a wide wool rug, a sleigh bed, a large mirror, and an expansive fireplace. The first thing Ralph did was to place his pet rock Jeremiah under his mattress (he befriended any rocks that he considered neat looking). He then proceeded to unpack the rest of his belongings, which speak quite well for themselves:

(1) Four-color Pen
(2) Rubik's Cubes

(I) Sound Effects CD

(I) Petri Dish

(I) Dress Shirt

(I) Magnifying Glass

(8) Gaming Books

(I) Set of High Elf Figurines

(3) (!) Slinkys

(I) Universal Remote Control

(I) Laser Pointer

(I) Flashlight

(3) T-shirts with Computer Puns

(3) Identical Black T-shirts

(I) Pair of Stonewashed Jeans

(I) Pair of Loafers

(I) Set of Day-of-the-Week Underwear

(2) Laptops

(I) Novelization of *Star Trek II: The Wrath of Khan*

As he finished unpacking and hung his shirts up in the closet, trying to shake out wrinkles as he did, he felt the gloom of the massive tree weighing on him. He soon fled its twilight and headed across a patio to the main castle. Gert was waiting in the foyer, staring at him through a warped glass window.

"Let me give you a tour," she offered.

"Thank you."

"I am so glad that you've come to stay with us," she said as they processed down a hallway, her hard-soled shoes resounding on the stone floor. "We're all going to have such a marvelous time. Usually we summer abroad, and the children were positively mutinous when we told them they would be cooped up in this musty old castle. Having you here will be such a nice diversion for them. Daphne is happy everywhere, Beatrice is unhappy everywhere, and Cecil's in the middle. He's fascinated by disadvantaged people like you, and having some male company will do him good. And of course, we're helpless trying to set up our 'internet connection,' or what have you. As soon as the kids are able to 'chat' with their buddies, I imagine they'll be at peace. Peaceful kids, that's all a parent can hope for, isn't it?"

Ralph nodded as if he, too, were a parent who had always hoped for nothing more.

"So, you've undoubtedly noticed that the castle — a manor, really, who are we kidding — is set up with three separate wings. The children like to think that they each have their own. Of course we're just humoring them with that. They don't seem to realize that the middle bit is only the entrance hall, which means that everything else — servants' quarters, dining room, the studies, all the closets, master bedroom, the garage, all of it — is actually scattered throughout their wings. But it's the Beatrice wing, the Cecil wing, and the Daphne wing. They're tyrants about it. Just tyrants. You should see Cecil trying to come into Daphne's wing. You can hear her protests throughout the castle. Very amusing. Do you have a 'lady friend'?"

Ralph shook his head as he tried to keep up with Gert's twisting monologue. "Not really."

"Wonderful," Gert said. "You're too young to be tied down yet. Not that you'll meet any available young ladies around here. We're quite isolated. You could follow Cecil into town when he's on the job, though. He's got this thing about working. He hates the 'aristocracy.' But you know teenagers — they'll always find an excuse to loathe themselves."

Ralph nodded, wondering in what way he loathed himself.

Gert stopped up short and took Ralph's hands in her own. He could see from the set of her eyes that she had grown weary of the castle tour, a full forty paces from where it had begun. They were on to deeper things. He felt afraid: Her impeccable kindness and charity made him certain of some inner wickedness. "Listen, Ralph, I want to be perfectly honest with you. I invited you over here because we could use your darling expertise, to be sure, but I also want you to know that I consider this a full invite to be an honorary member of our family. We *adore* you, we really do —"

Ralph blinked. He wasn't sure he had even learned everyone's names yet.

"— and I want you to know — we want you to know — that we all can imagine what it's like to have parents who are controlling and try to isolate you from any other family! I suppose I'm saying that I want to be a mother to you, too, if you'll let me. Like Mother Number Two, though I'd ask that you don't call me that."

"Actually, about that, Gert. My parents are great. I like them a lot. I didn't come here to get away from them."

"Oh!" Gert cradled Ralph's cheek in her hand. "Oh, of *course* they're great. I wouldn't mean to imply that they're holding you back from being special, or anything else like that." She laid one long-fingered hand over her heart. "They live in here." She moved the hand to Ralph's chest. "And in here."

"That, too, but they're also living in New Jersey. They're probably pretty worried."

Gert put a hand over her mouth and wordlessly embraced Ralph. Then she backed away, beaming a curdling force of affection. "We'll have someone give them a call," she said, then backed around a corner and vanished.

# CHAPTER VI

Gert left Ralph in a hallway dominated at one end by a massive window. He stared through the cloudy renaissance glass at a garden below and watched the bluebells bow before the first hints of rain. He did his best not to think about his parents.

Droplets began to strike the window. It was soon a deluge, turning the dust on the walkways to mud. Ralph took in the metal hooks set into the old brick walls, and the sky that was a different shade of blue everywhere he looked, though it never lost its substantial British grayness. He creaked open a small triangle of window and reached out a hand to feel the rain, the English rain, the lovely dreary water, bead over the back of his hand. He gazed at the wealth around him, a steerage passenger peering through a porthole.

"What are you doing?" came Cecil's voice from down the hallway.

Ralph pulled back his head, bumping the window frame as he did and nearly knocking his glasses off his face. Maybe it was the vibration of that shock, but he thought he saw a shadowy figure disappear behind the tree. "Feeling the rain," he said distractedly, scanning outside. The figure was gone.

"Does it feel like rain?"

"Yes."

"Jolly good. I've been sent to show you your gatehouse."

"I've already been."

"You have? What else am I supposed to do with you, then?"

"I don't know — ask your mom."

"I guess I'll show you my wing. I know more about it than your building, anyway."

Cecil's section of the castle was decorated in Che Guevara blankets, posters for arty bands whose names were whole sentences, and a suit of armor on which had been draped a camouflage helmet. At the far end was Cecil's turreted bedroom. "You see those signs?" Cecil asked.

"Yeah." On the wall were hung category divisions from a chain bookstore, suspended from rusty chains.

"I helped set up a new bookstore, because if you work just one job you can't make ends meet, which means I've had to work two to make it more realistic. Anyway, my coworkers looked the other way when I lifted some massive signage. Check out where I put them all."

TRUE CRIME was above the main door, SPECIAL NEEDS above the bathroom, SELF HELP over the bed.

"Cool, huh?" Cecil said.

"Yeah."

"I'm going into town now, actually. Do you want a lift?"

"No, I think I'll stick around here. Maybe take a nap or something. Thanks, though. Can I let myself out into the gardens?"

"Yeah. You should really check out the giant tree. It's been around for like a gabillion years."

By all traditional indicators of tree age, this specimen had indeed been around a gabillion years. Four people could stand at the compass points of its girth and not glimpse one another. Its network of thick leaves funneled the downpour into columns of water, leaving the rest of the area beneath its canopy in mist. Nothing grew under the wide circumference of its branches, besides toadstools and the occasional stand of wildflowers. Ralph dashed along a muddy path, past a vacant stable and through a stretch of dewy moss to reach the tree's wide trunk. He appraised it as a possible video game background, judged it evocative but hard to render.

"It's raining," said a little girl's voice.

Ralph turned and saw Daphne, holding her plastic scepter akimbo and staring quizzically at him. She was soaked through. "I was trying to find you," Daphne continued, "and I looked all over the whole castle. I didn't want to get wet, but now you've made me. Mummy's going to be upset with us. She was supposed to take me into town to get some new shoes before dinner, and now I bet she won't let me."

"I'm sorry," Ralph said.

"It's okay. Even though the shoes were pink and really nice. What are you doing?"

"I'm looking at the tree."

"It's very big, isn't it? It's way older than me."

"I'd say so," Ralph said. He wondered how to talk to a child. "Are you a princess?"

"I'm seven," Daphne said. "I know I'm not *really* a princess. It just gets so boring around here. My friends are all off in warm places for the summer where they can go swimming and stuff."

"I figured you had a good reason for dressing up."

"I'm seven," Daphne repeated.

"Do you know any magic spells?" Ralph asked.

"Don't be stupid."

"Have you ever climbed this tree?" Ralph tried.

"It's too old. It doesn't have any low branches anymore." She was right; the lower trunk bore only the scars of branches long since broken away. A person would have to be twelve feet high to begin a climb. Ralph reached a hand out and touched the rough bark.

"We're both wet," Daphne observed. Then she said, "Do you want to see something?"

Ralph nodded.

"You have to put me on your shoulders first," she said.

Daphne outstretched her arms and waited for Ralph to approach. He crossed the clearing, the toadstools making cardboard protests beneath his feet. When his knees touched the ground he became a new wet, a muddy and wetter wet. He watched the brown of the soil penetrate the fabric of his pants, felt its chill direct on his skin. Then he sensed a light pressure on his shoulders, and Daphne was upon him. He crossed his arms over her shins, and when he stood up they were one fantastic beast. Daphne hooted and slashed her scepter through the air. "Onward!" she cried.

"Onward where?"

"I'll direct you." Daphne gripped Ralph's ears and tugged them this way and that. She was agile with her fingers, and communicated to Ralph not only the direction she wished to go, but also the velocity. There was no delicacy to the impulses, however; he was directed by a jockey, not a dance partner. They left the tree's canopy and crossed a glade at the far end.

They passed over the meadow at a jostling clip, Daphne's hands slapped across Ralph's forehead, her weight no more than that of a knapsack. Once the grass eventually gave way to dirt road, her fingers directed Ralph to turn, then to turn again when they came to a trail.

"How much farther are you taking us?" Ralph asked. He imagined them getting lost in the deluge, arriving back at the house stricken with pneumonia, Gert buying him a one-way ticket back to New Jersey.

"Hush, noble steed!" Daphne instructed.

Ralph awaited further instruction.

Eventually Daphne flattened her palms against Ralph's ears, signaling him to slow down. When he twisted to peer up at her, she placed her finger mischievously to her lips and directed him toward a slatted fence. Ralph wiped the water from his eyebrows with the hem of her dress and approached.

A knot of wood had fallen from one of the higher planks, leaving an eyehole to which Daphne directed Ralph. The soggy splinters of the planks pricked through his shirt as he pressed against the fence. Daphne put her face to the hole and, after a moment, started giggling.

"What do you see?" Ralph asked.

"Men," Daphne responded.

"Men? What kind of men?"

"They're guards. Mummy had them set up all around the vale."

"What? Why?"

"I don't know. I heard her saying to the groundskeeper that we would need protection for a few weeks."

"And you have no idea why?"

"Nope. Mummy's crazy about stuff like that, though."

"You always come here to watch over the vale?"

"Yes. Sometimes I make up stories about the brownies and things."

"Let me see the guards."

"You can't. You're not tall enough. It's the same for Cecil, when he comes with me. I'm the only one who gets to see anything."

"I think you're making this up. There's probably some boy out there you have a crush on," Ralph said.

"Ugh, put me down. That's so not right. I don't like any boys. I'm not even *eight* yet."

"Sounds like I struck a nerve."

"You think you're funny. Let's go back."

Ralph headed back to the castle, Daphne remaining on his shoulders.

"You're as weird as all boys," she said after a few moments' silence, as they crossed beneath the canopy of the giant tree.

The burden on Ralph's back suddenly disappeared. He turned to see Daphne clutching a branch, her pink-tighted legs kicking in the air.

"What are you doing?" Ralph asked, dumbstruck.

"Playing with the tree."

"Come on down."

"No, never."

But her arms were tiring. Ralph stood beneath and caught her.

"What's wrong?" Daphne asked.

The tree branch was a dozen feet above their heads — there was no way Daphne could have reached it on her own. Staring a moment at the long, thick-barked branches that sawed at the sky, Ralph choked down his panic, then carried Daphne inside as the rain resurged.

# CHAPTER VII

Once they reached the patio, Daphne scrambled down and dashed ahead before Ralph could ask her how she had gotten into the tree. He started to follow her, then decided it was best to change into dry shoes before going inside and facing Gert. He hurled open the gatehouse door, whipped his wet hair out of his eyes, and sat on the bed. Maybe a nap first. He lay down, blinked at the antique ceiling lamp, then closed his eyes and tried to rest, though he soon found he was too unnerved to fall asleep. When he fitfully thrust his head against his rough linen pillow he heard the crinkle of a piece of paper. He extracted a note from beneath the cushion and propped himself up to read it.

Ralph,

Hope you've had fun exploring the estate! I've been work-ing in my office, which has a great view of the lands. I noticed you with Cecil earlier, Daphne later. I saw you at the far perim-eter fence — I assume Daphne gave you her usual fancy story about there being security agents. I'd ask that you please don't pay her any mind.

As for my third child, you'll get to know Beatrice soon enough. Forgive her for being a shade retiring; it was her mother we buried, you see. (Gideon's first wife, not me, of course!!!)

Would you have a chance to take an initial peek at the wiring before dinner? Not that I expect you to get anything accomplished yet, or would dream of telling you how to do your work. Still, thought you might like to get started. There's a mass of cables and gizmos behind the big wooden curio in the foyer. I imagine that would be a good place to start.

Gert

P.S. We'll have dinner formal-style tonight. Let me know if you'll need to borrow proper attire from Cecil.

Ralph pulled on an only-slightly-wrinkled dress shirt, changed his wet socks for dry, his sneakers for loafers, and dashed into the castle beneath the slackening rain. He threw open the door to the entrance hall, startling a maid and footman, who scurried away before Ralph could apologize. Behind a rustic curio he did indeed find a pile of ethernet cables, a half-dozen routers, a couple of dusty discs, the instruction manual to an air conditioner, and a half-eaten tart. He tucked his legs beneath him and got to work.

The yellow cables were tangled in with the blue and the red, which were in turn looped around a length of new black cable, still in its twisty-ties. The whole mess looked like a map of a subway. He knew he would eventually sort through the cables, but trickier was that the essential black cable was pinned beneath a leg of the curio. He braced himself and strained the display case an inch off the ground. Porcelain shepherds made a hushed slide on the shelves above.

He had finished untangling the cables when he heard a sob from somewhere within the house. He froze to listen, but the sob wasn't repeated. Then a few minutes later, as he was powering on a router, he heard another short wail. He set the contraption down and traced the noise to Beatrice's wing.

He stood at the edge and peered down a hallway done in black and red paint and leafy iron fixtures. "Hello?" he called, but there was no response.

Cautiously, Ralph made his way farther in, his footfalls resounding against the bare stone floor. All the doors off the hallway were of solid wood, heavily varnished and banded in dark metal, dust settled into their ridges. The cries — less hysterical but more frequent now — came from one of the higher floors.

Ralph mounted a creaking circular staircase, only to face a similar hallway at its end. He crept down. Though similarly decorated, this hallway didn't feel as gloomy; sunlight from the windows cast shining trapezoids on the ground. The decorations weren't as dusty; some of the doors hung open. The cries had lightened, too, and had begun to sound like expressions of both sadness and joy.

Ralph rounded the last stretch of the hallway to face a short balcony with a single door. It was ajar, and as Ralph pushed it he felt the air shift from the chill of climate-controlled indoors to the muggy warmth of the evening. Beatrice stood alone beneath the sky, leaning against a water cistern, worrying a piece of fabric between her slender fingers.

"I'm sorry," Ralph said. "I couldn't help but hear you."

Beatrice coughed and remained silent. Then, once she began speaking, her words spilled out easily. "Oh God," she said, running a palm over her red-rimmed eyes. "I'm so embarrassed."

"Don't be embarrassed. That's ridiculous."

"It's been an intense day. I'm sure you get it."

"I'm so sorry."

Beatrice sighed and pressed her fingertips together. "I bet you don't even know what happened. No one's dared say a word about it since we got home."

Ralph took a deep breath. "I understand your real mom just died."

"She's been dead awhile, actually. Gert dragged her feet getting the service together. My mum was in a coma for like half a year, and it's not like anyone ever had a doubt how it was going to end." Beatrice stared at him with bleary eyes.

"Mind if I stand next to you?"

Beatrice looked surprised. "No, go ahead."

Ralph leaned next to her, against the cistern. They watched the sunset. "I can't even imagine what it's like to lose a parent," he said.

"I bet you could imagine it. You'd probably come up with something like what I'm feeling. I feel like *I* can't imagine it, and it's happening to me."

"Oh."

"Wait. Where are your parents?"

"Back in Jersey. They don't talk to the British side. Something to do with wishes."

"Oh. That's weird." Beatrice shrugged. "It feels like I'm not feeling as much as I should be feeling. And that's weird, too. I lost my mum. And it's like I'm totally sad about it, but I'm also wondering what's for dinner. How am I possibly wondering what's for dinner?"

Ralph wondered what was for dinner, too.

"Her name was Annabelle," Beatrice said as the pinks of the sunset first started deepening to purples. "It's a name suited for dying, isn't it?"

Ralph frowned.

"I didn't know her really well," Beatrice said. "My father divorced her when I was little, and Gert's basically been my mother. But that doesn't change the fact that she's dead. It's so . . . strange."

"Your brother and sister don't seem too cut up," Ralph says.

"They barely knew her. Not that I did much more. Father met Annabelle in college. She kind of left me with him for a while, couldn't stomach the idea of raising kids when she was in her early twenties. So that was when he married Gert. None of us have seen my real mother for a long time. I used to talk to her every few months but it always felt odd, like some huge space was between us but we were supposed to pretend it wasn't there. Then she got in a coma and died. Why are you here?"

"Hold on. Hold on," Ralph said. Beatrice was so rapidly intimate. Maybe that was why she was so quiet; it must be tiring to be vulnerable with everyone.

Beatrice stared at him steadily. "What is it? Do you not believe me?"

"Of course I do. I'm processing, that's all. I'm not going all authenticity police on you."

"'Authenticity police?' You're such a geek. Look, I should get ready for dinner. Gert's always a monster when people are late. I'll meet you down there."

"Daphne told me there are guards set up around the castle tonight."

Beatrice looked up sharply. "She did?"

"Yeah. She was going to show me, but I wasn't tall enough. Have any idea why she would make up stories about guards?"

Beatrice sucked in her breath. "It's best we didn't talk about it. She's always going on that Mum's supposedly hired protection. Daphne's such a romantic; she's probably spying on us right now and getting excited."

"So she's definitely making it up, right?"

"Who cares?" Beatrice said, pushing back from the wall and rubbing tiny pebbles off her palm. "If there're guards, they must be doing their work. If not, then we didn't need them, anyway."

# CHAPTER VIII

Ralph returned to his cables. While he began to thread the yellow cable out from the others, he paused, sure he heard yet more sobbing. And these cries — tiny, really, mere whiffles of anguish — were right beside him. Ralph slowly turned, but he could see no one. It was as if the sobs were coming from the curio itself.

He moved toward the emanation point of the phantom cries, and there he saw it: One of the porcelain maids was crying. No more than two inches tall, crowded by piglets and paperboys, she was leaning heavily on her crook and weeping, her whole body shaking.

"What's wrong?" Ralph asked, before a half dozen far more vital questions sprang to mind.

She rubbed a sleeve across her red glazed lips and sat down, disappearing in the ceramic crowd. "I've lost my ducklings," she said.

Ralph slid a ceramic king over to better see her. "Where are they?" he asked, again censoring a number of more pressing questions (it seemed rude to question someone's very existence, or ability to speak, even though she was two inches tall; besides, this might be the way of all British home decoration).

The maid pointed her crook at Ralph. "*You* made me slide away from them, when you lifted the corner of the curio. They're over there, on the other side of the shelf, and I can't leave my pedestal to get them."

"All right, all right," Ralph said. And, with a scan to make sure he was alone, he pinched the maid's pedestal between his fingers.

"What do you think you're doing?" she cried.

"I thought —"

"You think I want to be back with them? I've been stuck next to those unmoving quackers for fifty-odd years!"

"Oh."

"They're so tiresome. How do you think it feels to listen to an eternity of squawks, to have your only source of physical pleasure be a weekly feather-dusting? You think I'm yearning to go back to the usual?"

"No, I don't think I was assuming anything," Ralph said, flustered.

The maid patted down the pockets of her apron, searching for something. Her movements were suddenly sluggish.

"You do realize that you're a talking knickknack?" Ralph asked.

"You're going to waste my last seconds of animation asking stupid questions?"

"Why only a few seconds?"

"Look, if you want more, you'd better talk to Chessie."

"Who's Chessie?"

"Are you serious? Your aunt — Gert and Mary's sister!"

"Oh. Is she here?"

"She'd like to be. Go and talk to her. You'll find her quite extraordinary. All young men do."

"Where can I find her?" Ralph asked. But by then the maid had stopped moving entirely.

✢      ✢      ✢

When Beatrice emerged from her wing, Ralph was staring at a couch cushion. She asked what was wrong, and he stammered something about jet lag and maneuvered to the subject of Chessie. He said he had overheard a servant use her name; he didn't go into any more specifics, as he wasn't sure whether having conversed with a porcelain milkmaid meant that he was insane.

Beatrice shook her head gravely. "Oh, I think I know. Daphne's guard stories make more sense now. Could be that Aunt Chessie's found out where we are."

"Wait. This isn't Chessie, the famous 'Duchess of Cheshire' Chessie?"

"You've heard of her?"

"Of course. She's, like, famous. She sells The Butt Sculptor in the States. Never seen her, though."

"That's the very Chessie. We're none of us allowed to see her. I used to think it was typical Gert snobbery, but now I'm starting to think it's something more specific. Especially if Daphne's stories about armed guards are true. I *knew* it was a matter of time before she found us again. Come on."

Ralph followed Beatrice downstairs to her favorite eavesdropping spot, a leaf-papered bench to one side of the window of Gert and Gideon's study. It provided a wavy view of the occupants inside and, as the stone around the frame was centuries old and crumbling, transmitted a good amount of sound as well. They watched the shadow of Gert talk on the phone, unloading on an unfortunate friend the vicissitudes of various falling investments and the difficulties of hiring a new groundskeeper.

"I sit here sometimes and listen to how ridiculous she is with other people, so that when she gets cross with me I can remember that it's nothing personal," Beatrice said.

"How often do you sit out here?" Ralph asked.

"Oh, a lot. I bring a book sometimes, and spend the afternoon. No one bothers me."

"Why does your mom want to avoid Chessie so much?"

"Surely you know! It's probably the same reason your parents have kept you hidden away in New Jersey."

Ralph shook his head.

"Chessie used to have a son. And seven years ago, he was suddenly *gone.*"

"Gone?"

"We were all there, though we kids were too young to remember much. They were playing some silly game for her son's sixteenth birthday. Chessie granted him a wish, and then the next day — *poof!* — he had disappeared. The papers said he was abducted, there was an international hunt — surely you heard about all this?"

"No, not at all."

Beatrice was about to ask a question but then raised a finger. "Wait."

They leaned in to spy better.

"— I will not have her anywhere near my children, do you hear me?" Gert was saying into the phone. "I don't *care* if she's driven all the way from London . . . and why *now*? . . . No, I will *never* be ready. . . . He *disappeared*, do you understand? It's all so *medieval*. I'm sorry, it's inexcusable. Stop her. Do whatever it takes, just stop her." Gert slammed down the phone.

"Looks like Chessie's coming to dinner," Beatrice said.

# CHAPTER IX

But Chessie didn't come to dinner. The meal passed uneventfully: The food was unappetizing but impeccably prepared; the conversation was guarded and political and dominated throughout by the Battersby parents; all present yearned for it to be over as soon as possible.

Only one incident is really worth noting. Just as the entrée was served, a great ruckus arose on the lawn, ending with what sounded like a gunshot, causing Gideon to drop his salad fork into his wine. When Daphne exclaimed and Cecil asked if he could investigate, Gert informed them that they could settle down and start their candied venison instead.

If you're wondering what Ralph was thinking at this point, we shouldn't really know, as he was being so polite that his face revealed none of his thoughts — or at least he thought it didn't. If we looked closely, though, we'd see that his expression was engaged but simultaneously a little distant, like your best friend's when your story's gone long. He was scared he didn't know how to behave in front of minor aristocracy like the Battersbys, or especially in front of a true royal celebrity like Chessie, and he wasn't sure if he especially liked Gert, or cared to find out whether he liked Gideon.

Beatrice looked closely enough to see these things on Ralph's face, and so did Gideon, who told his wife what he saw later that night as they prepared for bed. Not in the words I've set out, of course, but more like "not really our sort, is he?"

Gert, however ... Ralph withered beneath her solicitousness. She "couldn't be more fascinated" by Ralph's two little cats at home. She was "amazed" that he had been president of the Technology Awareness Club in high school. She found it "so very charming" that Ralph had never before left the United States, and that he loved his middle-class schoolteacher parents. ("It's *charming* of you, it just is, you darling!") He was suddenly lost, though, when in one breath she went from being "totally delighted" that Ralph liked his new quarters to crossly demanding that "all you children ignore that gunshot from a few minutes ago."

The children, as will do any children addressed in the plural, stared back balefully.

"Really, honey," Gert continued, "those kinds of things aren't nice to think about. Say something pleasant, Beatrice. Pleasant is pretty."

"My mum just got buried, Gertrude."

"Yes, of course, so she did. Let's get on with dinner. Where *is* dinner?"

After the meal, the Battersby children convened on the patio to strategize. Ralph and Cecil paced the floor while Beatrice reclined in a splendid pose on a chaise and Daphne worked out her nerves by swinging from an eave.

"Okay, Daph, that's enough," Cecil said, holding up his arms until Daphne dropped into them.

"So have you guys figured it all out?" Daphne asked, for a moment only white tights and crinoline underskirt as she struggled to the ground.

"We're pretty sure it was a gunshot," Beatrice reported.

"It's not even hunting season, is it?" Cecil asked.

"It's always hunting season," Beatrice said. "*Something's* sure to be getting killed."

"Why don't we ask Mummy and Daddy about it again, now that they're not all fussy because servants are around?" Daphne asked.

"No chance," Cecil said.

"Thousands of years of cultivated civilization, and ignorance is still the best way we British have come up with for dealing with problems," Beatrice said to Ralph, a trifle affectedly. She squinted. "But you know, that's probably not exclusively British at all, is it?"

"I don't think so," Ralph said. "Haven't really thought about it."

"Tell us more about *America*, Mr. Ralph," Beatrice said, throwing her pitch ridiculously low.

"Bea! Someone's probably been *shot*, and you're making boring talk!" Daphne squealed.

Cecil clapped his hands on Daphne's shoulders. "I'm sure no one's been shot, Daph. A bird, somewhere." He winked over her shoulder. "But it's certainly worth investigating, to make sure."

"I'll take that way, and you take that way!" Daphne said, pointing in random directions.

"Sure, whatever. You coming?" Cecil asked Ralph.

"Oh, I don't know," Ralph said, eyeing the chaise next to Beatrice.

"You should go with them," Beatrice said. "This is the only adventure you're going to get all summer."

"Don't you think," Ralph said, "that if a firearm has been set off, it's not wise for us to wander off into the countryside?"

"Ralph," Beatrice said, "what are you so uncomfortable about? We're in the country — there's always a grouse to be shot somewhere around here. If there was anyone dangerous around, those guards would have stopped them. Don't be so wimpy."

And so he went. Soon enough, he was enjoying his search of the twilit grounds. When he returned to Beatrice twenty minutes later, he found Cecil and Daphne already back and lazing about the patio. None of them had turned up anything, not a single clue.

"A hunter's bullet," Beatrice concluded. "Death of the usual variety, nothing to worry about."

Indeed, Ralph wouldn't turn up a single clue about that night, about the gunshot or the Battersby parents' reluctance to discuss it or the guards or even the funeral, for a little over a week. In the meantime he spent a large part of his days on the phone with British Telecom, or waiting for their servicemen, or holding wires in either hand in hopes that their currents would stop interfering. During his non-working hours he read with Beatrice on the roof, played squash (poorly) with Cecil, and taught Daphne how to shoot videos on her phone. One day he and Beatrice went into town to see a movie (an American blockbuster, which brought on an unexpected rush of pride related to frame rates and number of effects shots), after which Ralph hung out with Cecil in the stockroom at the clothing store and bought Daphne a clearance headband with two monstrous felt eyes wired to dangle over her bangs. It would be a great prop for the short films that Daphne the telephone filmmaker had taken to composing.

Every night Ralph double-checked the locks, morbidly certain that he was bound to have an intruder — it wasn't difficult to imagine someone breaking into his shadowy, isolated gatehouse. To keep his mind off the possibility until he fell asleep, he had taken to sitting up in bed, typing game ideas into his laptop, or composing the long apology email he would send to his parents once he got the internet working. Glancing about the spare stone walls lit only by the feeble glow of his laptop screen, listening to the scratches of his pen against heavy paper and seeing the reflected shadows of the giant tree's leaves pace the windows, he often wondered what he would do if someone knocked on his door. There was no peephole or door chain, no back escape and no one to hear if he shouted for help. His only defense would be to not answer the door at all, and that sounded feeble as far as defenses go.

His invader wound up not giving Ralph the option, materializing as she did at the foot of his bed, seated so her royal posterior rested in the space between his legs. Until her appearance, Ralph had been in a deep sleep, and it took him a few moments to click the light on and realize that there was, indeed, a famous duchess in the room.

Ralph's first impression of Chessie was a flurry of details: massive strawberry curls piled on a narrow head and held in place by strips of velvet, low-cut black evening gown interrupted by swatches of mesh and linen lattice, lips as wet and red as fresh-cut ruby grapefruit. Slowly the details formed together into what could only be his aunt Chessie.

"I was not expecting you to be here," she intoned, locking a cigarette into her curved mouth.

Ralph sat up, pulled his sheets about his bare waist, and stared at Chessie's lips.

"In fact," she continued, "I don't believe that was an error on my part. I do believe — correct me if I'm wrong — that even your parents probably don't expect you to be here."

"What are you doing in my room?"

"The way you say that makes me think you've already realized who I am. Otherwise, that would be the next logical question, no?" She pulled her cigarette away from her lips and examined it idly.

Ralph nodded. Just a few days before he had seen her ad in a newspaper flyer, mugging as she sipped a protein shake.

"I assume that the kids must have told you all about me. So now you inform me, if you will be so kind, how it is that you come to be alive."

And so Ralph stammered for a moment about how, to the best of his knowledge, he had never died, and could therefore only conclude that he was still, at least as of that moment, alive.

Chessie took a long drag of her cigarette and offered it to Ralph. He declined. "Those wily Stevenses," Chessie said. "They sent me a Christmas card a few years back saying you were quite dead."

"I bet they had a good reason," Ralph said quietly.

"Wishes, wishes, wishes," Chessie said, jumping to her feet and pacing the gatehouse. "All this fuss over *wishes*."

"What kinds of wishes?" Ralph asked, reaching for a discarded T-shirt and pulling it on.

Chessie pressed her hands against her cheeks, pulling her skin taut. "What do you see when you look at me?" she asked.

"Chessie of Cheshire. You're famous."

"For the wrong reasons. Do you know how it feels, Ralph, to be well-regarded, but not the way you want to be?"

Ralph nodded. He was seen as an adept geek, when he wanted to be fun, instead. He opened his mouth to tell Chessie so.

"I don't want to have to be a corporate pitchwoman," Chessie continued, barreling over his first syllable. "But unless I wanted to be a boring dignitary, a path that was never open to me for various reasons, I could find no other way to have a life that ... means something. And all I want is a life that means something. You can understand that, can't you?"

Ralph nodded, no longer even attempting speech.

"Tell me: I am the godmother to three immature children. Centuries ago, what would that have meant?"

"I'm very sorry, but I'm not sure."

"I would have been a fairy godmother! I would have granted wishes!"

Surprisingly enough, he had already considered that conclusion, but was afraid it would sound ridiculous if spoken aloud.

"Come," Chessie said, holding her hands out to Ralph, who stared at them. "Who says I can't cast a spell or two? Who says being a duchess can't come along with anything cool anymore? Look at my sister, Gert. Is she all you expect from aristocracy? Dry obligations and chilled heart? I'm of the old variety. I don't want to be elegant and unobtrusive. I want to have an *effect*. I want everyone to be at least a trifle scared to meet me, like I've got a poison apple secreted away in my purse. You're not scared of me, are you, dear heart?"

Ralph shook his head.

"Gert and Mary would have hated what I just said. They have an aversion to strongly worded statements, particularly those that don't originate from them. 'You know very well why we no longer partake in spells,' Gert would say, 'It's so *nouveau royale*. Five hundred years ago, fine. But not now.' We're so *polite* now. And while my other sister, your mother, wouldn't be as rude as Gert, she still doesn't have the nobility of soul to understand what I'm trying to do."

Ralph wasn't sure how to take this last bit. He had often called his mother strict, or annoying, but "nobility of soul"! The concept was beyond him, and certainly nothing he would consider attaching to his parents.

"But you get me in a way she never will, don't you?" Chessie continued. "Young Americans are always hankering for some fairy tale pizzazz."

Ralph remembered another of Chessie's ads, this one a photo of her hyping a treadmill while wearing a bathing suit of uncommon brevity. He didn't think of her as a storybook godmother. But, as he always tried to give the right answer when an adult asked a question, he said, "I guess we always do attach some magic to royalty. We don't have any of our own."

"You're a magician of your own sort, aren't you, dear?"

"No, I don't think so. Well. Depends on what you mean, I guess," Ralph said, secretly hoping Chessie was about to unveil a prophecy that would tell him what to do with his life.

"You and your game designing. Your mythmaking."

"How do you know about that? A few seconds ago you thought I was dead."

"I'm a *fairy godmother*, Ralph. I thought we went over this."

"Sorry. Please continue."

"Well, there's not much more to say. Just that we're after the same thing. We've got that American grit. You're a lot more like me than Gert's children are. I can see that much right away. Even back in the States, though . . . no one's ever really gotten you, have they?"

Ralph shook his head, suddenly chilled.

"We're magicians. Or at least, we both want to be. But your path hasn't been going too well, has it?"

"I don't know about that," Ralph said, hugging his knees to his chest.

"Dear, it's okay. I can help."

"How?"

"Really? Keep up! I *grant wishes*."

"Are you offering me a wish?"

Chessie nodded.

"Okay," Ralph said, spontaneously deciding to ignore years of his parents' warnings. "I wish —"

"No, no, not yet. It all has to be in the right sequence. I can't grant a wish to you before the Battersby children."

"Oh. Why?"

"Ralph, mere minutes ago you were fibbing and telling me you were dead. Wishes take preparation. I can't spring one out like a parlor trick."

"Well, when do I get my wish?"

"You must work on this selfish streak."

"Look! You can't show up in my bedroom, offer a wish, and then take it back!"

Chessie looked at him appraisingly. "Well! Plenty of ambition, after all. Surprising. You'll work hard for this, won't you?"

"Tell me what you want, and I'll make sure it happens."

"What I want is easy," Chessie said. "I need access to the Battersby children, even if only for a split second."

"I'll have to talk to Gert first."

"You haven't been following what I've really been saying, have you? No deal," Chessie said, and vanished, leaving behind one extinguished cigarette, its filter rimmed in red lipstick.

# CHAPTER X

When Chessie didn't reappear even once over the following week, Ralph feared he would never see her again. His anxiety became all-consuming — he would glance at the foot of his bed between each paragraph of his late-night reading, sit on the patio for hours and scan for a fairy carriage coming down the walk. But there was never a single magic duchess. To occupy himself he became involved in the lives of his cousins. Before long he was as close to them as he had been to any of his friends in New Jersey (which is, to be honest, not terribly close). With Beatrice he discussed his parents' wish ban. He told Cecil about his failure with girls, for which the suggested remedy was to ask out Cecil's assistant manager, who was folding socks. ("You're sweet" was her unpromising response.) And he had Daphne play simple games he had designed, for which she always managed to find the perfect sequence of keystrokes to crash the program. But Beatrice's indifference, Cecil's ill-conceived advice, and Daphne's game wrecking, though each a minor failure, hid within them a sort of familial tolerance, an unthinking acceptance of the crazy American cousin. Ralph interpreted this as affection. He found that, despite their essential ambivalence about his existence, the Battersby family was very pleasant company for a summer.

Of course, the Battersby family also included its magical and potentially evil aunt, who is certainly not gone from our story.

Had he been more attentive, Ralph would have seen a clear sign of Chessie's imminent reappearance: Sunday morning, the porcelain maid again took to sighing. But Ralph, distracted by the tantalizing possibility that he might have figured out how to make the wireless signal finally transmit into Beatrice's wing, rushed by the melancholy creature without noticing.

After dinner he came upon a much more obvious clue: While strolling past the tree with Daphne on his shoulders, she vanished entirely, reappearing hundreds of feet away on the castle roof, shrieking and hopping in astonishment.

We all behave differently on the occasion of witnessing our first teleportation: Some proceed as if nothing has happened, some faint, some develop a rare form of lockjaw. Ralph was a starer. He glanced at his shoulder, where Daphne had so recently been, then at Daphne on the roof of the castle, shouting incomprehensibly, then back to his shoulder, then back to the roof, as if waiting to see a zip line appear connecting the two.

Eventually he started toward the castle, but when he took a step he ran directly into the lacy flannel of Chessie's fairy godmother midriff. She had evidently been standing at his side for some time, watching in bemusement. She wrapped her gloved hands around Ralph's cheeks, kissed him on the forehead, and said, "That's magic, darling."

"D-Daphne," Ralph observed.

"Now do you see why I need your help? Gert doesn't like the old ways, sure, but she sees no problem in placing a protection ward on her children."

"Gert teleported Daphne away?"

"She probably isn't even aware that her Parental Protection Ward fired; she put them in place years ago. She won't let me see my own family, dear Ralph — and the teleporting wards are yet another way to block me."

"I'm sure she has a very good reason. If you'll excuse me, I have to go, you know, rescue Daphne."

"No, Gert really doesn't have a good reason. She's *unfeeling*. I'm certain the children still miss their silly aunt. Ask them to meet me. That's all I ask."

"If Gert's got some magic wards set up, how could I possibly be any help? If I even wanted to help, of course, which I'm pretty sure I don't."

"Because the wards are against *me*, not *you*. You can remove them for me. All I ask is that you give my nieces and nephew the choice. They've got their own minds, like you. Lay everything out before them, so they can decide like reasonable adults. If they don't want to see me, fine. But frankly I don't think that's likely."

"And if I do, and they do, you'll grant me a wish as well?"

"Once they all make wishes, you will be the fourth, yes."

"Why are you so desperate to do all of this?"

Daphne's cries on the roof intensified.

Chessie stepped back and held Ralph at arm's length. She was wearing a mass of rainbow flannel ribbons; he could really see her for the first time, and saw that she was gorgeous and powerful and maybe (he was aware of his "maybe," aware that he was fighting it into a "surely") good-intentioned. What could be the harm, he thought, of offering the Battersby kids the option of seeing their aunt? If Cecil and Beatrice decided it was okay, then he would have reunited them with a family member. And afterward, he could wish for his dream job at MonoMyth after all.

"What would I have to do?" he asked.

"You've met the milkmaid. She can tell you how to remove the Parental Protection Wards. Part of the magic is that I'm not allowed to tell you personally. The rules are a real bore."

"I'll see what I can do," Ralph said grudgingly, pulling away.

"Thank you," Chessie said, a single dramatic tear marring none of the magical foundation painted on her cheek. She batted her eyelashes expectantly (slowed as they were by heavy mascara, the batting of Chessie's eyelashes was a surprisingly involved process). "That's all I can ask."

# CHAPTER XI

As he approached the castle, Ralph saw Daphne disappear into the roof stairwell and figured that she had decided to find her own way down. He went straight to Beatrice, whom he found on the floor in her room, using a marker to ink black butterflies on her ankle. "Hey," he said, "I need the whole truth on your Aunt Chessie. Everything you know. Now."

Beatrice looked up at him and widened her eyes. "What kind of truth?"

"Um, let's start with whether she's good or evil."

"I don't know. I was a kid when I saw her last. Mom would definitely say that she's evil. The tabloids definitely think she's good. What a weird question." Beatrice capped the marker and squinted at Ralph. "You've seen her, haven't you?"

"No."

She squinted further. "Where? What did she say to you?"

Ralph buckled. "On the grounds. She wants to see you guys again."

"She's here? My God!"

"I know!"

"Tell me everything she said, right now."

"She wants to see you all. I told her that I'd have to ask your mom first, and Chessie didn't like that, so she disappeared. She approached me again. I told her I'd bring it up to you and Cecil, but that I didn't think you would be okay with it. Oh, and in the process Daphne got teleported away because of some Parental Protection Ward."

Beatrice stood up. "Where is she right now?"

"I think she found her own way down from the roof."

"No, Chessie."

"You're not really going to see her, are you?"

"Did she say exactly why she wanted to see us?"

"Granting a wish, apparently. What's that about?"

Beatrice scrambled out the door.

Ten minutes later Beatrice, Ralph, and Cecil were facing one another on a circular rug in the castle basement, a thick candle flickering between them.

"So what do you think?" Beatrice asked her brother.

"No way we're going to see her. The world doesn't need any more of this medieval self-indulgence."

"I wonder," she said, "if you could wish for an end of all wishing. Would that make it worth it?"

"Ugs, listen to me," Cecil said, nervously scratching at a blistering pimple. "It's not that I'm against the granting of wishes. I'm against the unreflective use of power. And this seems like such idle, mystical crap. Why should royal kids, who already have so much, be the ones to get wishes?"

"I know, but . . . I'm curious, aren't you?" she said.

Ralph watched the two of them and thought about how well-equipped to discuss these matters they both seemed. For his part, he was only barely able to restrain himself from running around the room and making googly sounds.

"Uh-uh. We've got to tell Mum," Cecil said.

"Gertrude?! She'd freak out that Chessie even approached Ralph, and then we wouldn't be allowed to leave the castle all summer. If we're safe because of the wards, why bother Mum about it? Let's at least get that possibility off the table."

"We tell Mum about it because Chessie *killed her own son*. You don't mess around with those kinds of people."

"You're as much of a snob as Gert. And we don't *know* that he's dead."

"It's not about snobbery, Ugs. It's about safety."

"I bet it was an accident. All she did was grant his wish. And somehow that led to his death. At the very worst, Chessie 'got her son killed.'"

Ralph found himself nodding emphatically.

"Even if it was an accident, do you want us to become another accident?" Beatrice said. "She's reckless!"

"I think we have to ask ourselves," Ralph said after clearing his throat, "why she's so set on granting us wishes in the first place."

"She's an old school traditionalist," Cecil spat. "That's it, plain and simple."

"If something went wrong with her son," Beatrice said, "then maybe she's looking for a vindication of the whole wish-granting system. That failure has got to be weighing on her."

"I thought of both of those," Ralph said. "But I also thought that maybe it could be that she hopes to get her son back through this, somehow."

"Oh," Beatrice said. "That's . . . almost sweet."

"So you're trying to say we could be doing a good deed at the same time as getting our greatest desires fulfilled?" Cecil asked, raising an eyebrow. "Sounds convenient."

"Yeah, I guess I am."

"Huh," he said, weighing the possibility with his eyebrows. "Huh."

"There's been a prohibition on wish-granting for years," Beatrice said. "We'd be doing something monumental."

"Why are *you* so into this?" Cecil asked.

Beatrice shrugged, and Cecil probably would have pressed further had Daphne not then burst into the basement.

"There you guys are! How could you hide from me, right now, when I got, like, *moved by magic*? I swear, Ralph was there — weren't you, Ralph?"

Beatrice drew her into her lap. "I know. We're discussing it."

"Sorry I didn't go get you down right away," Ralph said.

"It's okay," Daphne said. "I know how to use *stairs*. So what have we decided is going on?"

"How would you feel about —" Beatrice began.

"Don't even," Cecil said. "We can't. Don't even mention it to her, because we can't, and we aren't."

"How would I feel about *what*? You are *not* going to keep this from me!"

"Fine, you explain it," Beatrice said to Cecil.

Cecil toyed with the candle wax, dabbing a fingertip in and watching it cool.

"If you don't tell me, right now, I'm going straight to Mummy."

"An evil witch wants to put a curse on us, so we're going to ignore her," Ralph blurted.

"Oh."

Cecil held his hand out. "Everyone promise. We're going straight to bed, and not talking about this until we get up tomorrow. Our discussion is over."

Daphne visibly bit down on her excitement and placed her hand on Cecil's. Ralph and finally Beatrice followed, her fingers lightly resting on his wrist.

# CHAPTER XII

After leaving his cousins, Ralph had to pass by the castle study, at the entrance of which he stumbled into Lord Gideon Battersby. Gideon stood watching Ralph, the frames of his spectacles lost in the silver rays of his hair.

"Hello, Gideon," Ralph said.

"Ralph." He nodded. "Wouldn't you come in? I'd love to speak to you for a moment."

Ralph stepped onto the thick carpet. The library contained a few sloping desks, and short shelves filled with books with soft brown and green spines.

Gideon gave Ralph the sort of vigorous handshake generally reserved for bank presidents. "I was sitting in front of the window, examining one of my favorite books," he said, holding up a sun-faded tome with *The Fallacy of Magic* embossed on the cover, "and I couldn't help glimpsing, at the same time, that you were out on the grounds with Daphne."

Ralph nodded.

"Did you happen to notice whether the geraniums are due for cutting back?"

"No, I'm afraid I didn't," said Ralph.

"I also noticed," Gideon continued, "that while you were wandering with Daphne, my wife's sister appeared to you, dressed in some fairy godmother get-up, and caused Daphne to be teleported to the roof."

Though he tried to speak, Ralph stood mute.

"Let's discuss this like cool-headed men. I know I can't hold you accountable for my sister-in-law's behavior, but I can only imagine what she may have said to you. I have to request, in the interest of gentlemanly conduct, that you avoid dealings with her from here on. Lady Battersby and I have taken great pains that she shouldn't penetrate the boundaries of our family. Is that clear?"

Ralph nodded.

"Very good. Now, I have an international call to make before bed, but I wanted to make sure we had a suitable understanding first. There is little I can do to further curb Chessie's actions, but since you are a guest in my house, I'm afraid I have to insist on your proper behavior. These are my express wishes. I trust you haven't found me too emphatic on the issue."

"No, not at all."

Lord Gideon Battersby clapped Ralph on the shoulder. "So glad, so glad." He breathed a sigh of relief. "So glad we had this talk."

Once Gideon released him, Ralph went and found Cecil in his room, stuffing shirts into an army surplus bag.

"What are you doing?" Ralph asked from the doorway.

Cecil sprang up and slammed the door shut. "Shh! Daphne's bound to be spying."

"What are we hiding from her?" Ralph whispered.

"She can't know the truth!" Cecil whispered back.

"And that is?" Ralph asked, yearning for once to be fewer than two steps behind everyone else.

"Should I pack shorts?" Cecil asked, suddenly distracted. "Or face wash? Will there be showers?"

"Where?"

"Shh! When you made a wish back in the day, you entered a fairy tale where it got acted out. Everyone knows that. What I'm *asking you* is whether I'll need *shorts* and *face wash!*"

"Hold on — I thought no one was asking for a wish," Ralph said, feeling his neck grow hot.

"I don't want my sisters to risk themselves. But do you think I would actually pass up a chance to save the world?"

"Save it? From what?"

"Save it! Just save it! I'll figure out the details when I get there."

"Get where, exactly?"

Cecil paused as he was slinging the camouflage duffel over his shoulder. "I guess I don't know. Where's Chessie?"

"She's on the grounds somewhere. But you can't get close to her, because of the protection wards."

"Well, that can't stop me from trying," Cecil said as he dashed from the room.

It was darkly funny, really, watching Cecil stow his duffel on the patio, wander off into the woods, locate Chessie, teleport to the roof via the Parental Protection Ward, scramble down the stairs, run out into the woods, teleport back to the roof, scramble down the stairs, and so on, all with a steadily reddening face. Ralph hovered at the edge of the patio and watched it happening, wondering when Gideon would look up from his phone call in the study and start yelling.

"Come on, man, hold on a sec," Ralph said, but Cecil sprinted to the tree, raggedly panting, only to be teleported away again. Ralph could see the outline of Chessie's dress at the far side of the tree trunk as she waited for Cecil, could hear the distant moans of her frustration. He would block the door next time Cecil tried to pass, Ralph decided, would bar it with the couch . . . or he would go fetch Gert or Gideon, before Cecil fainted.

But when Cecil next ran by, Ralph did nothing.

He realized, then, that he had already made his decision: He wanted the wish to be granted.

He ducked into the hall, opened the glass door of the curio, and placed his face before the porcelain milkmaid. She was sulking in the corner, where she had propped her crook in front of her to keep the ducks at bay. "What do *you* want?" she asked.

"A Parental Protection Ward," Ralph said urgently. "How do I remove one?"

"Oh, you've come around, I see," she said, huffing as she stood. "Aren't you the morally ambiguous one?"

"Enough. Give me details. What do I have to do?"

"It's simple, really. A family member has to take something the child handled before the ward was ever placed, say he wants the ward removed, and mean it."

"That's it?"

"Well, it has to be in French. That was the official language of the English court when the Passive Magic Act was enacted."

"Do you know any French?"

"I'm a milkmaid, love. I don't even read English."

"Okay, I'll figure something out. I have to handle something they touched a long time ago, you say?"

"I'd suggest these iron ducks. They were all fascinated by them as kids. It would tickle me that I've been shepherding the keys to dispelling their protection. Come on, give me some irony to ponder in my lonely hours."

Ralph scooped all three ducks off the shelf, clenched them in his sweaty fist, and ran back to the patio.

# CHAPTER XIII

Ralph stood on the patio, gripped one of the metal ducks in his fist, and did his best to cobble a sentence from his memories of Mrs. Nelms's seventh-grade French class. He could remember how to ask whether the elevator went to the fourth floor, but little more.

As Cecil clambered past him toward the tree, Ralph tried *"warde pas, s'il vous plaît."*

The patio chandelier dimmed, as if someone had flipped on an air conditioner elsewhere in the castle. Ralph raced outside.

Chessie and Cecil were beside the massive tree. She had her arm about him, and he was whispering to her. As Ralph barreled out onto the patio, she smiled toward him — a quick, kindly parting of her lips — and ducked, with Cecil under her arm, into the gatehouse.

Ralph raced forward to join them, but then halted in shock.

The very idea was preposterous, but nonetheless he was sure of it: The giant tree had moved. It had taken him a minute's walk to reach it earlier that day, but now it dominated the clearing just beyond the perimeter of the castle, its trunk mere steps from his gatehouse. In the evening light the tree's form was a ragged black shape cut out of the sky, its huge branches galaxies gone dark within the swaths of stars. It swayed in a breeze Ralph couldn't otherwise detect, and those flicks of its branches seemed preparations for a grander movement, the pawing of a bull.

Ralph broke into a sprint toward the gatehouse, watching as the tree's rapidly doubling girth grew to meet him. He threw open the front door and dashed inside just before the tree's fluid trunk surrounded the gatehouse entirely.

The gatehouse interior was absolutely black. When he flicked on the switch by the door, no light came on.

"Hello?" Ralph risked calling. But there was no answer. He listened for footfalls — nothing. He wished, suddenly, that he had gone to the Battersby parents for help before dashing into the gatehouse.

He groped the dusty floorboards until his fingers curled around the flashlight he had packed (like any enterprising techie) into his luggage. He flicked it on.

Though nothing was missing, and nothing added, the gatehouse had nevertheless changed. The walls, for one thing. Where they had been perfectly vertical before, they now bowed in at the top, as if the rectangular house had recently made a slapdash attempt at becoming a cone.

Ralph did a visual circuit of the diminished borders of his room. The ceiling had been pinched closed like a pastry crust. The curtained windows had twisted and narrowed but not shattered; the bookcases — and, yes, Ralph gasped to discover, even the books on them — had shrunk at the tops. He gripped the flashlight between his teeth and opened a worn Forster. The book fell open with trapezoid pages. Even the dust he blew away from the top seam was a degree finer than that at the bottom.

It was unquestionably bizarre, but he wasn't totally unnerved. His life over the past week had twisted so rapidly that this latest happening seemed merely the next progression into oddity. But he did feel that if an adventure was so clearly beginning, he ought to change out of his smelly T-shirt before going any further. He donned his whitest pair of underwear, slacks, and a dress shirt, tried to brush his teeth until he realized there was no water (the bathroom spigot had pertly turned up its nose during the transformation), and applied fresh deodorant before trying the front door.

It wouldn't open. Not only wouldn't it open, but it didn't offer any of the slight budge even locked doors give. Ralph stared groggily at the offending door. How else did one leave a gatehouse, if not by the exit? There was the chimney, but peering up with the flashlight, he saw it had narrowed to a handsbreadth at the top, and that wherever the opening led, there was no daylight. That left the windows. Ralph approached one and threw back the curtain.

Wood.

It was dynamic, all waves and crests, like the tree had bubbled into the frame and frozen there. Ralph tried to open the window, but the warped panes of glass shattered and fell away. He reached a hand out to the exposed wood. It was moist with sap and as sharp as the end of a freshly broken branch. Ralph retreated from the window, huddled on the floor against a windowless wall, and hugged his knees to his chest, all the time nervously circling the room's dim corners with his flashlight.

Eventually he regained the presence of mind to use his cell phone. Of course there wasn't any reception from within a tree. Regardless, he wrote a text, using a macro he had programmed to have it sent automatically should the phone ever get reception:

BEAT/DAPH: SOS SOS IN TREE CHASING CECIL
AND CHESS COME HELP. RALPH

Much as he tried to control them, his breaths came quicker and quicker. He had seen Chessie and Cecil enter this very gatehouse, and if they were no longer here, there had to be *some* way out.

The only room Ralph hadn't investigated was the bathroom. When he carried the flashlight inside, raised the blind, and forced open the window, he found a narrow opening in the wood. It was like a branch turned inside-out, lengths of bark facing into an envelope-sized void. And at the end was a patch of stars, seen as if at the end of a telescope.

Ralph stood on the toilet seat and tried his shoulders against the narrow window frame. He would just fit. After rushing back to the bed and extracting his pet rock Jeremiah from under the mattress, he stuck his head in the tunnel, experienced a wave of claustrophobia, and decided to go feet first.

The shimmy out the window wasn't too unpleasant, actually — the tree helped him along in small contractions. By the time he was halfway out, though, he could no longer see anything of the gatehouse. Ralph was comforted by a breeze on his ankles. Once he could kick his feet in the air, he slid forward and let himself come free.

# CHAPTER XIV

He experienced a second's terrifying freefall. Instead of hitting earth at the end of it, as he had expected, he hit a branch. He fell heavily on his ribs and barely wrapped his arms around the broadly curved surface in time to prevent himself from falling again. He looped his arms more firmly around the branch and peered down.

The tree had gone from merely enormous to gigantic. The base of its circumference would now take minutes to walk around. The top of the trunk formed a horizon with the starry sky, disappearing at the limits of Ralph's vision.

The Battersby castle was gone, just gone. There weren't even ruined foundations where it had once been; it was as if the whole building had been sucked into the tower of wood.

A dozen feet above his head, he could see the ragged exit from his bathroom and then, even higher, a brick corner of the gatehouse emerging from between mottled bark lips.

He looked back down. The Battersbys' cars had been hurled to their sides next to the tree, submerged up to their hoods in the trunk. The gravel road twisted where it neared the chaotic scene, broken into shreds like the tines of a mashed fork.

Gazing back up, all Ralph could see was a highway of bark.

Steeling himself, he grasped the next higher branch. Once he had secured his footing, he grasped the next branch and nervously heaved himself over. The limbs came frequently enough that he would be able to climb the entire tree this way, proceeding from branch to branch, rungs on an overgrown playground toy.

His muscles soon began to ache (for few boys who set up wireless networks are also made for climbing trees), and by the time he was a half minute's fall from the earth, his arms and legs were burning.

As he continued climbing in the summer air, Ralph noticed the trunk narrowing — he was a mile into the sky, but nearing the top.

He looked up and saw clouds eclipsed by the silhouette of a large boxy building perched among the branches near the top. Cement and stones hung beneath its foundation like veins of a dismembered limb. The trunk swayed more and more violently as Ralph neared the Battersby castle.

By the time Ralph had struggled through a thin cloud layer to the bottom edge of the castle, he was swinging as much as a star slapped on a Christmas tree. He choked back vertigo as he crawled along a branch into a hole in the building's basement. After cautiously shimmying up the end of the bending limb, Ralph hurled himself onto the broken floor.

He breathed against the stone and mortar, enjoyed the swell of relief to once again be on solid footing.

The basement was freezing, and crossed by strong winds that snaked in through the hole in its side. Ralph backed away from the branch, crawled across the crumbling masonry, and unlatched the door to the foyer.

The central chamber was as he remembered it — draftier and much cooler, but mostly the same. The furniture was in the same positions, the internet cables still lay tangled in a corner. He began to call out "hello," but then stopped himself, realizing he had no idea what manner of creature might be inside. Besides, no one could probably hear his voice above the wind roaring against the walls.

An especially powerful gust struck the castle, pitching it to one side and back, like a ship in a tempest. As Ralph nervously mounted the stairs to the second floor, gripping the banister against the rocks and buffets of the castle, he passed into Beatrice's wing, and the sound of the wind subsided. He knew by the hollow echoes of his footfalls that there was nothing else still living in the castle. The children's bedrooms: empty. The servants' and parents' rooms: nothing but mussed bedspreads and scattered silk pillows.

Ralph called out as he wandered. But he never heard any response beyond the howls of the wind. He threw back the curtain and opened a window only once; when he did, the castle pitched forward and he was swaying over open air, clouds rolling against the castle, the ground distant below.

He sat on the floor for a minute, waiting until he could banish the sight of all the open space from his mind.

Once he'd calmed himself, he realized there was only one area left to try.

He creaked open the trapdoor leading to the roof, and in the narrow space he opened could see Chessie and Cecil standing at the battlements.

It was hard to make her out, as the freezing wind caused Ralph's eyes to water and warped everything he saw. She was dressed in full godmother regalia, hair done in a triple bouffant, with strips of stiff, colorful fabric girding her bosom. In her fist she clenched a smart-looking brushed steel wand that might have been purchased in an upscale cookware department. Cecil had donned a half-dozen sweatshirts, the necks of which collected at his throat like a turkey's wattle. Chessie had just finished saying something, to which Cecil responded, "Yeah, yeah, okay." Ralph craned forward to hear better as Chessie began to speak again.

"— has already prepared for it, but I need to hear it one official time, before the magic begins."

"Okay: I wish to help all the little people."

"Isn't that so charmingly proletariat? Fine. I do solemnly grant thee thy wish, dreaming, in accordance with the fine tradition of Royal wish-granting, that you find thy greatest desire, and in so doing come to know thyself."

"Uh-huh. So it starts now?"

Chessie rubbed an elbow and squinted. "Yes, I imagine everything must be ready by now."

"Is there a code word I can say to get back out, if I'm stuck or in trouble?"

"Um, no."

"And it just finishes once it's done?"

"Once you've 'helped all the little people,' yes."

"Who gets to decide that I'm done?"

"There has to be a fair amount of mysticism to all this, dear. I can't tell you everything."

Cecil ran his palms down the front of his pants. "So now do I get to start?"

"Yes, now you get to start."

"Can I bring —" Cecil's words were cut short as Chessie grabbed Cecil's waist, gave him a heave, and sent him hurtling over the side of the battlement. He didn't even have time to scream before he was gone. Chessie stood at the void beyond the wall and called: "Break a leg!"

There wasn't any thinking involved: Ralph just ran. With our greater leisure, we can see that he must have felt concerned that he had been the cause of this whole risky wish-granting. We also know that he had grown to hate the lack of wonder in his life. Both of these came together in the ooze of Ralph's skull to make him "unthinkingly" rush to the battlement.

There are three types of shocked silences: the kind when your uncle jokes about his ex-girlfriends at Thanksgiving dinner, the kind when you've seen what should have been an amazing sight and you fake astonishment so you don't seem hollow, and the kind when you experience something truly new and unknown. The third is the rarest and most precious, and was the silence of Ralph at the split second that he approached the battlement.

Below him wasn't the wide blue space that he had expected but the perfect simulation of a meadow in full daylight, somehow re-created no more than twenty feet below the skyward castle.

When Chessie saw him, her face contorted into an unnatural expression — or perhaps it was the first natural expression he had seen on her. Her normal mask soon came down, and she grunted and lunged for him. As he saw the ten flashes of red nail polish zoom toward him, Ralph leaped, plummeting onto a thicket in the grassy meadow.

After the head-rush and joint-tingling had abated, Ralph contemplated his situation. He was propped on a bramble bush, staring at grassland that was almost two-dimensional in its unblemished perfection: The cerulean sky hung flawless and even; the surrounding green hills rolled but never tumbled; the songbirds sang in complex harmonies. There was no more rushing wind. This is what it was to be magicked.

Ralph stood up and looked around. The only break in the verisimilitude of the meadow was above him, where the fuzzy outline of a battlement wavered, almost disappearing from view and then faintly reappearing. From over that wall glared a very ticked-off duchess.

He coughed.

Chessie unglazed. "You," she said, the word carrying as if over a long distance. "You!"

"Hello, duchess," Ralph called.

She pointed her wand threateningly, then sighed and let it drop to her side. "I suppose you've come to mess everything up."

"I want to help Cecil," Ralph said. Then, when Chessie only scowled in response, he added, conversationally, "So this is where his wish is taking place?"

"Yes." She sighed. "My nephew is questing even as we speak."

"So how does this work?" Ralph asked, shielding his eyes from the fluorescent sun as he squinted up at the duchess.

Chessie sat on the battlement and dangled her feet into the meadow, glumly resting her chin on her hands. "They make a wish, have a quest, learn a lesson, and when they return to the real world are further along toward being adults. Classically, that's how it would go. It's been years since I've done a wish, and I wasn't fully prepared this time. Gert keeps her children tucked away so thoroughly."

She fiddled with her wand. "By the time you convinced him to come talk to me — thanks for that, by the way, though you don't deserve any more gratitude than that, after this hysterical stunt you've pulled — I only had a minute to scramble all the necessary employees into the wish. These things take loads of time to arrange, and I'm afraid what's to come will be a little slapdash. We're all out of practice. The wish-granter — me — is supposed to hire actors to play the goblins and mentors and all that rot. I tried to call in J. J. Mucklebackit, the famous villainess from the nineteen-seventies — perhaps you've heard of her? — but she wasn't available on such short notice. So I'm filling in as the villain for Cecil's wish. It's time I got myself magicked in, too." She cracked her knuckles. "I think this may come off."

"If you're worried about Cecil's safety, then you're probably fine with me being here to help," Ralph said.

"Having a sloppy American running about takes away some of the poetry, I have to say. But yes, I could probably use assistance in making sure Cecil doesn't perish."

"How do I do that?"

"Stop him from falling into bottomless pits, that sort of thing. Oh, and this is very important — by rules of narrative economy, his wish has to finish within a hundred pages. If it doesn't . . . it has to finish in one hundred pages."

"Is this all being written down somewhere? How am I supposed to know when a hundred pages have gone by?"

"Yes, it is being written. The narrator is in the catwalks above. He's been tailing you for some time. If you squint, you can see him."

Ralph peered up to the sun, and could make out a hazy structure before its radiance, something like a wooden rainbow.

"Don't bother trying to communicate with him, though," Chessie said. "He's not allowed to interact with you."

"Is that what happened to your son?" Ralph asked. "Did more than a hundred pages go by for his wish?"

Chessie paused. "I don't know." She shook her head. "It's time to start."

Ralph spun around. "Where's Cecil?"

"Quests go at high speed. He got a big head start in those moments while you were jumping in."

"Where do I find him?"

"Ask about, be resourceful. I have to rush now — the boy's already been weeks in his quest without a villain, and he's sure to be at a complete loss. Now, before I dash away I need you to know something very important,

Ralph. We all change when we enter a wish. It's an essential part of the magic — we become more accepting of oddity, for one thing."

Ralph nodded.

"As for me, I'm going to be performing a role, and you will find my interpretation quite convincing. I suggest you flee if you come across me at any point. I will no longer be sweet Auntie Chessie, do you understand?" She bent down to stretch, touching her toes.

Ralph nodded again, amused at the idea that there had ever been a "sweet Auntie Chessie."

"Is that very, very clear? I will try to kill you next time I see you."

Ralph stared back at her.

Chessie screeched, hurled herself over the wall, and vanished before she hit the ground.

# BOOK II:
# CECIL'S WISH
## FAIRY REBELLION

# CHAPTER XV

Ralph stood beaming at the white sunshine, thinking it remarkably similar to everyday sunshine, only prettier (like sunshine frosting, really), when from around a corner of a path he heard the grinding of carriage wheels. He scanned about for a hiding spot . . . but idyllic meadows, he discovered, weren't ideal places in which to find cover. The best he could settle on was a large tuft of grass, into which he threw himself. Any observer could see that, while his head was neatly covered, the rest of his sprawled body was exposed. He was no better than a cat hiding in a rhododendron.

One side benefit of terrible concealment is a terrific view. Ralph saw that the approaching carriage was pulled by four black horses, chugging with all the unabating ferocity of miniature steam engines. Regardless of their labors, the horseman made cruel use of a fourfold whip, lashing all the creatures' stinging backsides with each flick.

The vehicle itself was Cinderella's pumpkin. Or, rather, it was Cinderella's pumpkin if glimpsed at a ball by a jealous royal and then demanded of an engineer whose previous specialty was torture equipment. Hundreds of orange metal surfaces were welded with the finest precision, resulting in what was either the most beautiful carriage ever to exist or a malevolent biscuit tin.

As the carriage neared, Ralph was surprised to discover that the horses were not horses at all, but unicorns.

About unicorns: More sentimental narrators possess three unwavering tendencies: 1) to follow "want" by "need" ("She wanted his love. She needed his love"); 2) to take time out of stories for young heroines to (positively) assess their reflections in mirrors; and 3) to make unicorns invariably white/gentle and in need of rescue by a dashing, nonthreatening hero — in short, horsey princesses. Her horn, set upon so eagerly by rapacious goblins, is a symbol of her innocence, and once it is pried from her she will become just a horse, as common as any other.

A crucial difficulty: Unicorns with horns aren't female. Just like rams and narwhals — none with a tusk or horn is female. The *Origin of Fantastic Species* confirms that unicorn horns are the evolutionary results of competition between males of the species, for while a horn doesn't do a unicorn a lick of good in fighting off a pack of Brimstone Hyenas, it is enormously handy in competing with other unicorns.

As far as our tale is concerned, suffice it to note that, given their glistening horns and foul dispositions, these four jet-black unicorns were doing nothing to draw Ralph out from his hiding place.

As the procession neared, the birds fled and the rabbits stopped chattering (disappeared entirely, in fact, into a nearby warren), so the only sound Ralph heard was the soon-deafening grinding of gravel beneath the carriage's wheels. Ralph debated calling out to the driver, in case he might get a friendly response. But the wild animals' reaction to the carriage cried out that whoever was inside was one hundred percent villain.

Ralph scrunched his eyes shut as the vehicle approached. Once the noise peaked and then began to fade, he knew he would soon be safe.

But he had forgotten his allergies.

And did Ralph have allergies! He'd sneeze crossing the grass median of a New Jersey strip mall. Generally, he kept them in control through medications. But of course, it is hard to remember to collect one's prescription drugs while fleeing a gatehouse-engulfing tree, so Ralph was caught without a single tablet. And this was bad news indeed, for fantastic worlds are homes to all sorts of pyrotechnically hyperallergenic pathogens. Among the more plentiful are griffon dander and cold-fused nuclear ragweed.

(And beyond mere allergens, Ralph had already been infected with a half-dozen mythically virulent diseases, all of which produced symptoms much more severe than sneezing. As he had built up none of the fairy-tale resistances of, say, your average miller's son, Ralph was already halfway to dead. The most virulent of these diseases had already permeated his bloodstream and had begun turning his frontal lobe the consistency of a tomato left in the sun. It was *distempus shamblis*, Shambling Mound Distemper. But for right now, the important thing for you to notice is that Ralph inhaled a mote of cold-fused nuclear ragweed.)

He sneezed.

At which point the sound of the wheels receding on the gravel stopped, the unicorns whinnied wickedly, and Ralph opened his eyelids to see ten spiteful eyes on him.

"What do you think you're doing?" the driver asked after an extraordinarily long pause, for it had taken him a few moments to come to terms with the oddly-dressed young man half-hidden in the grass.

Ralph sat up and blithely twirled a piece of grass in his hand. "Hi. Could you give me directions? I'm looking for my cousin Cecil, who's around here somewhere. I really don't know where I am, and I —" Ralph coughed. "Well, I'm sure, man-to-man, you could tell me where to go." Ralph coughed again. "Because I know this isn't *really* a fairy tale. Let's level."

The driver stared.

"I spoke with Chessie," Ralph continued nervously. "The Duchess, I mean. She'd be fine with your giving me some directions, I'm sure."

He continued to stare. The unicorns tossed their horns in the air, equine (and male) beauty queens.

"You seem like a nice guy. What's your name?" Ralph tried lamely.

The driver cocked his head at an odd angle, and it took Ralph a few moments to realize that he was receiving some sort of instruction beamed into his head. Eventually the man spoke aloud: "About five-eight, slender, awkward looking . . . Under authority Ten-A or Ten-C? . . . Please confirm that stiletto is most appropriate. . . . Thank you." He looked straight at Ralph. "You are not permitted to be here," he announced severely, and dismounted.

"Could you maybe pretend we didn't meet, then?" Ralph asked, scrambling to his feet as the driver approached.

"No," he said. "This isn't your wish." He brandished a unicorn-horn stiletto.

"Does that mean I can't be part of it?"

The driver lunged at Ralph. Ralph, who until now could name dodging a bully's punch as his most violent encounter, was entirely unprepared.

He was caught flat on his feet, a condition which would, alas, make his death all the easier.

# CHAPTER XVI

The blade was poised to penetrate Ralph's chest at the center, the squishy part below his sternum. It would be an easy crossing for a stiletto, as any conscientious medical student can confirm — the blade would enter where there was no bone, cross through a layer of upper abdominal tissue and lacerate the inferior vena cava before puncturing liver and hitting vertebra. The question of whether it was so well-aimed as to slide between the joints in the bone and sever Ralph's spinal cord is moot, as unicorn horns are naturally coated with anticoagulant, and Ralph would have bled to death within minutes.

Ralph's salvation came from an unlikely source — the same fantastic allergen that had undone his camouflage. Even as he watched the stiletto jab toward him, he felt another tickle in his nose (or rather, significantly more than a tickle; imagine staring up at the sun, with the sun then picking up its skirts and entering your nostrils) and suddenly he sneezed explosively. He bathed the driver's knife-hand in mucus and was rocketed backward by the blow, landing atop the bunny thicket.

The briar was dense and brambly, and it would take Ralph a few seconds to extricate himself. The driver would have had ample opportunity, therefore, to finish his stilettowork . . . had the mote of cold-fused nuclear ragweed not had some mischief left. The particle, having evacuated Ralph's system, thereby found itself dripping from the man's collarbone. Once it neared his chest it swam toward his skin.

If you've never directly contacted a mote of cold-fused nuclear ragweed, it's difficult to conceive. It's painful enough on mucous or other non-feeling tissues, but directly on your skin — well, it's like a pinprick, only with a touch of the entire continent of Antarctica to it.

So now the driver was howling, and the unicorns were prancing around him, and it was causing such a ruckus that the occupant of the carriage finally opened her window to find out what was going on.

"Oh, hello!" Chessie said.

Ralph picked himself off the thicket and bowed slightly. "Hello, Duchess of Cheshire."

"Please. Call me Duchess."

"Okay, sure."

Chessie waited patiently.

"Duchess."

"Very good. Now tell me — would you like to ride in my carriage?"

Ralph glanced at the four menacingly braying unicorns and at the driver, convulsing on the ground beside his unicorn-horn stiletto. Then he took in the sharp-edged carriage and Chessie, whose expression was filled with an intensity that he couldn't quite attribute to good will. "I'm not sure I do, actually, if that's okay," he said. And then, as Chessie's expression darkened, "Why did he try to kill me?"

"I'm sure I don't know. Now, come on, up you go, into the carriage." She threw open the door.

"Are you a good duchess or a bad duchess?"

Chessie squinted. "You are such a weird little Yank, aren't you?"

"Where's Cecil?"

"Up, up! Up into the carriage."

By now the driver had managed to brush off the mote and most of Ralph's fluids, and had regained his feet. Stiletto in hand, he started forward.

Ralph accepted Chessie's gracious offer and entered the carriage. She ordered the driver to tend to the unicorns and slammed the door closed, locking it soundly.

The carriage was quite roomy. Chessie had a six-room suite, including entrance hall, powder room (where the duchess excused Ralph to go clean up), bedroom, volleyball court, kitchenette, and sitting room, which was complete with a tea tray and fresh pastries. The tea was served by two fairy attendants, who were quite handy for pouring, since by hovering they were able to maintain a steady stream even during the carriage's frequent jolts.

Once Ralph had returned from the powder room, he sipped his tea, holding the cup far away from him as the vehicle lurched and bumped. It tasted like stones. The drink could very well be poisoned, he realized, but if Chessie really were a sorceress now, and really intended to kill him, she could have already done so in any number of ways. Even if the tea were poisoned, Ralph figured, it was better to die by hot beverage than by unicorn horn. Ralph drew the line at sampling the pastries, however: He saw one crawl forward an inch as he placed his teacup back on its saucer.

"This is a very nice carriage," Ralph remarked, as politely as he was able under the circumstances.

"It's not exactly palatial, but it does in a pinch. The roads through this forest are narrow, so I couldn't bring my larger one."

"That's too bad," Ralph said commiseratively.

"Tell me, have you been enjoying yourself?"

"It's very nice here, yes," Ralph said. He picked up his teacup, saw it was empty, and put it back down.

"Where have you been so far?"

"Well, actually I've just arrived. I think you know that," Ralph said.

"Just arrived! Well, we'll have to show you *everything*. How exciting."

"Umm . . . I got magicked into this quest. You were there when I came in, not ten minutes ago."

Chessie did nothing to mask her boredom at this tack.

"Thought I'd point that out. See if you had anything to say."

"I'm sure that's very good of you," Chessie said. She transferred two sugar cubes to her teacup. "A stirrer, Vermillion."

One of the fairies, who was indeed said color, produced a much smaller fairy, who stood stock-still as Chessie inserted him into her tea and swished about. When the stirrer emerged his face was bright red, and Ralph watched his little mouth form a pain-struck O as he was returned to a drawer.

"Oh dear, I forgot to offer," Chessie said. "Do you take sugar?"

Ralph shook his head.

"This must all be so strange for you," Chessie said.

Ralph nodded. They rode along in silence. Evidently no elaboration was coming. "Where are we heading?" Ralph finally asked.

"Oh! Sorry. We're heading to the capital of my kingdom. It's amazingly beautiful. There are all sorts of charming courtyards and little old shops — you know, spelled o-l-d-e s-h-o-p-p-e-s. You'll love it there. It's got all those things foreigners go crazy for."

"Am I going to live there?"

"For a time, if you like."

"Where is Cecil?"

"Rather far away, I'm afraid."

"Do you think you could let me out of the carriage, and I won't bother you anymore?"

Chessie flounced back on her antique sofa and threw her hands around a knee. "Honestly, Ralph, that seems a trifle rude. I haven't even said what I intend to do to you yet."

Not sure how to respond, Ralph looked out the window. They had entered a velvety forest; the woods drew close to the road. "Where are we now?" he asked.

Chessie glanced dismissively at their surroundings. "Chumpy Forest. Which means we're halfway to your beheading!"

# CHAPTER XVII

Ralph had already nodded civilly before Chessie's words struck him. He gave a strangled little noise.

She fondled a curl, then returned her focus to the passing forest. "It's a lot of work for an evil duchess to manage her kingdom. The overtaxing of peasantry, the foiling of marriage plots, the hiding away of prophesied jewelry — these all take a lot of effort. With this Cecil hero skirmishing with my forces and trying to unionize the fairies, I've been beside myself. Judging by your outlandish clothing and your acquaintance with this Cecil, I assume you are his cohort. Therefore I have determined that you must die."

"Okay. I can see your point, really I can. But I don't want to be killed at all. And a little while ago you said it was okay if I was here."

Chessie nodded sadly and parted her ruby lips to down the rest of her tea. Then her eyes suddenly lit up. She put the cup down and said, brightly, "I suppose we could kill you earlier rather than later, if you'd prefer!"

"No, that's all right. Thanks, though."

"You see, Ralph, I'm very sorry about all of this, but I can't brook having a hero plotting against me in my own duchy, threatening to overthrow my rule, monomaniacal as it may be. Cecil fights a dirty guerrilla war, picking at me from my forests, freeing fairies, and then scampering back to cover.

What better way to finally draw him into the open than to publicly behead his own cousin? It also happens to be an efficient way of dealing with your intrusion."

"Maybe we could have a fake beheading," Ralph suggested.

"What, an artificial head rolling into the basket? How would that work, do you think?" Chessie asked with genuine interest. "I'm not trying to insult your idea, I just want you to walk me through it."

"I don't know how you'd do it," Ralph said. "But I figure, well, if you have fairies in the carriage, and unicorns out front, then I bet you have whatever magic it takes to fake a beheading. It can't be too hard. Though I guess you have more experience with these sorts of things."

"I suppose I do," Chessie sniffed, suddenly remembering her position.

"How long do I have?" Ralph asked.

"Let me find out. Fuchsia!"

Fuchsia fluttered forward. Fairies don't generally wear clothing; Fuchsia was decidedly buxom but also a foot tall, pink, and winged, so Ralph found himself struck by a curious mix of feelings. He did his best to stare respectfully into the folds of the curtains. "Yes, mum?" Fuchsia asked.

"Where is Inexorable Pulse?"

"On break, mum."

In a flash, Chessie had Fuchsia on her lap, the little creature's neck squeezed between her thumb and forefinger. "I *need* the *time*."

"Yes, mum," Fuchsia croaked. Chessie released her, whereupon she flitted to the ceiling and coughed.

"*Now*," Chessie commanded. Fuchsia skittered out of the oil-paper window.

"Scads of fairies in this duchy, and these were the best I could find. Sweet creatures, but they can't predict a single need, and literally can't cook to save their lives. Those silly wings keep catching fire." Chessie stood and paced the carriage.

Fuchsia returned holding a nervous bespectacled fairy who turned a new color every time he grimaced. When the manacled sprite was delivered to Chessie's hands, he became a brilliant shade of blue, with an emerging flood of green at the front of his pants.

"Inexorable Pulse," Chessie intoned. "This is Ralph. He's asked the time. As he's about to be killed, you'll be doing him a special favor."

Inexorable Pulse pushed back his cuffs so they sat higher on his arms, and nudged his spectacles to the top of his nose. After ducking his head out the window and peering at the sun, he ducked back in and lost himself in his computations. He turned a brilliant shade of maroon. "It's two thirty-eight, mum, give or take forty minutes."

"Very good, Inexorable Pulse," Chessie said. She placed a steadying finger on his waist, slapped his legs, and watched him pinwheel. He let out a yelp as he spun, turning a myriad of colors while the sound strengthened into a scream. His little spectacles tinkled to the floor and shattered. Even though the colors of the torture were amazing — tie-dye on the spin cycle — Ralph dashed a hand out and stopped the spinning sprite. The fairy went limp and turned a shade of the palest yellow in his hand. One of his wings had ripped.

"You hurt him," Ralph said.

"I'm sure he's dying, the little fool. I'll hear none of it," Chessie snorted. "There are thousands more fairies. It's like mourning a sugar packet."

She poured cream into her tea, the silver stirrer ringing out against the porcelain. "And, by the way, you have twelve minutes to live. Well, probably eleven by now."

A beheading in the undetermined future — even when the head to be removed was his own — was something Ralph found himself capable of procrastinating out of his mind. But in eleven minutes! Once he had learned the precise timing of his demise, Ralph finally started to act sensibly. While Chessie was busy perfecting her tea, he dashed to his feet and tried the door.

It was still locked, of course.

Being unable to turn the knob seemed to Ralph the worst of all possible outcomes, but he didn't know the half of it. At least Chessie hadn't yet gotten around to planting a Copper-venom Spider on the underside of the handle. At least the Acid Asp draped over the threshold had fallen asleep. At least the lever to activate the trapdoor was out of her reach.

She cursed this last oversight as she regarded Ralph. Of course she remembered who he really was, though in the magic of the spell she had to obey my commands and couldn't let her performance reflect it. It seemed a shame to kill him. He was sweet, if addled and unromantic and entirely unsuited for questing.

Still, she had to make this work. Her nephew had asked for a simple wish, and she had a responsibility to buoy the dwindling supply of royal mystique. As the monarchs lost power in politics it became all the more important to exercise it in myth. The days of true enchantment were gone; she couldn't hope to compare to, say, the Russian czars before they got clobbered, but at least she could grant her own bloody nephew's greatest desire.

Wish-grantings had never been simple, logistically — the Royal Narratological Guild had a full-time staff of twenty who recorded and collated all the stories, and scores more who were in charge of getting all the necessary temporary employees in line. And they were expensive — five percent of British GDP was spent on extras and animal trainers and magicians and the like, though much of that was recouped in book and film royalties (sales of wish narratives being, incidentally, the origin of the very term "royalties"). Chessie couldn't very well have the first wish granted in eleven years put at risk by a young American who wasn't meant to be there.

No, it was unavoidable that Ralph should die — that was the long and the short of it. Preferably publicly, to get Cecil fired up, but if Ralph was going to keep causing this much trouble, a private execution would do.

I'd hoped not to have her perform any more magic in front of Ralph. Foreigners always tended to get unnerved when confronted by a good old Buckingham spell. But I figured that Ralph had already been subjected to unicorns and fairies, so what would some real wizardry matter? She raised her fingertips — she could have shot her arms to the sky, but one needn't be tawdry — and magically ripped away Ralph's shirt.

If it seems an odd move, I agree. In fact, it seems frankly predatory, in the TV-movie sense of the word. Chessie had that salacious image, after all. Famously caught cheating on her husband, always wearing skirts a little too short, dyeing her hair the color of tomato sauce, giving the image of having been fantasized about. She shouldn't go around ripping teenage boys' shirts off — it could easily be misconstrued. But regardless of what she should have done, this is precisely what she did.

Other narrators might fudge events to smooth over politics with their employers. But I'm a narrator with integrity.

Besides, it's not as though Chessie removed any other article of Ralph's clothing. Except his pants.

The shirt and pants danced in front of Ralph, then the shirt split cleanly and soundlessly, as if the fabric had been a pool of water through which Chessie had drawn an inky finger. Then Chessie magically bound the two halves over the struggling boy's wrists, and used the jeans to bind his ankles.

She rose to her full height (she was a tall duchess) and shoved him to the ground, this time with her own hand. He fell heavily and stared at her with wide eyes. Then she raised her palm, whereby a plank of wood removed itself from the carriage floor and placed itself over his torso. She lowered her palm, and he gasped as the plank warped over his chest and pinned him to the floor. He heaved against the restraint, but he couldn't budge it, nor could he slide out from beneath.

"Don't struggle!" Chessie snapped. She could sit through interminable royal processionals, endless knighting ceremonies, and prolonged state weddings, but death scenes made her crotchety. She called out for Ten P.M. Black.

A fairy emerged from a storage closet and flew into Chessie's outstretched hands. He was muscular for a fairy, and his color was a bruised purple. The edges of his wings glinted silver. When he laid his arms at his sides and clasped his wings, he made a fine approximation of an executioner's axe. Chessie hefted the fairy axe a couple of times. On each swing he beat his wings, adding speed to the slashes.

For practice, she cleaved the teapot neatly in two. It didn't shatter; it merely parted for the razor edge. The contents, however, spun out in a hot globe, scalding Fuchsia and Vermillion and the prone Inexorable Pulse. They gave fairy gasps and fled to the ceiling.

Ralph struggled, but each spasm only served to clamp the plank of wood down harder.

Chessie leaped about the carriage, swinging the axe. She cut loose great pennants of curtain that fluttered to the bumping floor; she sliced an unfortunate fairy guard in two on a backswing.

Meanwhile Ralph continued to struggle, and the plank continued to press down harder, until he could no longer breathe. His vision turned gray at the edges as he gasped against the floor. Soon he could see only the most colorful things in the room — the flashing silver of the axe, the wings of Vermillion and Fuchsia hovering near the window. Maybe it was his vision slushing as he passed out, but he saw them begin to beat their wings very oddly. Vermillion held Fuchsia's hand, but flapped twice as fast; they bobbed with the irregular pitch of their flight. He was lulled by the pattern as he fell into unconsciousness — red, red, pink, red, red, pink. Then he saw Fuchsia peer searchingly out the window. At the very moment that Chessie whipped her hair out of her eyes and approached Ralph with Ten P.M. Black held high, there was a great neighing chaos and the carriage came to a screeching halt before creaking, listing heavily to one side, and finally tumbling through open air.

# CHAPTER XVIII

As any aeronautical engineer will confirm, fairies do remarkably well in unicorn-drawn carriage crashes. Their strategy is simple: Keep to the center of the carriage and fly with equivalent speed against the rapidly decreasing velocity of the vehicle.

Prisoners magically trapped beneath planks of flooring do moderately well. The otherwise death-hastening wood serves like the lap restraint on a roller coaster.

Axe-wielding duchesses, however, make out substantially worse. And unfortunately, an axe-wielding duchess careening about a carriage is a problem for everyone.

The ceiling became the floor, then it was the ceiling again, and then it was back to being floor. Ralph, pinioned beneath his restraint, had a comparatively stable vantage point from which to catalog his repeated brushes with death. Ten P.M. Black whizzed before his face uncountable times. Ralph scrunched his eyes and waited to lose an arm or a nose, but his closest shave with the fairy axe resulted only in wisps of his hair joining the tumult.

Chessie clawed at him with her painted nails whenever the carriage's tumble thrust her close enough. She would near and then be hurled away, fairies and candles and cloven teapots beating around her.

The carriage eventually made its final bounce and came to rest on its side. Those fairies who were able to flew out immediately, and as their great thrashing flock rose into the air, Ralph realized there had been more of them in the carriage than he'd first thought. Fairy feather dusters, fairies whose wings had served as doilies, fairy platters, and fairy forks all swarmed from the wrecked carriage.

Ralph struggled against his restraint and gasped in pain. The wood was leaving deep abrasions on his chest, and he had begun to sniff his own blood. Then there was a heaving sound at the carriage's door (now its roof, incidentally), and the wood splintered as it was lifted off its hinges. When light flooded the suite of rooms, Ralph saw a figure he recognized silhouetted against the blue sky.

Cecil lowered himself into the carriage and set to work releasing Ralph from his bonds. The plank came away easily in Cecil's hands. "Thank you," Ralph said, before promptly plummeting to the bottom of the carriage. "Ouch," he concluded.

Cecil dropped to Ralph's side and boosted him to a bookshelf handhold. "We're not out of this yet," he said as he raised another gloved hand to push Ralph up to the door.

It hadn't occurred to Ralph to determine Chessie's whereabouts, and he realized his error as he emerged from the carriage and heard lightning bolts popping about his head. He rolled over the side, landing in a ravine. Cecil plopped next to him soon after, his knee landing on Ralph's chest and knocking Ralph's breath out for the third time in as many minutes.

There are some phenomena narrators consider difficult-to-near-impossible to describe for readers who haven't already had direct experience: childbirth, for example, or being flayed by dragonbreath. Similar is an aerial battle in which the two forces are a telegenic lightning-spouting duchess and a gaggle of fairies. Chessie's lightning didn't move in streaks but rather in spheres, globes of sizzling energy that engulfed anything careless enough to be flying within a few yards of their trajectory, then impacted the ground in dramatic explosions of light and soil and fairy parts. The fairies had numbers on their side, yes, but the sum potency of their offensive power was akin to a box of matches igniting. No matter what their volume, when foot-tall creatures battle an angry superduchess, the battle can only have one outcome.

Cecil unsheathed a wooden sword. "Fight me, not them!" he shouted.

Chessie paused in her lightning hurling long enough to scrutinize Cecil. "You hope to take on a duchess, boy?" she screeched.

"Do you refuse?" Cecil called.

Chessie replied by yelling at Ralph. "You," she howled, "are not supposed to be alive." And with that she hurled a lightning dart at his face.

Ralph cringed before what quickly became a searing heat, until Cecil flashed out with his sword and parried the sphere of light.

Chessie conjured a flaming shield to sizzle the half-dozen fairies who had thought to take advantage of her distraction. Charred, winged husks raining about him, Cecil yelled out again, "Do you yield?"

Chessie laughed and continued to incinerate fairies.

Cecil ordered the retreat.

He, Ralph, and the handful of surviving fairies fled to the cover of the trees.

# CHAPTER XIX

Maintaining decorum is essential to any royal's self-respect. It's one thing to engage in a little firefight on a country road, rising above the masses like a demigoddess, simultaneously showing off your figure and your magical talents. It's quite another to scrounge through the forest grubbing for little boys and fairies.

So when Cecil and Ralph plunged headlong into the woods, they were unaware that Chessie had turned her energies to summoning a new magical coach, one that wouldn't do anything so improper as be attacked and fall down a ravine.

That said, quivers of lightning bolts exploding around one's head tend to elevate one's fight-or-flight response. When Cecil and Ralph led the charge into the cover of the forest, it was with the gusto of children fleeing punishment.

"Run as fast as you can for two minutes," was Cecil's screamed order to his compatriots.

It wasn't a terribly sensible command, for a number of reasons. Among others: The remaining fairies were flying, not running; at that precise moment Chessie was picking mud from beneath a French-manicured nail; fairy watches all ran at different speeds; and two minutes of fleeing would lead most of them out of Chumpy Wood and into the Water-Warlock Dragonhunter-Damselfly Coven.

Of course, Ralph wasn't aware of any of these pitfalls. All he knew was that Cecil barked his command very forcefully, and having one's life nearly taken by a unicorn stiletto, a fairy axe, and a ball of lightning in rapid succession makes one highly susceptible to the suggestions of anyone who isn't confirmedly intent on one's own death.

So Ralph ran like he hadn't run since fleeing Johnny Keenes in fifth grade. He ran like he hadn't run since the New Jersey GameCon Festival was giving away free *Campaign Quixotica* demos. In short, he ran like he was fleeing a witchy duchess.

Trees whizzed by. The ground was alternatingly firm, soft, wet, and dry, but he never felt it. He kept seeing pulsing lights, but was unsure whether they were from Chessie's lightning, some local ambient magic, or the blood pounding through his veins. He burst through spiderwebs and giant lichen. He ran heedlessly through a nest of Invidious Centipedes (thankfully the non-electric kind), and easily outran the centipede guard dispatched to prevent him from squashing through the second nest, which he promptly did. He shook centipede juice from his shoes, then jumped a lava pit and splashed through a puddle of Gnomefreeze, which would definitely hurt later. He ran until he was a good hundred feet deep into the Water-Warlock Dragonhunter-Damselfly Coven.

He stopped short, not because he spotted a Water-Warlock or a Dragonhunter-Damselfly (though there were plenty about), but because his lungs felt gashed. He bent over and heaved in air. It was then that he noticed the ground. Or rather, noticed that there wasn't really any. There were only wiggly larvae, each no bigger than a fingertip. The grubs blindly thrashed about each other, and about the soles of Ralph's sneakers. He shook off the larvae that had climbed onto his socks, and started walking in place, listening to the squishing sounds until he could make up his mind what to do.

Paths led in two directions:

To the right, the larvae thickened in quantity, forming dunes and drifts to the side of the trail. Distantly he could spy the cheerful colors of damselfly wings.

To the left, the grubs gave way to clear, rocky ground. He could glimpse at the turn of the path, however, a loose length of dirty cloth flapping eerily at the entrance to a cave. From far down the path came muted howls and the snapping of bones.

He glanced back the way he came. Chessie was undoubtedly still hunting him down. What should Ralph do?

If he should head down the safer (if gross) Dragonhunter-Damselfly Path, turn to page CV.

If he should investigate the Cave of the Water-Warlocks, turn to page CVI.

Ralph had never been particularly squeamish about bugs. And he figured a known danger was better than one ominous and unimaginable. So he decided to head down the Dragonhunter-Damselfly Path.

A potentially offensive note: Here you are, with a chance to finally find out what a Water-Warlock is, and you choose to read about damselflies.

Your *cat* catches damselflies.

But I'm being unkind. Especially since you'll soon see that the path you chose for Ralph is actually far more perilous. Honestly, I'm not a prudish narrator — I hope you know that — but going into what happened to him would require more delicate use of language than I'm capable of. Bear in mind that Ralph wasn't wearing a shirt or pants, and that his skin tone happened to be the same color as a damselfly female in estrus, and that the particular Dragonhunter-Damselflies you've decided to force Ralph to contend with are eight-foot-long males with poor vision, as I quote from *National Geographic* (April 2006):

> 88 to 100 percent of all females had holes in their heads, caused by a male's iron hold. The aptly named dragonhunter (*Hagenius brevistylus*) earned the dubious distinction of inflicting more severe damage than any other dragonfly: The spines of his appendages gouged the female's eyes, punctured and split her exoskeleton, and pierced her head, so that a "maximally damaged" female had as many as six holes of varying sizes punched in her head.

THE END

Ralph decided that increasing quantities of larvae could only mean bad news, and headed instead for the Cave of the Water-Warlocks. He figured he'd only get the chance to be in Cecil's wish once, and who wouldn't be curious to find out what a Water-Warlock looks like? Sure, he might brush with death, would probably end up strapped on some Warlock Gurney and experimented on, but he'd undoubtedly find a clever yet self-effacing means to outsmart his foes.

Ralph crept into the forbidding cave and surprised the Water-Warlocks precisely as they were sitting down for sausages and ale. Since it had been a rainy spring, they had plenty of grog to mix from their distillery (the distant howling he had heard at the crossroads was escaping steam, the crunching the settling of giant grog barrels), and were delighted to invite Ralph to join them. They were even more delighted, afterward, to point Ralph toward Cecil's base camp with their watery, warlocky fingers.

# CHAPTER XIX (CONTINUED)

It's a very sensible decision for fairies to live in trees. Any creature who flies should consider it — you're safe from land predators, you have a good view of the surrounding countryside, and don't underestimate those consistently breezy evenings. For obscure reasons known only to the race, however, fairies prefer to live *between* trees. Their houses are constructed of four different varieties of lumber and carefully suspended between trunks by lengths of Invidious Centipede silk. These tree-homes are lovely to look at, but so intricate that fairies spend almost all of their waking hours building and maintaining and getting lost in them. Which is a shame, really, since that leaves them so much less time for gamboling about meadows, visiting wishing wells, leaving money in return for teeth, and such.

The fairy village, normally a setting of great cheer, was almost silent as Ralph passed through on his way to Cecil's camp. The only sound he heard was the mewing of orphaned fairy young.

Ralph, for his part, couldn't have been less concerned with the sociology of fairy tree houses, or, frankly, the horrible events that had led to the piteous crying. He shambled through the forest, willing himself to ignore the centipede juice that had dried on his ankles like lacquer. He was also, now that the adrenaline of his flight from Chessie was fading, concerned that this royal wish-quest was going to lead to his rapid demise.

He checked his phone again, and found he still had no reception. Though — yes — at some point there had been enough that his emergency message to Beatrice and Daphne had been sent.

Adventure was well and fine, he decided, when there was a way to break away at any time. Video games could be powered off, after all, which is why their errand missions were more pleasure than drudgery. He could think of nothing better, right then, than shutting this particular quest down and sitting at his New Jersey kitchen table, leafing through Sunday advertising inserts or peeling string cheese.

He wished he'd had a chance to talk more to Cecil before he'd gotten lost, or (ideally) never been separated from him at all. He knew he could count on Cecil to plot with him how to escape. They would build a device to send a signal to the outside world, perhaps. All it would take, Ralph decided, was a sufficient power source and a GSM-compliant device with a transmitter that could be jiggered for alternative power sources and could command enough bandwidth —

What he wanted most, he suddenly realized, was not to be alone anymore.

Ralph crept between the house-festooned trees, stopping every few feet to listen for friends or predators. For a long time there was nothing but his own footsteps on pine needles. As the day dipped toward twilight, his heart sank. He didn't relish spending the night in an unfamiliar wood in an unfamiliar world, hunted by a now-unfortunately-unfamiliar duchess. Thankfully, though, he eventually heard a smattering of tinkling sopranos and one recognizable baritone.

He found Cecil conferring with the surviving fairies around a campfire. "Ralph!" Cecil said, extending a hand. "Thank God."

Ralph said hello back, though it seemed a ridiculously normal thing to say before five ashen-faced fairies and a hero dressed in a fashion-forward leather jerkin. Ralph stood back, arms outstretched, and waited for Cecil's flood of queries.

But Cecil seemed as calm as when he'd picked Ralph up at the train station. He introduced the fairies — among the survivors were Vermillion and Fuchsia, whose arm was in a sling, making it doubly hard for Ralph not to stare at her bosom. Inexorable Pulse, it turned out, had perished beneath a carriage wheel. He was mourned, and three other fairies were introduced, their names too rapidly announced for Ralph to catch. They were a size larger than Vermillion and Fuchsia, and significantly uglier.

"Wild fairies," Cecil explained after seeing Ralph's focus, "are natural stock, not bred into lines. They're the domestic shorthairs of the fairy world."

"Huh, fascinating," Ralph said. "So you're buying into all this?"

The fairies stared at the crazy human in boxer shorts.

Cecil laid a firm hand on Ralph's back and guided him out of the clearing. They stood under a tree house in the next clearing over. Cecil accidentally bumped it, and set it spinning like a piñata. "What do you think you're doing?" he asked, his meaty breath coming over Ralph in waves. (Cecil hadn't, Ralph quickly realized, packed his toiletries after all.)

"You're mad at *me*? You're sitting in a forest with *fairies*."

"Watch your tone. They have good ears."

"They're not real. All this is made up to fulfill your wish."

"I hear what you're saying, man, I do, but they seem plenty real to me. Tell me those tears they cry aren't *real*. So leave off."

"What's gotten into you? Chessie tried to kill us, and you're playing it off like 'no big deal, all in a day's work for a hero!' We have to get out of here. We die, and we're *dead*. And I've come across a good thirty ways to die so far."

Ralph was shocked to see tears standing in Cecil's eyes. "Look," Cecil said, "if you're not going to be into this, lie low and keep out of the way. This is my wish, the only one I'm ever going to get, and it's *extremely realistic*, and I'm totally into it. So I don't need you to go poking holes in the best thing that's ever happened to me."

"Oh," Ralph said quietly.

Cecil leaned his sword against a tree, sniffed, and dabbed his eye with a leather sleeve. "Now I feel like a moron," he said, his voice cracking.

"Don't feel like a moron," Ralph said. "You're right, this is pretty fantastic."

"Have you noticed my cool new threads?" Cecil asked.

"Yeah, it's like Runway Robin Hood," Ralph said. "And are you bigger? You look jacked, man."

Cecil looked at his arm and shrugged. "Yeah, the fairies have some crazy ambrosia — it's like the highest-protein drink you could imagine. And don't worry about the clothes — I'll hook you up with some in a minute."

"Rescue any damsels?" Ralph asked.

"I would, if I came across any. But I haven't met a single one. It's like Chessie didn't cast any hot women."

Ralph laughed. "I guess she doesn't want the competition."

"Come on, let's go," Cecil said. "I'm going to properly introduce you to the fairies, and you're going to stop being a jerk about all of this."

# CHAPTER XX

Once he was dressed and introduced and applauded, Ralph found a space of log next to Prestidigitator, a stout fairy clad in moon-emblazoned blue robes and a floppy hat. From nowhere she announced, in an almost inaudibly high-pitched voice, "Fairy husbandry has been going on for centuries. City-folk *breed* us."

"It's nothing more than fairy slavery," Cecil spat.

"Even worse," said Fuchsia. Ralph dutifully concentrated on her hairline as she spoke. "Because most of us are used as objects."

"Ralph understands slavery, as an American," Cecil said. "Maybe he can explain how people think they can do something like that. That can be your role in the team: You'll explain things. We'll call you Explainer."

"Can we consider other options?" Ralph asked.

"Recently the city dwellers have developed fairy farms," Cecil said darkly, "which have resulted in a massive burst of production. Fairies live off the morning dew, so they don't have to be fed. There's virtually no cost to raising them. So that means fairies are cheaper than any animals or building materials. In the cities there are houses built of fairies, fairy-wing writing tablets, easy-care fairy houseplants. It's gotten outrageous. And do you know who's behind it all?"

"Yes! It's Ch —"

"Chessie," Cecil continued unabated. "She pretends to care about the people, but she's just another blue blood, siphoning everything she can from the powerless. She's making money off fairy frailty!" Cecil paced around the campfire. "I've been trying to do what I can, but she's put a bounty on my head. I've nearly been killed at least a dozen times."

"I'm sorry."

Cecil nodded proudly. "In only two weeks, I've become an underground hero. The peasantry has bestowed on me any number of magical items — ancient swords, fire wands, some really brilliant armor — but I still don't stand a chance in open rebellion. So I've fled here to Chumpy Forest. The Dragonhunter-Damselflies keep the royal militia away, and this is also the largest surviving population of wild fairies."

"*Was* the largest surviving population," Forest Keeper added glumly, "until today."

"I'm trying to raise an army. Admittedly, today we took a huge hit — though at least now we have you to aid us, Explainer." He clasped Ralph's hand. "Can we count on you?"

"Of course. Tell me what you need. But first — how long have you been here?"

"It hasn't been more than a few hours since we ran from Chessie, if that's what you mean."

"No, I mean 'here,' here. In your wish."

Cecil scratched his shoulder in irritation. "I don't see why we need to get into all this inconsequential stuff while zillions of fairies are suffering." The fairies nodded grimly.

"I . . . okay, fine." Ralph crossed his arms.

Cecil shrugged. "Jolly good." He clapped his hands and turned to the rest of the fairies. "Okay, let's get on with the specifics. We're down to five of us, since Fuchsia needs to stay here and care for the orphans. I'm going to take the bulk of the remaining fairies, and we're going to do our best to band up any others we come across against the royal oppression. That leaves Explainer and Prestidigitator as our strike squad."

"I can make sparkles," Prestidigitator offered.

Cecil unrolled a map that had been silk-screened on a fairy wing. The fairies blanched, but Cecil blithely pointed to various locations printed on the veined membrane. "Now, here's the capital, where the river divides. I'll be approaching by the most direct route, along the path that skirts the Water-Warlocks' cave."

Ralph nodded sagely. "Try the grog."

Cecil gestured to a distant point on the wing-map, at the crest of one of the fairy sinews. "Now, I need you and Prestidigitator to go here. It's the largest fairy farm in the realm. Tens of thousands of them. If you can find some way to release the poor souls and lead them to us, we have a decent chance of taking the capital. Now, I see you still have a watch. Does it work?"

Ralph looked down at his calculator watch, a birthday present from his mother (he had already lost his second watch, which he had kept set to random time zones for the learning opportunity). Shockingly, the LCDs were still displaying. He nodded.

"Okay, good. I've got one, too."

Gasps from the fairies. This was indeed a divine turn of events.

"Chessie addresses the people at noon every fourth morning in front of her castle balcony. Which means that we need to have everything in place by tomorrow at eleven."

The fairies cheered. As there were only five of them, it was a sad, squeaky business.

Ralph thought for a moment. "Wouldn't it make more sense to have it all in place five mornings from now?" he proposed. "Then I'd have more time to get my part of the mission done."

The fairies' cheering stopped. They stared balefully at Ralph. Lame.

Cecil grimaced, stood, and addressed him. "As we have seen this afternoon, the perilous path we walk is not without peril. But that peril comes with great value. When the lives of an entire people have been devalued, only great loss of life can return that value. In summary, danger is not easy."

Ralph, trying to tie together the pieces of Cecil's speech, found the high-pitched fairy cheer was over long before he thought to join in. He watched Cecil as he prattled on. What fascinated Ralph was not that Cecil had matured much, but that he had managed to maintain his hipness in a fantastic land. His five different sweatshirts had been switched for five different doublets, a V-neck wool jerkin, and a leather shirt. His warrior sandals were carefully worn and frayed. His multiple silver necklaces had been replaced by an equal quantity of rawhide lengths. The crossbow and quiver on his back had brand names emblazoned on them. As the fairies cheered him and reached out to caress the fringes of his leather pants, he looked like he had finally become a reality show star. Even so, his weeks without drugstores and showers hadn't done wonders for his skin — his face was covered in acne of an almost volcanic intensity.

Cecil finished his speech on a suitably rousing note, climaxing with "Tomorrow, the capital!" When the fairies leaped into the air to cheer, Ralph leaped convincingly along with them. Then Cecil and his crew bid their farewells, with Fuchsia leaving to tend to the fairylings. Prestidigitator stood at Ralph's side, waiting for him to herald the commencement of the Great Fairy Rebellion.

"Um," Ralph said, his voice cracking, "gee. Okay!"

# CHAPTER XXI

As she had noted, Prestidigitator's greatest gift was for sparkling. Her array was more ferocious than what six-year-olds produce on Independence Day, but only slightly so.

As Ralph and Prestidigitator had to travel through the night to get to the fairy farm, her gift was more helpful than one might first imagine. Ralph held on to her ankles and brandished her like a torch, sparkles emerging from the roots of her teased hair. They passed out of the Chumpy Forest, through the Forty Streams, and around the circumference of the Cast-Iron Tower Jungle. At each segment, Prestidigitator's pyrotechnics cast a thin sphere of illumination over the near landscape.

Fairies make journeying very easy for their traveling companions. Prestidigitator was an adept scout, consumed no food, made an amiable (if dim-witted) conversation partner, and attracted all predatory attention away from Ralph. Indeed, she found herself very sought-after by the monsters they passed during the night.

Within a few paces of their starting out, she lost a toe to the chomp of a carnivorous fern. Then it was on to the onslaught of the Forty Streams, whose spherical, conical, and ellipsoid blasts of water regularly extinguished

Prestidigitator and left them sputtering in the dark. The Cast-Iron Tower Jungle would have been a respite if it weren't for the abnormally large (even by magical wish standards) bats roosting in the eaves. Prestidigitator lost a necklace and a good deal of self-respect within one of their slurpy mouths before Ralph could extract her. Regardless of the danger, she insisted on continuing to serve as torch.

By dawn they had reached the Arcadian Fields, which are famously serene, if one overlooks the mass subjugation of fairies occurring within. Ralph checked his watch as he and Prestidigitator approached: six o'clock. Since, per Cecil's advice, it would take at least four hours to reach the capital, that left one hour to free a few thousand fairies.

Once, when Ralph was much younger, a wanderlusting miniature schnauzer had jumped into his arms in a mall parking lot. Immediately, he had begged his parents to get him a dog. Mary had said "we'll see" in that tone she always took on when she had already made up her mind in the affirmative, and Steve had checked out an armful of pet care books from the library, bookmarked the pages about the pitfalls of dog ownership, and left them on Ralph's bed.

The next Sunday morning they piled into the family station wagon to visit one of the biggest breeders in the country, out on Long Island. Mrs. Shirley Wilbefore operated Schnauzer Ranch, an estate they approached along a winding road shaded by rows of manicured maples. After they got out of the car, Ralph rode his dad's shoulders to the white picket fence of the ranch's border. Fenced into its rolling meadows were hundreds of schnauzers. They were of all sizes, from the equine giant schnauzers to the rodent-class mini-minis. A dog sergeant barked, and twenty puppies leaped a hurdle in unison. Another pack of puppies growled and chewed one another's ears, closely tended by Shirley Wilbefore herself, who sported a crew cut and a nanny uniform.

The fairy farm was much the same way — except, of course, that there were no dogs, only fairies. And instead of cavorting merrily, they were penned up, one atop the other, in cages stacked thirty feet high and topped by spurts of black fire.

"It's terrible," Prestidigitator squeaked from their hiding place behind a bluff. "Look at them — they've gone mad! They're chewing each other's wings."

"Really? You can see that far?"

"Yes. Oh, Ralph! They're all gray and limp. It's like they're only half-alive."

"Maybe this batch is destined to be used as roofing tiles," Ralph suggested.

Prestidigitator nodded glumly.

"How many do you think there are?" Ralph asked.

Prestidigitator took a moment to count. "Forty thousand, two hundred."

"Presti! That's phenomenal."

She looked at him and blinked. "Not really. I meant that there's either forty thousand or two hundred. I can't tell."

"Oh," Ralph said. "Let's hope for forty thousand, then."

"Yes," Prestidigitator agreed solemnly. "Forty thousand freed fairies are better than two hundred freed fairies."

"Any guards?" Ralph asked.

"Hmm . . . there are some fairy guards. They've got yellow tartan wings, which makes them Acolytes of the Dokapi. That clan's always been infamous turncoats . . . if they turned on their own kind once, they should turn back without too much convincing. Give me a moment with them, and I can get them to come back to our side. Otherwise there's not much in the way of defenses. Except for the Hellacious Hellhounds."

"Are those very dangerous?"

"They're fine." Prestidigitator smiled unconvincingly.

"What's up, Presti?"

"Well, they're no bother as long as they don't eat you. And as long as you don't look at them. Well, specifically, if you don't look at the pentagram of silver fur on their backs. Because if you do, you're transported to a random layer of the Abyss."

"So let me get this straight: You can face their front and be eaten, or face their back and be sent to the Abyss?"

"Yep."

"How many of them are there?"

"Two. Well, at least I think there's two. It's hard to tell, because they're generally invisible."

Ralph gulped. "Anything else I should know?"

"Nope. Just don't get eaten, and don't look at them."

Ralph shifted in the mud. He and Prestidigitator were in the positions of those green plastic soldiers he never knew quite what to do with when he was little, the ones that can't stand up because they're on their bellies with their arms propped up in front. Mud was seeping into the front of the designer doublet he had borrowed from Cecil, and Ralph was aware he wasn't likely to come across a fresh one any time in the near future. "We need to get started," he said. "We only have an hour left."

Prestidigitator nodded solemnly. "So what's the plan?"

"Well, first we have to get over the fence."

"That's easy. We'll fly."

"I don't have wings."

"Then *I'll* fly."

"But that means I won't be there."

"Right."

They lay in silence.

"Can you zip over and open the gate?" Ralph asked.

"There doesn't seem to be a gate."

"Oh."

"What if *you* open a gate and then *I* fly over?" Prestidigitator proposed.

Ralph stared at her. Then she spoke again: "Scratch that. I think I see a blue-green wingspan on a clear body. Which means we've got a Quencher Fairy in one of the cages. I've got it! I'll fly over, convince the Dokapi Acolyte guards to turn coat, somehow free the Quencher, then get him to extinguish a piece of the fence-flame so you can climb over. That's when we'll free the rest."

Ralph envisioned snoozing under his comforter back home, reading a novel about an Orc King while hugging a pillow to his chest and sniffing to determine what his father was making for breakfast. Then he shook his head and nodded at the same time. "Sounds like the best plan we have."

"All you have to do," Prestidigitator concluded, "is distract the Hellacious Hellhounds while I fly over."

"Okay," Ralph said bravely. "I can do that."

"If they're interested in eating you, they'll yap at the fence. If they're not hungry, they'll be sensible enough to turn around, and you'll go to the Abyss. We have to pray that they're hungry."

"Okay," Ralph said.

"Let's do this!" Presti said. "Are you ready?"

Which is when Ralph slumped over, dead.

# CHAPTER XXII

You see, the *distempus shamblis* Ralph contracted when he first appeared in Cecil's wish had finally run its course. Shambling Mound Distemper isn't an unpleasant way to go, actually. The infection blooms first in the colon, and once it ruptures (a symptom Ralph would have noticed far earlier had he bothered to eat anything recently), the microbe scampers up and down the digestive tract, leaving little piles of mystical messiness until one is so clogged that one has no option but to expire. The supernatural microbe executes all of this with administration of localized anesthesia, which allows for an oblivion of bodily functions. As I said, it's a most pleasant way to die, if, of course, one must die at all.

Prestidigitator had already raced into the sky by the time Ralph died. Looking down, she was dismayed to observe that Ralph had decided to nap right in the middle of their plan. She returned, saw the greenness of Ralph's corpse, and immediately figured out what had happened. She may not have been overly intelligent, but she had far more experience with Shambling Mound Distemper than you or I.

She considered carrying on with the plan. A dead Ralph would distract the Hellacious Hellhounds just as well as a live one. And though she was tenderhearted, she would have done whatever it took to free thousands of her brethren. But what stopped her was that she realized her role in the operation hinged on Ralph's being alive — what was the point of quenching a flaming fence, if there was no Ralph to climb over it? So she returned to Ralph's side, doing her best to blot out the infernal barking of the hounds.

At this point Prestidigitator's limited capacity for planning had run its limits. She was distraught: Ralph was dead, she was miserable to see so many of her kind in cages, and she was finding it very taxing to ignore the baying of the hounds. So she cried. Her sobbing formed a great fountain of tears and sparkles, a mixed deluge that alternately singed and bathed Ralph's still face.

Prestidigitator cried and cried, until finally one especially large and dramatic tear slid down her face and dropped onto the crease of Ralph's lips, the very spot where a sparkle from her flaming mane soon fell.

He remained dead.

She kept on crying.

Until something remarkable happened. You will be amazed to know that Ralph came back to life.

Seeing Ralph sit up and embrace Prestidigitator, we could be tempted to speculate that her compassion, her genuine sorrow at the loss of her new friend, brought him back to life. But this would be overly sentimental and beneath us. As my friend the pudding-maker often says, the proof is in the narration.

"I'm not dead? What, do people not die here?" Ralph asked Prestidigitator, after coughing up a small mound of refuse.

"Only by magic," the fairy remembered.

And that was the truth. In a wish, when one is pursuing one's greatest desires, one isn't killed by microbes. One is killed by monsters. That's what makes it so great.

# CHAPTER XXIII

Ralph's rapid death and rebirth seemed an occasion for tears and introspection. The monsters at the fence, however, allowed for no such luxury.

Seeing him stand, the Hellhounds increased their baying. Their ferocious howling brought all the Dokapi Acolyte guards to the fence, where they chattered angry words at one another and trained their fairy blowguns on Ralph and Prestidigitator.

"I'm going to admit we've lost the element of surprise," Ralph observed as he and Prestidigitator sat in the mud and watched the evil forces lift the Quencher and break him in half right before their eyes.

"Yup," she said.

"You'd think whoever built this farm would have put in a gate, so that in a case like this the guards could come destroy us."

"Oh, Hellacious Hellhounds can pass through physical objects. And the Acolytes of the Dokapi are great high-fliers."

"So why aren't they coming after us?"

"I suspect we're not important enough," Prestidigitator said.

"That hurts more than dying did," Ralph said.

\*      \*      \*

They rejoined Cecil's party on the highway that approached the capital. Cecil's gleeful reaction on seeing them crest a nearby ridge quickly fell into despairing fury once he realized the limited extent of their Army of Liberation.

"What happened?" he barked.

"We weren't able to free the fairies," Ralph said. "But we did find these." He held out a family of bunnies he and Prestidigitator had been transporting in a picnic basket.

"You're not serious."

"They burp fire," Prestidigitator said indignantly.

"Fantastic."

"What have you got?" Ralph asked.

"You wanna see 'what I got'?" Cecil asked. He led Ralph to a rise and gestured at a horde of fairies neatly grouped into battalions. "Meanwhile, you've left thousands of fairies imprisoned and tortured, and suggested that we burp on our oppressors."

"Okay, fine, you did better that we did. Is that what you want to hear?"

"He had more help," Prestidigitator consoled, stroking one of Ralph's fingers with her little hands.

"These peasants look up to me as their hero, Ralph. How can I be their savior if I've left a whole bunch of them stuck in tiny cages?"

"Sorry," Ralph said.

"You're making me look so bad."

"Look! I said I was sorry. We only have an hour left. Let's get going!"

"There's no point. We've got an army of hundreds, not thousands. There's not going to be a glorious procession to take the capital anymore. Even with your stupid fire-burping bunnies."

"So you're going to send them all home?" Ralph asked.

"No, of course not. We'll see this through to the tragic end."

And so the greatest fairy army ever assembled continued its final march to the capital. For the greatest-ever fairy army, it wasn't extraordinarily impressive; they barely turned the heads of a herd of goats they passed. It would have been a much greater army, Ralph was very aware, if he had done his job right. He cursed himself as he and Prestidigitator took up rear guard positions.

Much like chickens, fairies can burst into flight for short stretches but don't make for very good long-haul aircraft. Cecil therefore ordered them to walk, but as they found it hard to restrain their exuberance they hopped into flight every few yards. The fairy march was, therefore, quite a sight. At any given moment, a handful of troops were popping into the air, a column of kernels marching across a hot stove top.

The capital, fortunately, wasn't far off. Cecil dropped back to Ralph's position to confer as they approached. "So," he said gloomily, never quite meeting Ralph's eyes, "the Oppressor speaks at noon, in the main square. She'll then slink back to her mansion. We'll wait until she's done with her address and then attack. We don't stand a chance of getting at her directly when all of her guards are around, but if we surprise her we can force her to retreat inside. You and me'll follow her into the mansion and lock her in. That's where we'll stop her once and for all."

"What about the fairies?"

"They'll have served their purpose."

"Oh. Okay." Ralph looked at all the fairies jubilantly marching before him, all ready to serve their purpose. "You know, Cecil," he said, "we could take this army of fairies to the other farms instead. With a force this large, we could easily liberate them all."

"Then the Duchess would be forewarned. No way."

"You wouldn't have to attack Chessie. The fairies could all go live in that Chumpy Forest."

"And what then?" Cecil scoffed. "We wait until the day that those with all the power decide to come track us down? We live lives half-lived, hoping for the miracle of acceptance and liberation to wander upon us? That's no way to carry on, Ralph. I'm not going to work within the system."

"I get it," Ralph said. "This is your chance to right some wrongs. And you're certainly doing it in the most dramatic way possible. But you're taking all these fairies down with you. The most powerful among them makes *sparkles*, Cecil. If Chessie has more than two guards, we don't have a chance —"

"Now, I think we can both agree that's an overstatement —"

"What I'm saying is, if those unicorns survived, if Chessie is present and alive and ready to oppose us, then we're already at even odds. And if we're heading to the *capital*, she's probably got hundreds of guards. All sorts of other monsters, too. Dragons and stuff."

Cecil spat. "Don't be ridiculous. There's no such thing as dragons."

Ralph looked at the pixie train before them. They were singing songs to the birds, passing notes when they thought their captains weren't looking, struggling to take wing under the weight of pencil swords.

"This seems to be a lot more about your own stardom than their welfare."

Cecil growled and cuffed Ralph on the shoulder. "Take that back! They want to save their kind. I'm giving them hope."

"You're ridiculous." Ralph said. "Turn them around right now."

"This is *my* wish," Cecil sniffed. "And if you can't take that, we don't want you with us. No one invited you along, big boy. Go home and work through math problems all night, or whatever you do for fun."

A number of fairies had surreptitiously worked themselves toward Ralph and Cecil, to eavesdrop better. Cecil maneuvered to block Ralph from their view. "Look," Cecil said, dropping his hand to his sword hilt. "I don't want to do this, but I can't have a dream-killer on my march. Their spirits are already so low. They don't need you making them feel hopeless."

"Okay, okay, I'll be quiet."

Sneaking a look around to confirm he was being watched, Cecil reared back and punched Ralph hard on the chin.

"What was that for?" Ralph yelled, suddenly on the ground and clutching his jaw.

"I will not tolerate anything but total success," Cecil called loudly. As he and Ralph had been marching at the end of the column, when Cecil quickened his pace to join his fairy underlings, Ralph found he was fully alone.

# CHAPTER XXIV

Alone, of course, but for the basket of fire-burping bunnies. They cooed and nattered from beneath their gingham blanket, their sweet gibbering only making Ralph feel all the more lame. He sat beneath a tree and spent half an hour feeling very sorry for himself.

His thoughts swirled in a depressed spiral, descending from his rejection by Cecil to the plight of the fairies, to his own death by Shambling Mound Distemper, to his inability to get out of this wish even if he wanted to, to his parents and his cats and his old friends, to the fact that he didn't get a MonoMyth job, to his getting teased way back for creating Sir Laurelbow, which was the same time his parents informed him about their now-very-sensible wish prohibition, which was what made him curious enough to get into all of this in the first place. He wondered, as he pondered the list of failures: Was he an eternal loser?

Ralph got himself sulky indeed. Even the bunnies' loving nibbles on the fringes of the jeans beneath his doublet did little to pluck his spirits. I wish I could tell you that he eventually came to some revelation that gave him the courage to go chase after the fairy army.

But he didn't. He just got tired of being gloomy.

Ralph gathered the bunnies (they had wandered from the basket to feast on the sweet grasses nearby), placed them in the basket, and bounded down the road toward the capital. Realizing that he looked silly skipping along with a basket of bunnies, he switched to a cooler gait, a sort of fist-clenched jog.

The castle was as castles are envisioned on film: turrets made more for moony princesses than for siege defense, a moat filled with alligators whose sole job seemed to be to open and close their jaws, grass-lined streets that might well have been cobbled with sugar cubes. In the center of it all rose a multicolored keep, with a neatly tiled rainbow roof.

Lacking the requisite army for forcible entry, Ralph joined the line of peasants filing across the lowered drawbridge. "Hello!" he called to the scrutinizing guards, and pointed obscurely at the basket of bunnies. They let him pass; apparently the combination of jeans and bunnies was too odd for a troublemaker.

Some of the homes were of older construction, Tudor buildings of wood and white plaster, but the remainder were made of fairies. Those constructed of dead fairies were bad enough — sprite legs and arms roped together to make beams, wings knitted to make roofs if they were opaque, windows if they were clear. Some of the buildings showed a perverse sense of humor — welcome mats composed of fairy feet, knockers fashioned from molded fairy fingernails. Others were of a simpler style, thousands of corpses roped together in clean lines.

But the buildings made of live fairies were worse. Since fairies take their nourishment from the ether in dew, a builder is saved the trouble of poisoning or beheading the lot if he works with them live. Roped or cemented in place, they stand still and stare out at the world, doing their best to keep their feet and wings out of one another's eyes.

Ralph kept to the shadows as he followed the crowds streaming toward the keep. Minarets rose from its confectionary walls like baubles of multi-hued glass. Ralph arrived at the central square just as the duchess had begun demonstrating, of all things, how to use an exercise ball.

She was wearing an oversized tiara and a long-trained lavender gown, which she had hitched up to mid-thigh in order to straddle a fairy-size sphere. In fact, Ralph craned to see, the ball was one obscenely fattened and de-winged fairy.

"As you can observe," Chessie said, her words echoed and amplified by a fairy microphone, "the exercise is easy to accomplish. Simply squeeze your legs" — the fairy turned purple as she demonstrated — "and as you feel more comfortable, intensify your pace. The sensation will spread all the way up your legs. Oneandtwoandthreeandfour" — the fairy turned deeper shades, culminating in indigo — "and then release." The fairy's color returned to normal as he deflated, pitching Chessie forward. She kicked him, and he took in his breath again and held it.

The crowd — a few hundred strong, many of them armored — cheered. Ralph scanned about for Cecil and the fairies, and was dismayed to find they were nowhere to be seen.

Have you ever lain upon the grass and thought yourself very much alone, staring at the shoots and blades for an age before seeing the many small creatures who have made a home there? A similar feeling came over Ralph as he stood in the courtyard. Gray fairies were camouflaged against the stone of the walls; red fairies had spread their wings along the fabric of the royal canopy. A popsicle vendor, Ralph noted, had a supply of wares that twitched and giggled. And that cloaked vendor, he was delighted to discover, was Cecil. He caught Ralph's eye, paused for a tense moment, and then winked.

Ralph made his way toward him, careful to avoid Chessie's line of sight, leaping from the shade of one large man to another, crossing them like so many stepping stones.

"Cecil," Ralph said as he discreetly sidled next to the vendor. "I'm so glad I've found you. Look, I'm sorry for what I said. This is your quest, go for it."

Cecil wavered a moment and then nodded. "Welcome back, man. Now, back into the shadows. You're drawing attention."

Ralph secreted himself in the chilly confines of Cecil's fairy-lined popsicle cart.

"We're set to begin," Cecil said, his lips just visible within his cowl.

"Excellent. Still the same plan?"

"Yep."

And then, though they were about to commence an intricate assault, Ralph and Cecil found themselves with surprisingly little to say to each other. Ralph still felt deeply ambivalent about Cecil's motivations, but his loneliness left him no choice but to join with him. Together they mutely followed Chessie's weight-loss propaganda, Cecil gripping the hilt of his concealed sword, Ralph gripping the wicker handle of his bunny basket.

"Where did you find those bunnies, by the way?" Cecil asked.

"Along the road."

"Just sitting there?"

"Yes."

"And the basket?"

"They were already in the basket."

"So these bunnies were sitting in a basket on the side of the road, waiting for you to pick them up?"

Ralph nodded.

Both leaned in to inspect the bunnies. They were snoozing in concentric circles, each bunny's snores only slightly ruffling the cottontail of the bunny before him. Then a bunny startled from her sleep and chittered at the sky, before quickly resuming her bunny slumber. Upon seeing her eyes, Cecil gasped and Ralph dropped the basket entirely. The rabbit's expression had been pure malevolence. And pure malevolence is a depth of evil rarely encountered; merely glimpsing it scars the cornea.

She was a perceptive bunny and, soon realizing the ruse was up, took action. First standing up on her hind legs, she scanned about, spat in Ralph's face, leaped up to eye level, and then dive-bombed Cecil's mock-fairy-popsicle cart.

"Fire-burping bunny" is perhaps a misnomer. Compared to their more noteworthy feats, the burps are but a charming idiosyncrasy.

The exploding rabbit flung dead and dying fairies into the air in a large-scale version of that snakes-in-a-can trick. The crowd became a jumble of flailing limbs covered with peasant blood and fairy-wing confetti. The remaining fairies camouflaged about the courtyard took to the air in a chorus of terrified squeaks.

Cecil found himself beyond the radius of the bunny's initial blast, and was only knocked off his feet. Ralph, however, was flung a hundred feet into the air, and survived the fall back to earth only by crushing a dozen fairies similarly launched. The basket of bunnies came skidding to rest on its side near him. Ralph staggered toward it through the slurry of wings and tiny limbs. The bunnies had emerged crawling with mechanical determination. At the exposed bottom of the basket was a note:

———

*XOXO,*
*Evil Duchess Chessie*

———

Another rabbit sprang into the air, this time exploding in a nova over the crowd's heads. Peasants and bits of peasants — a mixture of fairy and human varieties — went flying. A third bunny prepared to leap as Ralph held his ground against the stampeding mob. He grabbed the rabbit, shoved it back in the basket, and wrapped the gingham blanket snugly around the mass of them, their eyes glowing through the fabric.

The haze of vaporized fairy juice had thinned enough in the air that Ralph was able to locate Chessie. She had retreated to her mansion door, against which she had barricaded herself with a phalanx of armed guards. The orders she barked at the soldiers were lost under the tumult of the crowd.

Ralph dipped his hand into the basket, pulled out the first bunny he reached, cocked his arm, and launched it. It soared into the air, little rabbit limbs splayed, all four lucky feet pointing to the corners of the courtyard, and disappeared from view in the cluster of guards.

Nothing happened.

You see, bunnies will not tolerate being treated as hand grenades. They are creatures of free will — and no creature likes to blow itself up unless it has come to that conclusion on its own.

Ralph, unaware of the intricacies of bunny psychology, launched rabbit after rabbit.

Chessie realized Ralph's plotting and, screeching all the while, frantically fitted keys into the mansion door as the bunnies continued to rain. They impacted the walls, bounced off the steel helmets of the guards, came to rest in roof gutters. But still no explosions. Ralph was down to his last bunny when he saw Chessie finally wrestle the door open. Her escape route secured, she paused long enough to shoot a victory bolt of energy from her palm, aiming straight at the center of Ralph's chest.

But while her magical bolt was sizzling into existence, Ralph launched his final projectile. He lifted the last bunny by its struggling hind legs, swung it once around his head, and let go. It screeched as it flew on its collision course, for its rabbity intelligence afforded it all too much knowledge of its destiny. When it struck the bolt of energy, a fireball erupted that seared the nearby guards to the ground as easily as ladlefuls of pancake batter.

If the explosion of one fire-burping bunny was calamitous, a bunny chain reaction was Armageddon. The courtyard became so instantly hot that the heat turned into sound instead. By the time the mass of explosions was over, every living creature in the courtyard had been hurled to the ground and deafened. The armored guards were unable even to stand, the plates of their armor were quaking so intensely.

Ralph quickly shook off his daze, as only heroes are capable of doing. The front hall of the royal mansion had blown off, revealing singed parlor furniture and a checkered hallway leading into a labyrinthine interior, all of it burned to sepia tones.

Ralph dashed toward the smoldering entrance as a cloaked figure stole across the courtyard to intercept him.

# CHAPTER XXV

The figure stood in front of Ralph and pulled back his hood. It was Cecil.

The spectacular demise of the bunnies left the capital in silence, except for the buzzing of sound-flattened corpses. The surviving citizenry were passed out on the ground, dreaming of heavy metal concerts. Their livestock were licking their wounds and gazing nervously at their own bellies. The fairy militia had been all but obliterated. Ralph and Cecil stood before the smoking husk of the mansion entrance, steeling their courage.

They nodded at each other and started into the mansion, scrambling single file. Shortly after they disappeared down the long hallway, a third figure picked her way over the rubble and followed them, unnoticed.

In Cecil's loudly voiced opinion, the mansion contained far too many rooms. He went to great lengths to liberate the fairies in each chamber they came to, but he could only suffer through so much untying of fairy knots and ripping of wings free from varnish before he grew bored. After rescuing a set of personable fairy twins from a life of bookendry, Ralph suggested that Cecil consider delegating to them the more mundane chores of sprite liberation.

"I suppose so," Cecil conceded, then gave the twins a rundown of what the task involved.

As they proceeded through the palace, Ralph and Cecil were compelled to ignore the pleading cries of the fairies and weakly inform them that help was on the way; but, as Cecil pompously reminded Ralph, thus was war.

When choosing to decorate her home in resentful fairies, a drawback Chessie ought to have considered was the abundant information they would eventually provide about her whereabouts. Cecil learned from the exhortations of a duster that Chessie had ascended to the second floor. Once there, a polished-fairy mirror informed them that Chessie had the moment before fled yet higher.

As they proceeded through the palace, the supply of fairy informants began to dwindle, until they reached the seventh-floor ballroom, where they were shocked to find no fairies at all.

The entire level was a broad dance floor, lit on one side by a bay of windows. It was empty, and there were no stairs to a higher floor.

"Do you think she's here somewhere?" Ralph asked.

"I'd be surprised if she could climb this far up. She's a lazy aristocrat, after all," Cecil panted.

Ralph was sure he had something pertinent to say in return, but his words vanished entirely when the floor was suddenly illuminated in radiant colors.

A cloud had moved above, allowing sunlight to pass through a skylight and fill the ceiling with blues, yellows, and luminescent blacks. Ralph stared upward and saw they were standing beneath what seemed a giant stained-glass ceiling. But it was unlike any glass Ralph had ever known — the ceiling was a patchwork of colored gases, hovering at a uniform height and overlapping one another to create ever-shifting shades at their borders.

From the center of the multicolored cloud hung a wavering teal ladder of gas.

"Shall we?" Ralph asked.

"Not sure we have much other option," Cecil muttered.

It may be difficult to imagine how one climbs a gas ladder. But one must remember that a gas is just a solid whose atoms are spaced farther apart. Even as your narrator, I can't speak with total surety, but my theory is this: If you try really hard, you can be sure your atoms are in the right position to rest on the gas's atoms, and you can climb a gas ladder as you would a ladder of the more conventional variety. You just have to concentrate. Birds and moths know how to do it every time they fly. Trees know how, when they use the sky to pull themselves toward the sun. You were able to do it back when you were a baby growing into the air. You could do it still, if only the gas ladders around you were as obvious as this one.

And so Ralph and Cecil climbed into the floating colors.

When they broke through the gas layer, a film of color cascaded around them (crimson in Ralph's case, yellow and green in Cecil's).

Stepping directly onto gases requires an even higher level of concentration than does mounting a gas ladder, but when Ralph channeled his energies and tried a foot on the floor, the molecules held him. After Cecil stepped off next to him, they held each other's arms and experimented with how best to keep steady. As they hobbled toward the edges of the gas dome, every step was as if on a balloon. The effect of the light show was so stunning as to be deeply unpleasant. Ralph kneeled, put his head between his knees, and felt he might be sick.

They did a circuit around the vault of color, but could find no exit. The gas had even expanded to fill in their entrance hole. "I wonder what we should do now," Ralph said.

"I don't know," Cecil said crossly. "I wish she would show herself. I think I've done everything I was supposed to so far. I've been an admirable hero — why this rainbow chase?"

Ralph sat down on the gas. He realized it had been a long time since he had last rested. Sleepiness might be the wicked intention of all this, he suddenly realized — and surely it wasn't a good idea to nap in a room full of magical gases.

Cecil pressed his face against a pale yellow swath of the wall. "I think I see solid ground on the other side," he reported, "but I can't be sure. It's way too murky."

"We can't pass through, can we?" Ralph asked.

Cecil pushed with his fingertips, which sank into the misty edges of the gas and then stopped. "I don't think so." He blanched and put his hand over his mouth. "Ugh. I don't feel too good, man."

At which point Ralph temporarily lost concentration and, fittingly enough, passed gas. At first Cecil seemed not to notice, but then Ralph saw Cecil's nose twitch as a luminous mixture of fragrant sea green gas floated up from the seat of Ralph's jeans and diffused into the air.

The combination of embarrassment and pride Ralph always felt when he farted faded as he realized that he had farted in *color*. "It's in us," Ralph said, swiveling around. "The color is *in us*. We have to get out of here."

Cecil smirked. "Agreed."

Ralph joined Cecil at the wall, and together they pressed against it. But as their atoms continued to align with those of the gas, they couldn't break through.

# CHAPTER XXVI

Ralph was finding it harder and harder to think straight. A few minutes earlier, walking on gas had seemed most logical. Now he couldn't help but revert to his old everyday way of thinking, and it started to seem a trifle odd. Very odd, actually. He gave Cecil's arm a drunken punch. "Hey, bud. How are we even *standing?*"

And then, as soon as he said it, Ralph sank a foot into the gas. If he kept slipping, he realized, he would dash himself on the ballroom floor below.

"Crap," Cecil said, and tugged at Ralph, pulling him back up easily. "Of course you can stand on it. It's *colored.*"

"Oh yeah?" Ralph slurred. "Why does color mean you can stand? I don't think it's all that . . . clear." He giggled and, as soon as Cecil released him, sank away. Cecil grabbed his shoulders just before Ralph slipped through to his death.

This time Cecil had to really heave to get Ralph back up, as he too had begun to merge into the floor. "Man," Cecil said, "I can't keep hauling you up if I start sinking, too."

"Well, you can't let me fall through. I'll be a puddle on the ballroom floor. Splat splat splat." Ralph giggled again.

"Shut up! Let me think —"

"Wait, I have an idea!"

We'll never know what Ralph was thinking, because Cecil evidently had settled on his own idea first. He seized Ralph's left arm and leg, spun around twice, and let go.

And, with a giant squiff of multicolored air, Ralph whooshed through the wall and landed in the next room.

This chamber had a solid stone floor, which hurt keenly for a second and provided sweet relief afterward.

"It's a real room!" Ralph called. "Come on over."

Cecil grunted in affirmation and then tumbled forward. The tricky part was that he fell through the gas floor and stumbled through the wall at equal speed. Ralph saw only his chest emerge, right at floor level. It looked as though a bust of Cecil had been placed in the corner.

Ralph grasped Cecil's forearms and heaved. After a minute's struggle, he and Cecil lay gasping on the solid stone.

"That was ridiculous. A rainbow gas room was not where my wish was supposed to lead. If I am going to die, it should be at the hands of an evil giant, something like that, but not this weirdness," Cecil said.

They shared relief of being on a normal floor again, of breathing air that was as clear as air should be. Then Ralph looked closely at Cecil for the first time and laughed.

From chest down, Cecil was colored. Clothes, flesh, everything: a perfect rainbow.

Since there was nothing to do about this, Cecil and Ralph positioned themselves on either side of the only exit from the room, a plain door that had been fitted with a plaque:

*Evil Duchess's Secret Quarters* — **DO NOT ENTER**.

*(If You Must Enter, Please Extend Simple Courtesy of Knocking First.)*

They clasped hands. "Ready?" Ralph asked. Cecil nodded.

"So," Cecil said, drawing a big breath. Then he scratched his head. "Who's going to knock?"

Ralph pushed open the door.

The Duchess was reclining on a throne at the opposite end of a large chamber, watching the entranceway with a fiendish yet disengaged glare, to all appearances bored at an execution. She wore a sheer white gown with a gold circlet around her waist.

"I suppose you think you're going to stop me," she said. "All that heroic nonsense."

"Hello, Chessie," Cecil said.

"Duchess." Ralph bowed.

"Welcome to my Hall of Treasures." Chessie gestured about her. Ralph saw that the chamber's name was apt. Grand bookcases and curios cluttered the room and obscured the walls. They were filled to capacity with trinkets: porcelain elementals, stoneware ogres, matching griffon/ hippogriff salt and pepper shakers, all lined three or four deep on bowing shelves.

"You will release the fairies you've been cruelly breeding!" Cecil proclaimed, in a tone that would have been most threatening had his voice not cracked at the end.

Chessie waved a hand. "Got it. But you're ignoring all sorts of diplomatic procedures for these things."

"The people say the kings who ruled this land before you were kind and just. They took only the fairies they needed. They were sporting — but you have been despotic! I will not bargain with you."

"*Despotic*," Ralph thought. *Nice word.*

Though she maintained her scowl, Chessie was unable to hide a shine of glee at how seriously Cecil was taking his wish. "Commerce is commerce. My kingdom is doing fantastically well, thanks to those fairies." She sucked in her breath and stood up. "By 'diplomatic procedures,' I mean that you're not supposed to go off ranting yet. There are some common niceties to observe first."

"Oh." Cecil bit his lip, then spoke up again. "What are these niceties? How would I observe them? If I decided to, of course."

"Oh, a 'how do you do, how have you been' would have been nice. But beyond that, I have an offer to make that will render all of your bleating unnecessary."

"I'm listening."

"You would both make fantastic ornaments. Has anyone ever told you that?"

Cecil and Ralph shook their heads.

"I've been far too busy, you see. My collection hasn't been updated in some time. So that's the crux of it: I want to turn you into trinkets."

"That's your *offer*?" Ralph asked.

"No. And I will tolerate no more of your interference, Ralph. Let's fast-forward past all your classless wheedling. I am speaking to my gallant nephew only. Now, Cecil, it is my grave duty to inform you that your older sister, precious Beatrice, has been transformed into one of these trinkets."

"You're lying," Cecil said. But he obviously believed her. For that matter, Ralph believed her, too — Chessie had plenty of chances to be duplicitous before, yet had been remarkably up-front. This was the same woman, after all, who had so considerately given him advance notification of his own beheading.

"My offer is this: I allow you one guess as to which trinket is her. If you succeed, I will free her, you, Ralph, and all the fairies. Everyone! If you fail, however, you will become a figurine. Mother-of-pearl, I suspect."

Cecil unsheathed his sword. "And if I choose to fight?"

Chessie melted his sword so it bent over like a dandelion left in a jacket pocket. "Not a terrific idea."

Cecil slapped his wilted sword to the ground and nodded solemnly. "I accept your challenge."

Mustering up courage, Ralph put a restraining hand on Cecil's shoulder. "Now *Beatrice* is involved?" he asked. "What in the world does she have to do with this wish? Chessie, you don't sound like an evil duchess anymore. You sound like Chessie of Cheshire, Gert's sister."

"What's the bloody difference?" Cecil spat.

"I think Cecil's completed his quest, and I don't think you're being totally fair. I don't know what's going on right now, but it doesn't feel right. I repeat: What does *Beatrice* have to do with Cecil's wish? Why put her in jeopardy?"

"Beatrice was caught trying to sneak in," Chessie sniffed. "She's foregone all rights to complain about anything."

The text message. Beatrice had come to try to rescue him.

"So you've punished her by turning her into a trinket?"

"Ralph! I warned you — there's nothing holding me back from destroying you. There are centuries of wish precedents you know nothing about. I am in full rights to use an intruder as I see fit to raise the stakes of a wish. The Royal Narratological Guild gives full pre-authorization."

"Fine. I at least demand the same opportunity to rescue Beatrice, should Cecil fail."

"Absolutely not, lover boy. This scene is the culmination of billions of pounds sterling worth of narrative craft. I won't have you fiddling with the poetry of Cecil's wish."

"You allowed me in here. You said I could help."

"I did?" Chessie asked, surprised. She pointed a finger at Ralph, the manicured nail fizzing with blue magic, then some glimmer of her old earthly self flashed across her face and she shrugged and returned the finger to her lap. She scanned the thousands of trinkets and laughed. "Okay. Everyone gets a guess. But you risk the same penalty. And your statuette will be made out of dung."

"You don't need to do this for me," Cecil said to Ralph. For a moment he seemed to have lost his new heroic proportions, and Ralph couldn't resist slinging a comforting arm over his shoulder.

"I'll be honored to," Ralph said.

Cecil threw his arm off, and screwed his mottled face into proud disdain. "No! Seriously. *I'm* the hero here."

"I'll be happy not to interfere," Ralph said. "You just have to guess correctly."

Cecil stepped farther into the Hall of Treasures. The quantity of trinkets was boggling. Tens of thousands of pieces covered the chamber, stacked floor to ceiling, some as small as fingernails, some grazing the ceiling. Chessie reclined in her throne, her fingers gleefully hitched in her gold circlet.

Cecil began his slow circuit of the room.

To the typesetter's delight, I will excise from this narrative Cecil's lengthy choice-making. It lasted eleven and a half hours, long enough that Chessie lit the lanterns, baked and consumed a chicken with lemon glaze and porcini mushroom reduction, and invited Ralph to a game of Go Fish (which Chessie won, though Ralph suspected she cheated). The plot highlights of this half day include Cecil's near choice of a porcelain dryad, and his near calamity of knocking a sandstone seahorse from a shelf.

Throughout it all, Cecil returned to one piece over and over. It was placed high enough that, when he finally chose it, he had to mount a rolling ladder to retrieve it. Cecil gingerly cradled the treasure as he passed down the rungs, and when he reached the bottom revealed to Ralph and Chessie a jade princess with real human hair coming from her head and twisted into a necklace, hair that was the very color of Beatrice's.

# CHAPTER XXVII

Cecil proffered his choice to Chessie.

She closed the pendant in her fist and shook her head. "No, sorry, that was the long-dead Contessa di Hourata. Sad story, really. Some creep made her into a perfume at the age of fourteen. Most clearly younger than Beatrice."

And suddenly Cecil was gone, replaced by something shiny and no bigger than a child's palm. It clattered to the floor. Ralph gingerly picked it up and saw a portrait of Cecil carved onto an oyster shell.

"I'll summon Maudlin Décor to find a place for it later," Chessie said. She watched Ralph as he walked to the center of the room. "I'm intrigued now," she said. "Cecil's lost. It happens every once in a while, kids make a wish that doesn't pan out. Raises the heart rates of the rest of them. Technically I should call it a loss and let everyone go home." She looked up as I made a "keep rolling" gesture from the catwalks high above. "But you . . . I have no idea what will happen now!" She suddenly squealed. "What suspense! This is more fun than I've had in years, *years*."

Ralph choked. "You can't kill Cecil!" he yelled. "After your own son died. Is this to make things even? How can you be so heartless?"

"Go on, don't let me stop you: choose," Chessie prattled on. "Do you like the display of chess pieces? Maybe she's one of *those*. Let's go take a peek."

"Make it end. Where's the exit?"

"The only way out is to finish Cecil's wish. I'm giving you the same option I gave him. Find Beatrice."

Ralph had watched Cecil as he examined the room, of course, and had considered every option along with him. I am happy to inform you that Ralph's selection process was, therefore, blessedly brief. He brought over a wooden tiara, the perfect size for Beatrice's head.

Chessie took it into her hands and scrutinized it. Then she shook her head, and Ralph, too, was turned into a statue.

She wasn't lying about fashioning it out of dung. Since dung can't see, we're going to have to leave Ralph's head and watch the scene that follows from the ceiling, where I've been directing and recording. Come with me.

Ralph's incarnation was strangely lovely, a sort of scarab fashioned from some extinct animal's ossified poo. Chessie picked up Ralph's and Cecil's figurines, and from our perch above she looked quite regal, like a true queen arranging the gifts of visiting dignitaries.

She placed them on a low shelf, then was suddenly struck by a fit of passion. She let out a maniacal howl and lifted the trinkets over her head, preparing to smash them into the floor.

# CHAPTER XXVIII

Until, that is, she was interrupted by a high-pitched voice from the far side of the chamber.

"Stop!"

Chessie had no idea who this cheeky intruder was; all she saw was a little creature pertly rising into the air. We, however, recognize her as Prestidigitator. "Oh, *do* remove yourself," Chessie said. "I'm busy destroying the heroes."

Yes, Prestidigitator! She must have survived the bunny blast. She must have adventured through the keep to the highest floor. She must have passed through the ballroom and the rainbow gas chamber. She must have been in this hall the whole time, hiding above the door frame. She must have heard when Chessie said everyone present could have a guess, and she demanded hers.

Chessie held the trinkets high and considered dashing them against the floor, anyway. Then — for though she may have been diabolical, she was a stickler for rules — she lowered them. "Make it quick," she said. She didn't shrug this time; she licked her lips nervously. (Chessie knew what often happened to fairy-tale villains once a third guess was made.)

As the newcomer zipped to the center of the room, Chessie kept prattling. "Blast. This is truly annoying. I'm going to end up with yet another crystal fairy figurine, and I've already got thousands of fairies. Literally. *Thousands.* Bor-ing."

Prestidigitator didn't stop at the bookcases. She didn't stop at the curios. She didn't stop at the jewelry cabinets. No, she zipped right up to the Duchess herself.

"What do you think you're doing?" Chessie said.

"I'm saving the day," she squeaked.

"That's ridiculous. Even if you had a weapon, which I have divined you don't, I'm protected by spectral armor. Even if I hadn't already disarmed all enemy magic in this chamber, all you would be able to produce is a sparkle. I'm most curious as to how you're planning to 'save the day.'"

The little creature eased closer and closer until she was hovering in the air right before Chessie, her lips almost grazing her cheek.

"What are you doing?" Chessie said anxiously, uncertain how naughty this fairy might be.

Prestidigitator gripped Chessie's golden circlet. "I choose this belt thing," she said.

"Nonsense," Chessie said, drawing back. "I never said objects on my very *person* were permitted."

But Prestidigitator held on tight, flapping in front of Chessie as the duchess began to dash about the room. "I don't care," she tinkled. "It's in your chamber, and I choose this belt thing."

"But you *can't*," Chessie wailed.

But she could and she did. And no matter how evil a duchess might be, a fantastic promise is a fantastic promise.

Cecil and Ralph were suddenly sitting on the floor again, human and whole, smelling only faintly like the sea and poo, respectively. They glanced about dazedly, then shouted with relief. For Beatrice was sprawled on the floor between them. She was dazed but healthy, staring at them open-mouthed. In the transformation her jeans rode high enough on her legs to display the black butterflies she had inked on her ankle days before.

The golden circlet, which had sported an engraved representation of a sullen girl's face, an engraving that only the smallest eyes could see, had vanished entirely.

"Beatrice!" Cecil cried, hugging his sister.

She stared numbly at her brother, until she took in the Hall of Treasures and gasped. "Where *are* we?"

Prestidigitator gave Beatrice a hug. Shocked, she reacted with stiff limbs.

Chessie ripped the fairy from Beatrice, threw her to the ground, and kicked her in the ribs. The duchess stared down at the creature and chewed her nails.

"What are you —" Ralph yelled as he clutched the stunned little fairy to his chest.

"She's no fairy. No wish actor can interfere that way. It's against contract. Tell me, little demon, who are you?"

"It's Prestidigitator," Ralph said. "She's been with me the whole way." But, now that Chessie pointed it out, there was something odd about Presti. She was a lot bigger than he remembered. Her face seemed to sag, somehow, and her clothes seemed ill fitting. She looked more like a Prestidigitator blow-up doll than the real thing.

"*Daphne?*" Beatrice asked.

"Daphne!" Ralph said.

Presti reached around to a zipper at the back of her neck, removed her magical uniform, mechanical wings and all, and was revealed as Daphne. How she fit that puffy tutu into a fairy costume, no one will ever know.

"I can explain," she said, clutching her ribs and eyeing Chessie nervously. "Beatrice and I came to save Cecil, but right when we were going to get inside we got caught — well, Beatrice got caught — but I had worn my fairy costume with the wand that Mum got me from British Home Stores, so I guess when I entered the wish no one stopped me because it looked like I belonged here. I know the costume doesn't fit me perfectly and I'm very sorry but I just meant to help my brother, so don't kick me anymore. Please."

Chessie looked up at me meaningfully. "It's as you say," she barked. "The real Prestidigitator got blown up by a bunny not half an hour ago."

"No!" Ralph cried, wondering if that meant the actor who had played Prestidigitator had been blown up, too. "How do the special eff —"

But at that very moment his voice was drowned out by a massive rushing sound.

"What's that?" Daphne hiccupped, looking reproachfully at Chessie.

"The fairies," Chessie cursed. "You've done it, now, Cecil! All the fairies of the kingdom have been freed."

Have you ever seen a pigeon trying to roost and unable to find a spot to land? The sound he makes is a collection of desperate thrashings — his wings beat against the air, against the walls, against the ground, against each other. Imagine a million pigeons trying to do the same, accompanied by murderous screeching. Then put it all on the other side of thick walls. This is what was heard in Chessie's sanctum.

Chessie put her hand to her throat. "Millions of fairies. Billions of fairies. Coming to kill *me*."

She looked up at me pleadingly. "Make it stop, darling! Now!" But she knows what I can and cannot do.

"They can't get in, can they?" Daphne moaned into Ralph's chest.

Chessie screeched. "Does anyone have a cell signal?"

Beatrice and Ralph pulled out their cell phones and shook their heads. "Oh, don't worry about *yourself*, dear," Chessie snapped to Daphne. "They'll love you. You're practically half fairy, yourself."

The stones of the wall appeared to breathe against one another. Then one was knocked out and fell to the ground. The daylight creeping through the resulting hole was fettered by the horde of fairies outside.

Chessie put down her wand and gestured for the others to surround her. Her manic demeanor dropped away; suddenly she was no longer Chessie the evil duchess, but the mortal Ralph remembered from the Battersby grounds. "Okay, listen up, children."

Cowed by Chessie's change in manner, they obeyed.

"Look, Cecil," Chessie said rapidly. Her eyes darted between her nephew and the growing hole in the wall. A fairy leg could now be seen, kicking about and trying to gain a foothold. "I granted your wish. I think I've done a bang-up job, actually. You've freed all these fairies, and they'll glorify you forever — and that has been the *real* point of all this, hasn't it?"

"Of course not —" Cecil started.

"No time. Argue later, dear. But I planned only up to this point. Honestly, what's supposed to happen now is that we all vanish away once your wish is completed. You go back to your ordinary life changed and broadened, and la-la, all's perfect. But something's gone wrong. Cecil failed, and Daphne succeeded, but this wasn't supposed to be her wish. There's too many fairies. I can't *believe* this is happening again."

The walls started to buckle, and Daphne screamed.

"Again?" Ralph asked.

"Enough!" Chessie said. "Listen to me, Daphne and Beatrice. The only way out of this will be another wish. Anyone who truly loves Cecil can wish to save him — and save all of us in the process. But I'll warn you — I thought we were orchestrating Cecil's wish on the fly, but if one of you wishes us out of this, it will be your only wish, and it will be truly spontaneous. The narrator won't be able to guarantee anyone's safety, even less than he's been able to here. Do you understand? This is no longer a game."

"I was turned into poo!" Ralph said. "This was *never* a game!"

Daphne stopped crying long enough to nod at Chessie. She wiped her nose, then started wailing all the louder when a chunk of plaster plummeted from the ceiling and sprayed shards about her.

"Now! One of you wish!" Chessie said.

"I want my Mummy and Daddy! Can't we go home?" Daphne cried.

"No!"

"You can't be serious." Cecil said. "Of all the irresponsible adults I've ever known, you —"

"Shut up. We're done with you."

"You're going to kill us so we learn a lesson?"

Chessie sniffed. "The killing part was unplanned."

Cecil rolled his eyes.

"I'm *teleporting you away from your doom!* Do you want to keep trying my patience?"

"Just get on with it," Ralph urged.

"Beatrice, make the wish!" Cecil said.

"I . . . I was going to wish for something else. I already had something in mind."

"I can't believe this. Selfish until the end."

"IwishtosavemyselfandCecilandRalphandChessieand —" Daphne said.

Chessie released her breath. "I do solemnly grant thee thy wish, dreaming, in accordance with the fine tradition of Royal wish-granting, that you find thy greatest desire, and in so doing come to know thyself." Chessie huddled them all together.

"Wait, one thing," Ralph said. "She didn't mention Beatrice by name, does that matter?"

"Enough!" Chessie said crossly. "Daft boy. I will hear no more from the geek."

"That doesn't sound very nice —"

"I said enough!"

The ceiling began to quake and heave. "Oh my gosh, oh my gosh," Daphne said, wedging herself between Ralph's and Cecil's legs.

"Silence!" Chessie said. "I need to concentrate, you little goblin!"

"Please!" Ralph said, "What about Bea —"

But then, with a barked "sorry if this doesn't work out," the wish was granted. Chessie, Cecil, Daphne, and Ralph were all gone. Just in time, too, as right then the ceiling buckled and dropped its tons of rock to the floor.

And Beatrice? If the mass of stone hadn't killed her (which it did), the flurry of gemstone and porcelain shards from the shattered figurines would have. No, she was dead forty times over within a split second.

# CHAPTER XXIX

Yes, she really died. Just like that. Abandoned and squashed.

Quit your crying.

# BOOK III:
# DAPHNE'S WISH
## THE SNOW QUEEN

# CHAPTER XXX

Ralph awoke in a bed, which is a very appropriate place to do so. Someone had tucked stiff and fragrant cotton sheets tightly around him and cradled his head in scratchy embroidered pillows. A patchwork bear regarded him from the foot of his straw mattress. He rubbed his eyes and took in more of the room.

Doilies and dust, everywhere. Woodcut geese hung on the wall, suspended by lengths of raffia. A candle burned nearby, even though the daylight was strong enough to set the window curtains glowing. A hanging needlepoint proclaimed the RULES OF THE GENTLE HOME, which were too far away to read, and would have been massively boring even had he been able to.

"Hello?" Ralph called.

There was no answer, but in the quiet that followed he could hear footsteps from somewhere beyond the closed door.

He threw back the sheets; he wanted to be alert and standing whenever his host (or captor) came into the room.

Someone had changed his jeans and doublet for an old-fashioned nightshirt, stitched with flowers at the hem. Even with a geek's sense of fashion, he knew he looked pretty lame. He forgot about the nightshirt, though, when he swiveled and lowered his feet to the floor. He gasped in shock. The air may have been warm, the window sunstruck, but the floor was icy.

Gritting his teeth against the cold, he tried to stand. His legs buckled under him.

He caught the edge of the mattress before he fell, and hurled himself back into bed, sinking deep into the thick sheets and prickly straw beneath.

The footsteps stopped at the other side of the door. His eyes darted as he watched the latch raise and release. He envisioned what kind of foul creature might barrel forth — a bugaboo with furry limbs and a beak, a human-sized lizard with curved yellow nails.

She had lost her hairstylist and cosmetic dermatologist, apparently, and was suddenly an old woman; nonetheless, it was Chessie. Her hair fell limply about her face, streaks of gray instead of her old frothy blond highlights; the skin beneath her eyes sagged. As she rubbed her hands down a simple dress she regarded Ralph with imperturbable eyes.

When she neared, Ralph saw her irises were remarkable — how had he never noticed them before? — a white-water blue that shone as if lit from the other side.

"My name is Regina," the woman said. Her voice was the same, but the accent was different. It was as if Ralph were meeting Chessie's twin, separated at birth and raised in the eighteenth-century countryside.

"Chessie, it's Ralph. What's going on? Daphne said she was going to rescue us, didn't she?"

The woman-who-increasingly-was-not-Chessie-at-all stared back.

"I'm sorry," Ralph said carefully. "You look like someone I knew."

"I haven't a clue what you're talking about."

Ralph muttered, not loud enough for her to hear: "I think you do."

"I suppose you'd like to know how you got here. I've been caring for you for a week," the woman said, in the babbling manner of fairy-tale exposition. "You had quite a nasty fall — I would suggest you not tax yourself. I will ask you no questions, and suggest you do the same of me, at least for the moment. To keep you from going crazy, and all that." She fixed those eyes on Ralph, and she liked something she saw there; her expression brightened. "Would you care for something to eat? I've been preparing pumpernickel toast daily since you arrived. It's wound up slop for the hogs every morning until now. I would love to bring some out."

Ralph put a hand to his stomach. He wondered: Was he hungry? As soon as he thought of it, he was famished. "Thank you. Some toast would be great," he said.

Regina left. Ralph scanned the room for any sort of weapon, but he had come up with nothing by the time she returned with a tray, holding a few hot slices of brown-black toast, a broad knife, and a ceramic jar of butter. She watched with pleasure as Ralph bit into a thick piece, steam rising over his face. "Where am I?" he asked once he had finished, trying to remain cool. Which was indeed a difficult thing to remain, tucked into an antique bed alongside a teddy bear.

"You're in my home. It's so rare that I have guests at all, that I must say I was so happy to come across you. You dropped from the sky, right over my coop. Fell right through the thatch and crushed my best-laying hen and four of her eggs."

"I fell from the sky? I killed a chicken?" asked Ralph, impressed despite himself. Wait until he posted *that* online.

"Yes," Regina said, winking. "I've known a few Water-Warlocks in my time. You undoubtedly wish to work your magic in secret. Well, your secrets are safe with me."

"I promise, I'm not a warlock, or wizard, or anything. I'm from New Jersey."

Ralph knew a great many things, among them:

- His home IP address
- C++, UNIX, Pascal, Java, BASIC, ASCII, HTML, and CGI Scripting
- The names of the three major temperature scales and the boiling point of water in each
- Elvish (both Quenya and Sindarin)
- His Jedi name
- His age in binary code

. . . but he didn't know one lick of magic. Nonetheless, Regina nodded sarcastically. "*Of course* you aren't a magician. You just *happened* to be flying in the sky."

"I mean it. Come on, give me the real Chessie for a moment. I need some help — I can't use my legs!"

"You'll find a bedpan under your bed," Regina announced, looking at Ralph pityingly as she opened the door. "Your mind was obviously weakened by whatever dropped you out of the sky; I'd suggest you get as much sleep as you can. I'll be outside tending to my flowers."

After Regina left, Ralph lay back and stared at his new quarters. He wanted to explore, to open the drawers and throw back the curtains, but he simply couldn't get his legs to move. Or maybe Regina was right, and his mind was weakened. His brain could be becoming mush, mush, mush.

The room was perfectly still. So still, in fact, that he could hear the wings of a fluttering fly. Ralph watched the insect hop around the room, explored his surroundings along with it. The fly spent some time investigating a worn bureau, flitted to the stuffed bear, walked the perimeter of a small mirror on the wall. Ralph grew bored, lay back and stared at the thatch of the ceiling. Then the fly entered his vision again. Until now it had avoided the borders of the room, but finally it landed on the ceiling. The moment it did, it dropped directly to the coverlet and lay motionless.

Ralph waited for it to buzz away again, but it never did. He lifted the poor creature to his eyes, and found it was quite dead. Rimmed in frost, its wings were winter panes of glass. The corpse thawed in Ralph's hand. He dropped it to the floor, then watched in horrid fascination as it frosted all over again.

Ralph shrank into the bedding and pressed his eyes closed.

# CHAPTER XXXI

He was awakened by the noise of a text message being received. Delighted, he patted the pockets of his nightgown — but no phone. The ding came from somewhere below him. Ralph leaned far over the side of the mattress and saw, sure enough, that the pair of jeans Cecil had given him had been wedged far under the bed. He placed a hand on the freezing floor — touching it was like handling ice cubes, deeply uncomfortable but not impossible — and reached for the pants. By stretching his middle finger out, he was able to graze a denim belt loop. He seized the jeans and rooted through for his phone.

It had low batteries and one bar of reception — not enough to place a call, but enough to receive a message, from an unknown number:

RALPH NEED SOME HELP JUST ASK FOR IT.

Ralph placed the phone back in his jeans pocket, rolled them up neatly, and hid them under the bed. How was he supposed to ask for help? He certainly couldn't ask Regina, given that Chessie had held true to her warning him that she would be out for his blood.

I can see him, silently mouthing the text message's words and chewing a fingernail, as puzzled and anxious as if he were indexing his rock collection.

Let us hope that Ralph doesn't decide to ask for help aloud. For narrators must come when requested, and a story with two narrators can only be confusing to us all — crap, he did it.

*Hello, Ralph,* responded a voice broadcast from far above even me. *Maarten Sumperson on the line. How may I help you?*

Nuts.

Ralph bit his lip. He wasn't sure if he was supposed to talk back to booming voices from above, if that would mean he was irrevocably crazy, like a prophet or something.

*Ralph. You asked for help. Surely you have some bidding?*

Despite its volume, Maarten's voice is soothing — soft, with a slight Dutch accent. "I need some help, please," Ralph whispered.

*Yes, Ralph?*

"I don't know. What's going on?"

*You're in the retelling of a story. 12,455 words. First narrated in 1845, by yours truly. Commissioned by one Hans Christian Andersen.*

One narrator is surely enough, Maarty.

*He requested help. I'm not trying to cause trouble.*

Sure, Mr. Look At Me, I'm Maarten Sumperson! I Have *Seniority!* I've Worked With Some *Famous* Authors! It doesn't mean you can butt into *my* story, which *I'm* telling —

*No. You've moved onto Daphne's quest now, which is a re-telling. Check your handbook, if you want —*

Take it away, Maarty. Don't you worry about me and my self-esteem.

"Mr. Sumperson," Ralph asked, "sorry to interrupt you, but could you tell me more about why I'm inside another story?"

*It's a popular record in the log. Hold on, I'm new to the computerized system. . . .*

Ralph heard the distant clacking of keys.

*Let's see . . . story was originally requested by Mr. Andersen as a souvenir of the wish-granting of a little girl of his acquaintance named Gerda. Common name: "The Snow Queen." He came up with the setup, of course; I engineered it and wrote it all down.*

"And why is that important now?" Ralph asked.

*Well, let me see . . . the tale record has most recently been accessed by a Duchess Chessimyn of Cheshire, exercising her rights under the Kelling Provision to log on to our Royal Narratological Guild database under her official authority as a wish-granter. It seems she's adopted the tale as a starting point for Miss Daphne's wish. Godmothers often do this sort of thing when they haven't had time to properly plan. Though it's hardly ideal to plagiarize, it isn't exactly frowned upon. While "The Snow Queen" was developed by an expert narrator, namely myself, the new version will be modified by the same apprentice narrator your tale has had so far, and catalogued as a lesser incarnation of a masterpiece.*

Really. Want to say that again, jerk?

*You want to stop working against your own main character for your utterly transparent "secret" reasons?*

"I'm sorry, what? And I thought Hans Christian Andersen wrote 'The Snow Queen,'" Ralph whispered.

*He did, in a manner of speaking. But even so, he employed a narrator, someone who was actually telling the story, and that wasn't Mr. Andersen. We narrators are the ones who actually do the work, up there in the catwalks, making sure the story unfolds properly. You've undoubtedly read many of my tales before, though you never saw my name. It's quite thrilling to finally be known, really —*

"I'm sorry to interrupt, but I bet Chessie is going to return soon, and I'd really like to know what I have to do. Where is Daphne, and how do I find her?"

*She wished to save you and Cecil. She's off doing that.*

"I need saving?"

*Yes, very much. You've been imprisoned by the Snow Queen herself. She'll have you dead within a fortnight.*

"Yipes. So how do I find Daphne?"

*You can't. You're too weak. You're the damsel in distress.*

"Do I have to be?"

*You tell him, Mr. Official Narrator.*

All right, enough attitude. Why don't you retell him the original Snow Queen story, Maarten, since that's what Daphne's lived so far? Condense it, though. And stop after the capture of the young man — that's where I want to go in new directions.

*Ready, Ralph?*

Ralph nodded and nestled deeper into the sheets, shivering as he glanced at the door.

Storytime.

# CHAPTER XXXII

*Once upon a time,* Maarten began, *in a distant city, three children named Daphne and Cecil and Ralph lived with their families in cramped rooms in neighboring buildings.*

"Wait, this is really Daphne? And Cecil and me?" Ralph interrupted.

*Get a sense of metaphor, you literal-minded American. This is her internal state. It doesn't have to be* exact —

"Okay, okay."

*Besides, I'm telling you the original version. It hasn't really happened in this case, but she believes it has, so it may as well have* —

"Sorry, sorry, calm down."

*It's just this modern crisis of imagination, I . . . okay. To continue. All this time the snow was falling fast. Winter in this land isn't like it is in New Jersey, Ralph. The snow is thick and never stops. It never lingers on the ground, but it's always tumbling, with flakes that are so broad they blind you when they hang off your lashes.*

*One time it was so snowy that Daphne couldn't even see Ralph or Cecil* — *when she looked for them, all she could see were snow creatures flying at the window.*

*The snowflakes have a queen* — *whenever they come so close that you can't see past them, that's where she flies. She's the largest snowflake of them all, but she's also more than that; when she peers in the windows, the flakes freeze in the strangest patterns, like flowers.*

"Iterated fractals," Ralph murmured, geekily. "Cool."

*The Snow Queen, you see, is made of ice! She's the most beautiful creature you've ever seen. She dresses like a lady, in the finest white gauze, and she glitters from millions of little flakes that live deep in her skin. Fragile and grand, all at once. But even though her eyes shine like stars, there isn't any peace in them.*

*As for Daphne's Ralph and Cecil, they grew to love sledding more than anything else in the world, spending their mornings in the town square with the other boys, tobogganing through the streets. Daphne would miss them so much, but they would always come back to play with her in the afternoon, later and later each day.*

*Now, some of the boldest boys would fix their sleds to farmers' carts or big dogs' tails to be carried around the town. One morning the biggest sleigh ever imagined appeared. White all over, it was, and driven by gray horses. In it sat the whitest figure, muffled in fox fur.*

"Just like in Narnia!" Ralph exclaimed.

*No. That's the White Witch. The Snow Queen came first. Pay attention. This figure drove her sleigh around the main square, and all the boys tried to catch her. But most of them couldn't manage it. The bigger boys were too clumsy to get their sleds attached; the littlest boys were nimble enough, sure, but their legs were too small, and they couldn't run fast enough. No, only Cecil and Ralph could. They were old enough to catch up, and young enough to slip their sled-ropes over the hitch. Away they went. They rode the giant sleigh through the square again and again, the other boys cheering and hooting the whole time!*

Clock's ticking, Maarten. Ralph will be killed before you finish your rambling.

*Then, when the sleigh came to a quiet spot, the driver lifted the boys off their sled and placed them right next to her. Cecil sat closest. He could only see her face, but even so he knew she was the most beautiful woman he had ever seen. When she looked at him with her ice-perfect eyes, he couldn't speak. Whatever she said to him, he nodded.*

*"Are you cold?" the Snow Queen asked Cecil. "You must be frozen. Crawl under my fox fur cloak."*

*As soon as she said it, he knew he was very cold, so he did as she said.*

*They were going so fast now, all through the town, that before they knew it they were in the countryside. The boys got scared when they saw how fast they were going past the hedges and streams, so they shrank into the Snow Queen's warm fur cloak. Then, suddenly, the giant flakes around them had turned into great big birds pulling the sleigh through the big sky.*

*"You're still cold," she said, and then she kissed Cecil. Her kiss was more chill than ice, and he couldn't break free. He felt like he was dying for a moment, and then he was colder than the air and the snow, and he felt as comfortable as if he were at home with his own mother.*

*"I will not kiss you again for some time," the Snow Queen said, "for I could kiss you to death."*

*Once she had finished kissing him, she grew even more beautiful in his mind. He crept closer and reached his arms around her.*

*They flew all night, over the lakes and forests, and then over the frozen seas. The storm winds screamed about them; but the whole night there was the great moon, bright and silver, for the boys to look at whenever they got scared. By the time the sun came up, they were asleep at the Snow Queen's feet.*

*And somewhere, now far away, was the little girl they'd left behind.*

Thank you, Mr. Sumperson, that will be plenty.

# CHAPTER XXXIII

When Maarten had begun his booming story, Ralph felt he could listen for hours. But by the time his alter ego was falling asleep in the Snow Queen's sleigh, Ralph could barely keep his own eyes open.

Much later, Regina opened the door. She was wearing what would have looked like a nun's habit, had it not been fashioned of stitched paisley patches. While Ralph was dozing, she threw back the gauzy curtains and filled the room with bright and chilly light. Ralph cracked open his eyes to see a smooth blue exterior wall, with the hints of a dense flower garden at its boundary. The sky beyond was an even, brilliant white.

"How long have I been sleeping?" he asked.

Regina looked up sharply, a glare all the more alarming for her generally docile manner. "Don't worry about how long. Just worry about sleeping enough to get better."

"I don't feel any better," Ralph said. While he had been listening to Daphne's story, he had pressed his legs to find a fracture. But they weren't broken or even bruised; they were simply weak. Trying to use them was like trying to make a fist right after waking.

"Oh, you will get better. You simply *must*." It was the least convincing performance she had yet given.

Regina left Ralph with a tray of scones, each labeled with a little card. The batch encompassed a variety of fantastic flavors: pumpkin curd, sweet rampion, Valhalla rhubarb. They smelled fantastic. But, despite his grumbling belly, despite the scones' warm and flaky fragrance, he didn't pick one out. Instead, he lay in his bed and thought.

Perhaps Regina was poisoning him. He could think of no reason for her to do so, but old women in secluded cottages were known to do such things. But if she wanted him dead, she could easily have offed him already. He didn't seem to be getting any *worse*, at least, and although his legs were as weak as ever, and being awake was enough to put him to sleep, his mind seemed alert.

Why keep him an invalid? If Regina thought he was a warlock, then perhaps she had some wicked use for his sorcery. But surely he'd need to be healthy for that — wouldn't a bedridden warlock be useless?

He couldn't resist; they smelled so good. While he finished his last scone (this one the flavor of a pineapple-and-ham pizza) and washed it down with lukewarm tea, he heard another text message come in on his phone. He pulled it out from under his bed.

RALPH. HAVE ACTIVATED BEAR. YRS TRULY MS

After unsuccessfully trying to text back and then hiding his phone away, Ralph decided he didn't dare fiddle with the bear at the foot of his bed, in case Regina was somehow watching. He had memorized the timing of Regina's visits (once each for breakfast, lunch, Irish teatime, British teatime, Russian teatime, and supper), and he knew his safest stretch to risk a peek would be after lunch and before Irish tea. For a long time he watched the creature stare back at him with its bead eyes, and wondered what Maarten's latest text meant.

The bear was one of the jointed variety that parents adore and children find scratchy. Once the safe interval came, Ralph turned him upside, downside, offside, and was about to turn him inside out when he noticed a loose piece of thread on the animal's lower paw. When he tugged, it unraveled freely. Once the worn velvet pad had fallen away, a mirror was revealed beneath. Or it seemed to be a mirror, only it didn't show Ralph at all, but rather a girl slogging through snowdrifts. When he tilted it, it showed a different part of the picture, like a spyglass. He squinted closer. The girl was Daphne.

He heard a squeaking sound, and discovered that it originated from the bear's upper paw. When he held the stuffed animal to his ear he found that he was listening to a perfect reproduction of the sounds of a winterscape — the howling wind, even the ragged sighs Daphne made as she struggled through the snow. And alongside he heard a voice, a young man's voice, a most ideal and mellifluous voice, describing it all.

And so, by wrapping the bear around his head (like a virtual reality headset as engineered by a nineteenth-century child), he was able to follow Daphne's story.

Daphne was trudging along a winter trail. She wasn't sure when or how that started. She wasn't sure of terribly much, actually. It was like she had always been an olden times little girl, but she had blacked out on the specifics of why.

She spoke to herself (as little girls tend to do when alone in fairy tales — they also tend to weep bitterly, which you'll notice she will do with regularity). "I miss my young man and my brother so much. And they're gone forever."

"No," said the sunshine. "I do not believe it."

"We agree! We do not believe it! It can't be true! It is not so!" cried the winter songbirds, who never knew when to finish making a point.

Daphne wondered what to do next. She remembered having long ago been with her parents, and her brother and sister, and an American boy named Ralph, having some episode in a fairy castle that ended violently, and then suddenly having lived an entirely different life in which she was a Danish girl who lost both her brother, Cecil, and her best friend in the world, a young man named Ralph who made her heart pump a little faster whenever she imagined his face.

She felt peevish, actually. Part of her relished this world of talking sunshine and songbirds, and part of her found it uncomfortably sweet, like eating handfuls of sugar.

Ralph, being so very smart, would understand exactly what was happening, and Cecil was so decisive that he would know precisely what to do about it. And Beatrice would be the compass to make sure everyone came to the right conclusion. But Daphne didn't have any of them, and didn't know how to find them, and wept all the more bitterly thinking about it. Her tears fell to the snow's surface and were lost.

# CHAPTER XXXIV

What Ralph had glimpsed of Daphne's tale so far, though minimal, had been way too cutesy. Ominously cutesy, like happy music in a sci-fi movie. He knew that Daphne was bound eventually to get herself into serious trouble. In order to help her, though, he'd first have to find Cecil (who was bound to be imprisoned nearby) and escape. He found himself unable to determine how to do so while incapacitated and locked in a small room, however. Were he designing this moment in a video game, he would have two options: A small creature would come by to give him a means of rescue (the closest he had come to such a benefactor was the fly, which was unfortunately still quite dead) or he would press some combination of buttons to free himself (as he hadn't a controller, doing so would be tricky).

Ralph was sure Daphne was about to go through a charming sequence of events that would make for a precious story. But he found it hard to concentrate, knowing he was trapped and going to be "dead in a fortnight" . . . only he couldn't remember how long a fortnight was, and he wasn't able to get a phone call through to his parents, whom he suddenly missed very much.

"I'm sorry," Ralph called up toward my position in the catwalks, "but do you think you could speed Daphne's wish along? I don't have time for 'cute.'"

Absolutely not.

"I'm *dying* here." Ralph's voice caught. "Please. I can't stand this sweet nonsense."

I'm not taking orders from a character.

"Then I'm not listening to my narrator."

Fine. Let's take this narrator out for a spin and see what he can do, then.

The picture in the magic mirror suddenly went dark. Ralph's heart quaked as Regina opened the door to the cottage and vaulted in, toting Cecil behind her. Death was in her eyes.

# CHAPTER XXXV

Regina shrieked as she slammed through the door, dragging Cecil behind her. Ralph quickly realized that something was off. He was gray-blue, his features lined in purple, hair thick and shiny on his scalp, like Halloween hair. Dead. Unmistakably dead.

"What did you do to him?" Ralph stammered as defiantly as he could. Defiance is a difficult emotion for geeks to pull off. Ralph hiccupped.

Regina advanced on him, and as she left the doorway, he could see that she had a heavy stone cleaver in her fist. He shrank behind the coverlet.

"I've got a new bedfellow for you," Regina hissed.

"Look, Chessie, this has gone far enough. Daphne's seven; she's terrified and alone. I know you're poisoning me, and I know you've already *killed* Cecil, and how do you think you're not going to be arrested?" As he got more agitated, Ralph stood on the bed and clutched the sheet to him.

"Lies," she said uninterestedly, testing the heft of the cleaver.

"What possible good could killing him do?"

Regina stroked the dull edge of the heavy implement. "Cecil isn't dead. He's very ill, though. I don't have the time to travel between the two of you anymore, so you'll have to make room for him in your quarters. As far as your accusation of poisoning, you may feel ill, but that's only so you stay in one place and don't go wandering about and ruining everything."

"You want to keep me here forever?"

"She wished to save you. You're the object of her quest. So stay put."

Regina placed Cecil's body under the covers on the other side of Ralph's double bed, and wordlessly left the room.

Ralph stared at his new bedmate, to all appearances fully deceased. He reached a hesitant hand and felt Cecil's neck, and found it slightly warm. Every few seconds, Cecil drew a shallow breath. Whenever he exhaled Ralph could detect the slight aroma of baking soda and dates.

Scones. The boy had been done in by scones.

"Don't die, Cecil," Ralph said. "I'm sorry I allowed this all to happen." He grasped Cecil's chilled hand.

Ralph's only other experience with death was in sixth grade, when the school's whistling janitor, Petey, was discovered laid out flat in a side hallway by a student out on a bathroom pass. The kid had run into the Chorus classroom and summoned the teacher, whom Ralph and the rest of the class followed. What surprised Ralph was that, even after dying, Petey was still the same old janitor; he was still in the same outfit, had the same thick cowlick. He just lost the more subtle Petey qualities. It was the same with Cecil's corpse — all of his parts were still there, but not the unknowable feelings that connected them.

All Cecil was now, was the hip medieval outfit, the awkward complexion, the arrogant and sensitive set of his features. Ralph stroked his hand and hoped for his mystery to return.

# CHAPTER XXXVI

Daphne was resting on an ice ridge that overlooked a snowy prairie. At the far side of that plain rose a tower. The Snow Queen's palace was savage and unnatural, like the exit wound of a cannon shot off from the center of the Earth.

"Why, it's hopeless!" Daphne wailed. "I'll never be able to reach them!"

Rescuing Ralph and Cecil was indeed nearly hopeless, but there was a benefit in that very fact. No one could bestow on Daphne a power greater than that which she already possessed: her very vulnerability. Any kind-hearted soul watching might decide to help her.

Daphne knew she would have to start moving, or risk losing courage, not to mention all feeling in her toes. So she threw herself off the ridge, rocketing through the packed snow, all the way to the bottom of the crest. By the time she slowed to a stop, she was soaked through, her skin red and chapped, and she felt more miserable than she had ever yet felt. And the Snow Queen's tower was still far off.

There were trees growing beneath the gray sky, she was certain. But all the greenery was blanketed in so much snow that their true forms were long-hidden — they might as well have been old men frozen in mid-step. Daphne eased between them in the eerie quiet, surrounded by a smooth whiteness broken only by her own footprints.

The swirls of snowflakes began to thicken into shapes that grew more and more pronounced. They did not fall from above, like proper snowflakes, but hurtled along the ground. All the singular loveliness of the flakes grew grotesque; no sooner had Daphne set her eyes on one than another ripped her attention away with fresh shivers of fright. The patterns thickened so transfixingly that a squadron of snowflake soldiers formed before she realized what was happening.

These were the Snow Queen's guards. Some were little men with spears and crystal bellies that you could peer through to the snowy landscape behind; some were bears with great silver teeth; some were birds with sharp, rhomboid wings. The scariest guards had no shape at all. They were rolling figures of ice that shifted to fit the landscape as they hurtled toward her.

Snow Guards cannot be effectively attacked by any but the most proficient warriors, for how can one kill something animated through magic? Cut off a foot and that foot will still float and advance, slice through a heart and the organ will function as well in two pieces, for snow creatures don't need anything hot and basic like blood to sustain them. That Daphne stood no chance against these creatures was obvious to any beings who happened to be watching.

And there were some very important beings watching.

Her tale had attracted no small amount of attention, as will the story of anyone who has great odds stacked against her. As I've transcribed this quest, pages have been nicked and spread throughout the wish's realm, and now all the fantastic creatures are clamoring for copies of pages.

Most of them will be of no use in aiding Daphne. But a group of retired golden angels has been following her story. They watched Daphne struggle with this cold legion of magical snowflakes. Though these heroes had once been speedy indeed, they were fat old men now, and it took them some time to fasten their hero costumes. It wasn't until now that they arrived, the very moment a guard was about to run Daphne through with his ice lance.

When they hurtled onto the scene, the angels were each no bigger than an egg, golden pellets that slammed, sizzling, into the snow. They swiftly grew to the size of vanity chess pieces, then finely featured beavers, and finally came to look like large men with wings and shields and spears and helmets that extended down to protect their noses. Their weapons were hot, which made all the difference — they smote the Snow Guards until the last one melted, screaming, into the snow.

Then the angels rubbed their hands over Daphne's numb feet until they began to feel warm and snug, as though she had her furry boots back.

The old winged men flew away before Daphne could thank them, for they, too, knew that her powerlessness was her best hope. She waved them farewell and trudged on to the Snow Queen's palace.

# CHAPTER XXXVII

The tower didn't have any doors. Instead, there was a gaping hole in the front. It would have been easy enough to stroll through, had it not been crossed by cutting winds. Should Daphne have tried to enter, her flesh would have instantly frozen and shattered.

It was frustrating, really. She could see deep into the palace's blue-tinged expanses, but she couldn't approach the entrance by more than a few feet before the cold grew too fierce. She teetered at the edge of the portal like at the tip of a diving board, gearing up the courage to dash through, even if it meant certain death. For what other option did she have?

She figured the less time she spent under the cutting winds, the better, so she backed up to get a running start. She started sprinting . . . and then stopped.

As she had begun to run, her feet had shifted on invisible currents of slippery ice, streams frozen beneath the snow. If she could only . . . and then she reached her hand under the snow and located one of the currents. She traced it back to where it began, halfway up the ridge. Then she blew on her little red fingers, curled her body up into a tight ball (a trick seven-year-old girls who have lost their boots and cloaks are particularly well suited for), and began to slide.

It was slow at first, but then how she did fly! A pink blur on the wide expanse of white, she was turning and spinning and rolling and wheeling until she had no idea where she was hurtling or even who she was.

What she *was* aware of, however, was that the cutting winds were bound to destroy her, no matter how fast she may be speeding when she finally crossed the threshold. It would be a very silly Snow Queen, after all, whose tower defenses could be defeated by a little girl, even an astoundingly quick one. As the blue ice and gray sky whirred about her, she gave in to the motion and almost began to enjoy it. This, she realized, would be her final fling.

But all that turning and spinning . . . soon she felt a pleasant buzz inside. Then the glow intensified until it was . . . not unpleasant, really, but rather so very pleasant that she wouldn't want it to last more than a few seconds.

She would have liked to get outside herself to see what she looked like, but unfortunately seeing outside of themselves is something seven-year-olds are unequipped to do. Warm pink flames came to bathe her until she was a meteor hurtling down the ridge, leaving behind a brook of yellow-green grass.

Her course was leading her nowhere near the palace entrance, as a flaming little girl rocketing down a hillside is a frenetic and directionless projectile. She veered every which way, zoomed down hills only to round the base and zip back up, flip into the air, and land half a mile away. As she went faster and faster, she crisscrossed the whole expanse of the Frozen North, going miles out of her way only to pass over an ice mountain and double back. Pinball would make an apt metaphor, if a narrator were earnest and modern and inclined to such descriptions.

Daphne reached the tower at the approximate speed of a thought. She missed the portal entirely and instead pierced the structure's icy hull, sliding easily through and leaving a clean hole, as though a chef had gone after the tower with a Daphne-sized cookie cutter.

She was lucky she didn't enter through the front entrance.

Not for the cutting winds, but for the bevy of Snow Dragons. The Snow Queen had stolen their hatchlings and lodged them in nets at the top of the chamber, which made the dragons cranky beyond their general orneriness. Behind the dragons were Ice Worms, any one of which could have swallowed Daphne in a mouthful. And Ice Worms, of course, never travel unless in the company of Sleet Mermaids, which aren't particularly menacing on their own . . . only, they refuse to travel without their Cold Trident Housecats, which would have been dangerous but not overly so if it hadn't been for their Deep Freeze Fleas. Oh, and the Snow Queen had ordered the floor ripped out and replaced with spikes of chilled aluminum. Whether frozen spikes would have been a danger to a pink-clad little girl rocketing at one-fourth the speed of sound is debatable, but that debate need not be joined, since Daphne did not enter through the entrance portal but rather penetrated a large closet sideways, coming to rest in a puddle of steam next to an old mop that had turned stiff and gray and had therefore been placed with the other items no longer useable.

It is taxing enough to rapidly decelerate from a speed of hundreds of miles an hour to zero. Add to that simultaneously dropping from four hundred degrees of body heat to ninety-eight point six, and slowing from spinning at four revolutions per second to not spinning at all, and you'll have an inkling of Daphne's disorientation. The mop she came to rest against was the most welcome companion in the world. She sank her lips into its nasty old fibers and clutched it like a teddy bear.

She wept bitterly again, but only for a moment this time, because she knew Ralph was near. Realizing that her entrance hadn't been overly subtle and someone was bound to come hunting for her, she threw open the icy closet door before some wicked animated snowflake could do it first.

Daphne, of course, had no idea of the most recent mayhem in the entrance chamber — as, I startle to report, neither did you. My apologies: Let me take you there now.

The Deep Freeze Fleas had discovered the Snow Dragon Hatchlings on the roof, and, as dragon hatchling blood is quite sweet, had flocked to them. The Snow Dragons had risen to protect their children, in the process spraying the Sleet Mermaids with frost and ticking off the Cold Trident Housecats, who are infamously fearsome when agitated. The resulting melee shook the walls of the tower and bathed everyone in crimson slush.

But since Daphne prudently avoided the entrance chamber entirely, we will return our attention to her closet.

The narrow door opened onto a large ice hall that stretched farther than she could see. There was no regular shape to it, just a cavern formed by the currents of snow. It was a wide open space, as gaping as the Snow Queen's heart and lit only by whatever glittering reflections of the northern lights managed to pass through the murky ice walls.

Daphne passed over the cold floor and found, once she reached the far wall, more caverns of a similar type. While she started out with determined footsteps, leaving steaming puddles beneath her angel-warmed feet, she eventually began to slow and lose hope. For while she had an idea of how to fight something that was there, how could she possibly fight emptiness?

Though it may seem dumb in retrospect, we shouldn't really fault the Snow Queen for placing every single one of her guards in the entrance chamber. There was only one way into the tower, after all — who could have foreseen that some obnoxious little girl would coast through a twenty-foot wall of ice and invade an unused closet?

The truth was that, for the first time in centuries of Royal Narratological Guild storytelling, the Snow Queen was worried. She wasn't fearful, mind you — she was far too powerful to be fearful — but she was undeniably concerned. Daphne had somehow escaped the Flint Robbers and made it across the frozen wastes, had then defeated the royal Snow Guards, who had never before been defeated — so the Snow Queen figured she was dealing with some weird and demonic gremlin, and placed all her minions in the entrance hall as the surest way to defeat her. A titanic initial offensive, if you will.

And it hadn't worked.

The door to Ralph's cottage prison opened. In walked the Snow Queen, her face drawn and stony.

"Matters have gotten worse," she said. "I'm afraid Cecil can't remain here with you."

"What are you going to do with him?" Ralph whispered. The Snow Queen's poison had been stronger of late, and he was too weak to move.

"You won't need to worry about Cecil anymore," she said.

Meanwhile, Daphne passed through a hundred chambers as empty as the one she first encountered. In each she found only eerie torches, their cold white flames illuminating little more than themselves.

As she trekked, Daphne came to realize that she was progressing through an ever-narrowing sequence of curved caverns that spiraled inward like the chambers of a nautilus. They shrank in breadth as she went, until she had no sooner entered a chamber than it landed her into the next. Soon the chambers were only a few feet of empty space until the next door, and then they were nothing more than doors, the icy surfaces grating as she opened one against another. Finally she skirted through a narrow portal and came to a door so imposing that it made all the others disappear. It was a tall slice of glacier, its doorknob a chill globe of brass barely within her reach.

Daphne slowly placed her fingers around the searingly cold metal. The portal shivered once and then opened.

# CHAPTER XXXVIII

She found a boy sitting at the center of a frozen lake, swaddled in thick white furs and staring into the surface of the ice.

Daphne stood in the midnight doorway, staring. The boy never moved, only stared at his reflection. Daphne leaned down and peered into the deep blue surface to try to see her own image.

But she didn't find herself. Swimming beneath were what Daphne first took to be fish, the kind you find in pet stores that would be completely see-through if not for the flashes of their scales when they turned. But then she saw they were actually words, glinting words. She couldn't read them through the scored ice, but when a word swam near the surface she would see an *f* tail curve, the twist of a backbone *V* before its owner shot away.

"Hello?" she dared to call. "Boy?"

He was too far away to make out clearly. But she recognized him somewhere deep inside. Her ribs gave a flutter when she first saw him; he was something grander than ordinary.

"Hello?" she tried again.

But he wouldn't look up, so she started across the ice.

The surface was solid, and scored enough that there was a bubbly roughness under her bare feet. She felt secure hobbling across as the swimming words flashed beneath her.

When she neared the boy, however, she saw the blue of the ice beneath her deepen, until she seemed to be crossing an invisible membrane across a night sky. The swimming words stuck to the shallower waters and didn't approach her anymore. She still had a dozen more feet to go to reach the boy, and beneath her was infinity.

"Look at me," Daphne pleaded. And then, fractionally, he raised his head. Daphne gasped. It was Cecil, so sick he could barely move, but staring back at her in feeble panic. His eyes were no longer the tangled molten brown long since fixed in memory, but the gray clarity of clean riverstones, of reason itself. And when his eyes met hers, the ice beneath their bodies cracked open.

# CHAPTER XXXIX

Plummeting through ice clogged with silvery words is like jolting awake and gasping after one of those falling dreams. Except, of course, that the shock lasts for whole seconds and is accompanied by syllables quivering against your cheek. And instead of waking up, you land in a cascade of ice onto a mirror.

Daphne and Cecil fell near each other on the glass but skated in opposite directions. Words carried in the deluge of cold water tumbled about them and lay flopping on the surface, their embedded letters warping as they gasped for air. As she tried to work through her shock, Daphne lay on an ice floe and stared at the gills of *BRINK* as it rose and fell in the steel light of the mirrored cavern.

She couldn't find her brother anymore, and no matter where she paddled her floe, no matter how loudly she called his name, there was no answer.

Daphne dropped a single tear. And when her tear hit the water the ripples it made, slight as they were, added just enough tension to the lake that the mirror beneath the surface shattered, and she tumbled through.

# CHAPTER XL

This fall wasn't nearly as peaceful as the previous one. First, she fell a long way — the length of a suburban home's driveway, say, if stood on end (presuming one could do such things to driveways). Second, she was falling through pure darkness. And third, the air around her lacked all warmth. It was so cold, in fact, that if she had fallen much farther, say the length of a cul-de-sac, she would have perished from the chill and then shattered at the bottom.

But as she fell a shorter length and struck a thatched roof rather than a hard floor, she survived. She and Cecil whipped through the musty hay and tumbled onto a bed.

And, of course, they toppled on top of Ralph. He had watched their plummet on the bear's paw, eventually decided that the cottage they were heading for was his own, and scurried to hide under the bed. He stuck his head out so he could stare at the roof. It was as frosty and motionless as ever, until it disintegrated in a flurry of hay fibers. The two Battersby youths fell hard, struck the bed, and were flung by the protesting springs to the far corners of the room.

Once the hay had settled, Ralph saw Cecil clutching a bedpost, and Daphne hanging from a tapestry.

"Daphne?" he called. "It's me, Ralph!"

Daphne had the admirable presence of mind to nod from her perch.

"Thank God," Ralph said, trying to get to his feet and then collapsing, shivering on the floor. "I've been following you this whole time; I saw everything, and we have to get out of here!"

At which point Ralph tried to pull himself back into bed and fell, winded, onto the freezing floor. "Or at least you have to get out of here. She keeps feeding me those scones, and they make me weak."

Daphne disentangled herself from the tapestry, hit the cold floor on her angel-warmed feet, stood, and straightened her pink dress. Ralph felt her eyes on him.

"I missed you," she said.

Ralph was about to say thank you when a woman's voice boomed from above.

They peered up through the torn roof at the full radiance of the Snow Queen.

She was Regina and Chessie and a goddess. Gone were the lines of pearls and the masses of ringlets; gone were the practical cap, the apron, the hovering demeanor. Instead she was a cold sun. Tendrils of her frost snaked around the walls and the sundered roof. When she spoke, she jerked about, propelled by the power of her voice.

"You have been wicked," she intoned. She slammed the ice wall on "wicked." It shivered and dropped shards that shattered on the floor, splattering Ralph and Daphne.

Daphne peered up, shielding her eyes against her aunt's chilly radiance.

"Come and speak to me," the Snow Queen continued. She pointed at the girl's rib cage and levitated her into the air heart-first, her head and limbs dangling. Daphne brushed through the thatch and was soon beside the Snow Queen.

"Auntie Chessie, what are you doing?" she asked.

"Who will love you like I? Who will expect nothing more from you than your presence, and will cherish you for it? I am the source of everything that keeps you. Your American playmate will move away. Your brother will drain your admiration and return you nothing. Why do you focus so intently on *them*?"

Tears stood in Daphne's eyes. "You're not my mummy. Don't be like this."

The Snow Queen stilled her icy tendrils and opened her arms. "Come here," she said. "Give your aunt a hug."

Ralph called out a warning. But Daphne was too far away to hear him.

She floated closer to Chessie, limply entered her embrace.

The Snow Queen folded her cold radiance around her.

Daphne cried into her arms. It had been a long, lonely quest, and it felt so peaceful to be crushed. "I'm done with my wish; let's go home," she said.

"Hush, hush," said the Snow Queen. "You've found Ralph and Cecil, so you can live with me in my tower now. You can be my child. Every day will be sunny."

It sounded like perfect peace, after so much tumult.

"Will I get to go home eventually?" Daphne asked. "Can I play with my friends again?"

"Of course," the Snow Queen said slowly.

"And my brother? You'll make him better?"

"You have rescued him and Ralph. Your wish is done, so they will be sent away."

"Will they be okay?"

"You won't need to shed a single tear for them."

Daphne looked down at Ralph and her brother, piped in Chessie's silver glow. "I want to be with them."

From his vantage point Ralph watched Daphne begin to glow. The tendrils of frost shied away from her.

"We'll discuss this later," said Chessie.

"No," Daphne said without lifting her gaze from Ralph below. "You must promise he'll be safe."

"I will not hear it, Daphne."

Daphne began to struggle in her aunt's grasp.

Ralph gasped, for he could see, distant in the darkness above, the squadron of Sleet Mermaids floating down, like jellyfish in a tide.

"You will stay," the Snow Queen said soothingly.

With a screech, Daphne ripped free of the Snow Queen's grasp and tumbled toward the cottage. The Sleet Mermaids brandished their ice-flamed fingertips and streaked toward the stricken trio.

# CHAPTER XLI

"You will have nothing to leave me for once they're dead!" screamed the Snow Queen.

Daphne shrieked as she plummeted. As she called out, she erupted into a golden explosion. When Daphne struck Ralph's bed, her warm globe enveloped him and Cecil.

The Sleet Mermaids who weren't able to check their fall in time burst into clouds of steam as they hit the hot light.

Ralph and Daphne and Cecil basked for a moment in the sphere, and then watched its ruddy light expand. The Snow Queen and the Sleet Mermaids were hazy beyond its perimeter, like figures seen from underwater.

Outside the cottage window, Ralph watched the ice of the Snow Queen's tower disappear. Columns of water sprayed the golden dome as the frozen tower melted away. As the sphere expanded, he saw the Snow Queen trapped in its membrane for a horrible moment. Then, with a screech and a pop, she vaporized.

Ralph, Daphne, and Cecil clutched one another while the tower melted. And as the sphere dissipated, they saw that Daphne's heat had melted all the land around them — there was no longer any frozen wasteland, only damp plains.

With the Snow Queen's hold broken, they were able to pick themselves up and make a first few tentative steps over the muddy terrain. The group found themselves in a warmed but bleak land, without food or shelter; there was no time for mourning or mulling. His strength regained, Ralph propped up Cecil on one side and took Daphne's hand on the other, and together they began the trek to the borders of the Melted North.

# CHAPTER XLII

The Battersby children were in trouble. Deep, deep, trouble.

Gert's scolds resounded through the castle corridors. Provided the family ever found a way to get down from the tree, Daphne would be required to attend sixth grade at the Sacred Heart Scottish Girls Academy, a school that doubled as an anonymous lockdown for troubled celebrity children and was rumored not to even allow its students to own laptops. She would also be attending *Les Petites Filles* Etiquette Camp after school instead of participating in any school plays. All princess costumes and pink shoes were to be stricken from her closet.

Come fall, Cecil would be remanded to the Admiral Scribner Academy, in a location so dull that I can't recall its name. Once it became clear that the fulfillment of Cecil's wish meant that the servants had been released with full pensions, he lost car privileges, had his allowance reduced to one hundred pounds a week, and was grounded to his own wing until the end of the summer.

As Ralph wasn't, strictly speaking, a Battersby child, how to punish him was less clear. But, as Gert and Gideon saw themselves as the parental figures in his life until he could be lowered to the ground and sent back to New Jersey, they certainly thought it suitable to give him a lengthy admonishing. He was in a position of *authority*, the other children had placed an implicit trust in him, a trust that had been *abused*. He had been the *crowbar* that had allowed Chessie to *pry open* the family, and they knew they couldn't expect truly civilized behavior from him, but they had come to expect at least common *decency*.

The moods of the Battersby parents were aggravated, of course, by the matter of the missing Beatrice.

Lined up before the large window at the foyer (which enjoyed a rather spectacular view of leaves and open sky, as it was now in a tree a mile above the Earth), the children allowed themselves to be pried of every bit of information they had. Gert gasped to learn that Beatrice had been discovered sneaking into Cecil's wish from the ramparts of their very castle. She put her hand to her throat when she learned that Beatrice had been transformed into a circlet. She stood and paced when she found out that Beatrice, along with her other children, had been in a quaking castle chamber during a massive fairy rebellion. She fainted when she learned of the chamber's collapsing. Once she came to, she demanded to know everything they could tell her about what had happened to Beatrice in the chamber. That was when things started to get murky.

"I bet she left somehow," Daphne proposed.

"Yeah, she probably got out," Cecil said.

"Maybe she was in Daphne's wish with us, and we didn't run into her," Ralph proposed, his face ashen, realizing how feeble his suggestion sounded.

"Oh my child, my child!" Gert said, gesturing at the sky outside the window and falling to her knees.

Which was when Beatrice walked in.

She looked gorgeous and otherworldly, the way people in retouched photographs do; all the blemish and detail had been rubbed away, and she had been bathed in her own essence. Her white skin was paler than ever, and her severe black hair hovered in a floating frame for her face. Once he got over her sudden beauty, Ralph was struck by the oddity of Beatrice emerging from within the castle. Ralph, Cecil, and Daphne had woken up on the roof muddy and cold, but she glided from her own chambers as if she had just taken a glorious nap.

"Beatrice!" Gert said, rushing over with Daphne at her heels.

Beatrice fixed them with a severe look that stopped them in their tracks. "Mother, please, I'm fine."

"What happened?"

"I was in Cecil's wish, but I got out. I'm here, don't worry."

"You're in big trouble, young lady. We strictly forbade you from speaking to Chessie, and you —"

"I was trying to save my *brother*, Mum. If you're going to get mad at someone —"

"Don't you dare interrupt me while I'm talking to you." Gert tried to look stern, but the castle shifted in the stratospheric winds and she nearly lost her balance.

"He lied. He said none of us should talk to her, but he did, anyway."

"What?" Cecil said. "Do you have any idea what I've been through? And just because *I* wanted to do the world some good, instead of staring at my own navel like a self-indulgent goth, and because I was willing to risk everything for it, you're going to turn on me?"

Beatrice raised a hand tiredly. "Look, we're going to have to deal with this. Cecil got his wish, Mum, and Daphne made a wish to save him. They're back safe and sound, and I know you'd rather we hadn't wished at all, but it's worked out, and I'm sure we've had all the learning and life experience and so forth that a wish is supposed to provide. After all, we got the same opportunity *you* did when *you* were a child."

"You had a wish once, Mummy?" Daphne asked.

"Beatrice," Gert said. "Oh my Beatrice. I'm so glad you're back."

"I've brought someone with me," Beatrice said abruptly.

"Oh?" Gert said curiously, until she saw who was exiting Beatrice's wing. "No. Beatrice, darling, you *didn't!*"

"Mum and Dad, Chessie. Chessie, Mum and Dad. I believe you remember one another."

If Beatrice looked like a scrubbed clean version of herself, Chessie had slid in the opposite direction. Her ringlets fell limply around a sallow face. Her newly downtrodden appearance didn't make her a scratch less terrifying to Daphne, who leaped behind a couch and began to wail.

"Gert, Gideon," Chessie said, raising her palms. "Sister. Brother."

Gideon positioned himself in front of his wife and children. "You're not welcome here," he said.

"That's enough," Beatrice said, standing protectively in front of Chessie. "It's time we all had a talk about what really happened those years ago. We have little enough true family as it is. I don't want Chessie to be like my birth mother was, only barely connected to us. It's time we work this through. Let's hear the truth."

"She's turned you against us," Gideon said.

Beatrice shook her head, and then nodded. "If so, only through honest words."

Chessie stared at her sister. "Gertrude, I'm sorry to have made you suffer."

Gert sniffed. "Apology accepted. Now leave."

"I'm more sorry for what I'm about to say."

"That's enough!" Gideon roared. "No more!"

"No!" Chessie said. "You can't ask me to leave when we're a mile up in the air. I have a *right*, Gideon, a right to speak to my *family*. It's been long enough."

"She's right, Father," Beatrice said.

Gideon put his arm around his wife, who had gone pale.

"It wasn't Chessie's fault way back then," Beatrice began to say to Ralph.

"Let me, please," Chessie said. "Cecil, Daphne, Ralph, I must tell you something. My son was lost, yes. I had organized a wish-granting ceremony for him, yes, on his sixteenth birthday. When I heard what he wished for, though, I refused to grant his wish. It was too risky. But Gert granted it, anyway."

"You?" Cecil asked.

"Yes. It was *Mother*," Beatrice said.

"She loved the adventure she went on when her own wish was granted as a little girl, and thought all children should have their own. When I was hesitant, she went ahead behind my back. And when my son didn't return, it all changed. She was terrified I would try to get revenge, and she hid you away from me, barred me from seeing you."

For a moment Gert simply stood before them, at an awesome loss for words. She looked at her husband, then her own manicured fingertips. "I . . . I couldn't stand for you to see me after what I'd done, even my own sister."

"Why didn't you tell us the truth?" Cecil asked Chessie. "You could have sneaked a note to us; you could have told us while we were getting ready for our wishes."

"By hiding her guilt," Chessie said, pacing, "your mother — like Ralph's mother — went overboard in the opposite direction. She disavowed all wish-granting, and would have nothing to do with me. Besides, you love your mother. Your love for your parents will be the most uncomplicated love you will have. Why should I take that away from you? Doing so wouldn't get my son back . . . better you think me a villain than I turn you against your own mother."

"You see?" Beatrice said. "You see why I had to bring her? It's so *unfair*. You've been so selfish, Mum and Dad, messing up and then faking it, scape-goating Auntie Chessie when all she wanted was her family around her in the darkest moment of her life."

"I was the family tramp, Mary was the dullard. You were a little queen," Chessie said softly to Gert. "Our parents loved you the most. You had no idea what it meant to be disliked and opposed. And you took my son on a whim, because you thought the world could only be as kind to him as it had been to you."

"Stop, stop," Gert said, and sank to the floor.

"It's over," Chessie said, wrapping herself around her sister. "No more wishes."

# CHAPTER XLIII

Chessie finally got to come to dinner that night. Ralph, Cecil, and Daphne were all overwhelmed to sit down to dinner with a bedraggled and humbled duchess who had most recently appeared to them as a blazing demigoddess. Gert and Gideon, in the throes of navigating a shameful history long repressed, found it hard to make even their usual polite conversation. Beatrice, evidently not hungry, sat and stared at her plate. It was, all in all, a very unpleasant affair.

Still, Ralph found a new somber camaraderie in the group. Gert and Gideon, if desolated, at least weren't being insincere anymore. Gone, too, were Chessie's dramatics; she carried herself like a normal middle-aged woman. Daphne and Cecil were tired and vulnerable rather than restless and impulsive. Ralph enjoyed the quiet dinner, or would have if it hadn't been for Beatrice's peculiarity.

She was still newly luminous, and Ralph found it hard to wrest his gaze away from her and toward his roast beef, bites of which kept missing his mouth and falling into his lap. But she also didn't sit quite right in her chair anymore. He couldn't place it; nothing was technically wrong, but the subtle details were off. It was as if she were sitting in a distant dining room chair before a green screen and then edited in. She sank a little too far into her cushion, for example —

Beatrice noticed Ralph's scrutiny and gave him one long wink.

Ralph leaned over a dish of whipped potatoes with mint sauce to whisper to her. "What's going on?"

"I'm dead."

Ralph almost spat out a mouthful of peas. "Sorry?"

"I'm dead. I'm a ghost. Here, watch." She gracefully laid a fingertip on the back of Ralph's hand — and passed right through it to the tablecloth.

She then pressed that same finger to her lips, asking for Ralph's silence. Heart racing, he returned his focus to the roast beef.

After dinner, once the rest of the family had dragged themselves to bed, Ralph asked Beatrice to join him on a stroll through her wing.

"I died back at the end of Cecil's wish," she explained as they staggered their way along the swaying corridor. "And I'm in the Underworld."

"The Underworld?"

"Yeah. It's not too terrible, really."

Ralph shook his head. "How does being dead feel?"

"I don't know. You'd have to ask the real me. You're talking to my phantom."

"Oh!"

"I had no idea when I made my wish that I'd have my own ghost. It's a nice perk, really."

"Does Chessie know about this?" Ralph asked.

"Does she! She granted it. I wished to die, and I've been dead ever since, going about my wish the whole time you were helping Daphne."

"You wished to *die*? Really?"

"Well, I wished to visit someone who was dead. My real mother, Annabelle, specifically. And apparently being dead was a prerequisite." Beatrice wavered for a moment in Ralph's vision, like a signal that had temporarily hit interference. "Ugh, I don't know how long I can keep this up."

"What do you mean?"

"I keep fading more and more. You saw me sink into the chair at dinner. I'm afraid . . . I'm afraid that the real me is in trouble. I'm losing her."

"Are you sure?" Ralph asked. As he did, the spectral Beatrice stumbled, and when he tried to catch her, she passed through his arms and vanished.

# CHAPTER XLIV

Ralph knelt at the spot in the hallway where Beatrice had disappeared, staring stupidly into the stone floor. She was in need of aid; that was clear. He should go get help, whether from the Battersby parents or Cecil and Daphne. But could he really get them involved again? He had already risked their lives once, and they could have perished many times over back in the Snow Queen's realm. No — it would be safest to enter the next wish alone.

He headed for the roof trapdoor, pausing every few steps to listen for Gert or Gideon. His guilt doubled as he realized that his parents must be worried sick. He had been intending to squirrel away a moment to contact them. But of course there was no reception at the top of a giant tree.

As he turned the corner, he bumped right into Chessie. She fixed Ralph with an inquisitive look. "Where do you think you're going? And where's Beatrice?"

"You granted her a wish," Ralph said flatly.

Chessie nodded. "That was back in the heat of Cecil's quest. I'm sure I wouldn't have done it now, after that heartfelt reunion."

"Were you going to tell Gert and Gideon?"

"I knew I would have to tell them once Beatrice's phantom disintegrated. But surely you can understand if I'm reluctant to approach them.

Disintegrating phantom daughters are upsetting, and I'm already on shaky footing with them."

"You promised — no more wishes."

"Ralph, stop this prudishness. I have perfectly good reasons for granting it, reasons which I have no obligation to share with you. And you must remember that, once Beatrice's wish is finished, you get one of your own. Surely you haven't forgotten our bargain."

"They're right not to trust you."

Chessie sighed. "If you're going to be so tiresome, I'm heading off to bed."

"Surely you can call this off somehow."

Chessie dusted her hands. "That's it. I'm through trying. I expected more of a sense of adventure, after all you've been through."

"Will you come with me to help?" Ralph asked resignedly.

Chessie shook her head. "I'm pooped. It's fully under control, I'm sure. The narrator has gotten the hang of things."

Ralph glanced up at the trapdoor.

"I'm tired of telling you not to interfere, so I won't," Chessie said. "But I do ask that, if you get yourself killed, do it in the wish, rather than jumping off the wrong side of the castle. There are legal precedents for dying within a wish — it gets so much more complex if you perish on your way there."

Ralph shook his head in confusion.

Chessie sighed and pointed to another spot on the ceiling. "You're going the wrong way. Take the other trapdoor."

"Ah," Ralph said. "Thank you."

# CHAPTER XLV

What kind of narrator is this, you might wonder, who can't prevent a lame-o geek — a kid who once read *1001 Ways to be Funny* in order to make more friends, who was once rejected from an Oz convention, who once attended a *Lord of the Rings* marathon dressed as a hobbit — from worming his way into the last wish?

Truth be told, I probably could have. But I didn't see much of a need. Sure, I would have loved it if Cecil's and Daphne's wishes had been pure quest stories of the old variety. But that wasn't how it worked out, and so be it. I figure, what will it matter if Ralph wanders through one more wish? I'll be able to handle whatever he pulls.

BOOK IV:
# BEATRICE'S WISH
### THE UNDERWORLD

# CHAPTER XLVI

Beatrice died back in Chessie's castle, when a ton of fairy-propelled stone shards fell on her.

Done.

BOOK V:
THE PRIVATE LIVES
OF NARRATORS

# CHAPTER XLVII

You might be surprised to learn that I was born on a partly cloudy day in March. There must have been a twinkle in the sun's light, though, to mirror the twinkle in my mother's eye as she held me, swaddled as I was —

Are you listening?

Fine. As you wish. Back we go.

BOOK IV:
# BEATRICE'S WISH
### THE UNDERWORLD

# CHAPTER XLVIII

Forgive me if I skip some of the early events in Beatrice's wish. Trust me, I'm not going to tell you what happened in the first months for the same reason I haven't informed you of every snack and every poo. It's simply not crucial.

The vital facts:

When Ralph hopped off the roof, he found himself back where he had finished Daphne's quest, in the Melted North. His trek out took a long time. He passed by the cottage where Regina had once imprisoned Cecil, and there he fell into a wonderful story full of wolves and witches and animated glass monkeys.

Until he ran across a wily demon and died.

# CHAPTER XLIX

Why does it matter that the demon was wily? Did Ralph put up a fight? What are demons' preferred methods of killing, and did the demon have a criminal history or a social worker who should have been working to prevent such an act? All good questions. For now, though, we've left Beatrice alone for far too long, and as she is my favorite character in this book, I'm keen to rejoin her.

Ralph ran across a wily demon and died.

# CHAPTER L

Okay, fine, a brief sketch of the wily demon, since you may not care enough about my delightfully sullen Beatrice until we've settled exactly what happened to our "hero." Here we go.

Note that I never wrote that he was killed by a wily demon, I wrote that he "ran across a wily demon and died." This particular demon wasn't suited to slaying, as he was only a couple of inches tall. He crawled into the back of Ralph's shirt and proceeded to insult him, observing (rather aptly) that he was a classless, good-for-nothing brat. When the demon finally leaped out of his shirt, Ralph chased after him. The hunt for the imp took weeks, led him through a desert and around the inner rim of a volcano, finally culminating in a sojourn through the canopy of the speckled nimbus cloud forest.

At which point the demon mistakenly set off a trap laid centuries earlier by a now-extinct tribe, releasing a forty-ton walnut that brought down a dozen trees and squashed flat a nearby orphanage. Ralph was lucky enough (if we can attach the word "luck" to any part of this sorry episode) to have been knocked to one side and land in a giant spider's web, where he was advanced on by the only web-spinning tarantula demigod ever believed to exist.

Don't worry: Ralph will die in eight pages, but not yet. Considering the imp had just fallen over the tripwire that released the second walnut, which would have pulverized Ralph and the web-spinning tarantula demigod as well, the "disaster" that occurred next was actually an auspicious turn of events.

I don't know if you have ever come across a melting frozen tower. Even if you have, you certainly haven't witnessed an entire frozen continent melting. Once its tectonic core heats up, a massive tidal wave of water is released that washes out everything it comes across. Now, the melt of the continent happened a few months earlier and was initially contained in the Carp-Carpathian Mountain Bowl, but eventually it swept away the mountain range that contained the bowl, resulting in a tidal wave that spoiled the map, much like a toddler running amok with her daddy's blue highlighter.

This tidal wave roared through the cloud forest precisely as the spider was advancing and the second walnut was rolling. The imp drowned, and though the spider survived (*n.b.*: arachnid demigods are highly buoyant), it was swept far away. Ralph would have soon been killed had he not been caught in the web, which the water's force wrapped about him. His cocoon contained a nice-sized air pocket and floated, so Ralph bobbed through the world-flooding waters like a bath toy.

As reclining in a spider's web was comfortable (particularly without the spider attached), he wasn't sure he ever wanted to leave. Not being able to rid himself of the gruesome image of the walnut-flattened orphanage, he was convinced, perhaps accurately, that the world was cruel and not worth facing.

But eventually Ralph had mourned unknown children long enough and remembered that he still hadn't found (and saved) the dead Beatrice. He struggled to pick open a hole in his web shell, strand by strand (spider silk becomes much less cohesive when waterlogged), sat on top of his makeshift canoe, and looked around.

There wasn't much of anything to see, as there was no dry land anywhere on the horizon (nor, though he couldn't know it, anywhere at all). The sea was choppy and unending, its color gone gray for all the various rocks and swords that had been swept into it. Ralph munched the legs of a drowned beetle that had been trapped in the web (sure, eating a soggy insect is gross, but this was a survival situation) and wondered what to do.

At first, he tried paddling with his hand, but each time he leaned over the cocoon's side it rolled, threatening to dump him into the iron sea. Not sure what fearsome creatures might be lurking beneath the surface, Ralph decided that dehydration was at least a more distant death than being eaten.

He spent a day reclining in his spiderweb canoe, gazing at the sun and wondering when someone would come along to rescue him, or at least set him on a course of some sort. He started thinking of how little he knew of what might happen, and how he wished the narrator in the catwalks would fill him in.

Filling him in would be a gross breach of storytelling rules.

What did happen was that a robed skeleton approached on a boat.

Its dirty gray bones were covered in a silk robe, which it held tightly closed in its elegant metacarpals. The boat was a flimsy thing that would have rolled in the waves had it not been passing magically through and between them, cutting a straight line through the chop. Ralph watched the skeleton's approach with as much fear as his brain could muster, that emotion being recently much taxed.

The skeleton spoke. Skeletal voices are gender-nonspecific, and since Ralph couldn't get a good look at its hip bones, he hadn't a clue as to its sex.

Not that skeletons mate with any regularity, so gender is fairly moot even to them.

"You are Ralph?" it intoned. Ralph nodded.

"Are you aware that you are the last being alive in all the land?"

Ralph shook his head.

"You are. Are you willing to perform the duties required of you as said last being alive?"

Ralph shook his head.

"Are you willing to perform the duties required of you as said last being alive?"

Ralph shook his head.

"Are you willing to perform the duties required of you as said last being alive?"

Ralph nodded.

"Brilliant," said the skeleton as it sat down on the edge of its boat, momentarily flailing its arm bones to maintain its balance. "It makes all of our lives so much easier when everyone's assigned to a purgatory. Having someone not yet dead wandering around makes all the paperwork so much more difficult, all sorts of exemptions to file and such."

"I'm not dead yet," Ralph observed.

"Quite right," the skeleton said, slowing its speech to make sure this obvious numbskull understood. "But that's not to say you won't be dead shortly."

"Will being dead mean I can go back home?" Ralph asked.

"How many dead people go back home?" the skeleton asked.

Ralph wondered how to answer.

"No," the skeleton said dryly. "You won't go back home. Because you'll be dead."

"I think I'll stay alive, then."

The skeleton looked hard at the featureless sea, then politely returned its eye sockets to Ralph. "Forgive me, but I don't really see how you'll manage that."

"Look, I know this must have something to do with Beatrice. Let me meet her and get on with it."

Yes!

The skeleton looked confused. "Beatrice?"

"Yes. This is bound to be her wish."

"And you expect me to immediately recognize that name among the millions of dead?"

"I guess not."

"There are probably a thousand dead Beatrices in the various purgatories."

"I'm very sorry."

The skeleton sighed. "Let's give it a shot. This Beatrice is a male or a female?"

"Female."

"Known by you?"

"Yes."

"Likely cause of death?"

Ralph shrugged.

"Is she of a sunny or rainy disposition?"

"Rainy. Definitely rainy."

"Young or old?"

"Young. Ish. A teenager."

The skeleton nodded. "Gloomy teenage females are automatically assigned to Purgatory Main Isle. Very crowded these days."

"Is it hard to get to?"

"If you're alive, impossible. Flatly impossible. Even when you're dead, it's difficult. Before the Flood, PMI served as the exclusive entry terminal for the dead, but now we've had to farm our client load out to dozens of auxiliary purgatories. PMI's almost at capacity, so even if you died right now, you'd still be too late to have much chance of being assigned there."

"And it would be impossible to see her if I was in a different purgatory?"

The skeleton laughed, which caused its ribs to grate harshly against one another. "They're *different purgatories*. Yes. It would be strictly impossible."

"What's to be done, then?"

The skeleton shrugged, another unpleasant sight when no flesh covers the bones. "There are zoning exceptions, of course. If you die within a mile of any given purgatory, you can get a local waiver. But that's simply not going to happen for Purgatory Main Isle."

"Why?"

"PMI was formerly in the middle of the Acrid Plains, which were hard to reach, though not impossibly so. But after the Snow Queen's Flood, the Acrid Plains are . . ." The skeleton trailed off and gestured at the fathoms of dark water. "To make sure you were within a mile of PMI, you'd have to die two miles below the surface of this ocean."

"Maybe I could swim two miles down and then die," Ralph suggested.

"Swim two miles down? Good luck. On top of the physical feat, which you seem to be of too geeky a stature to accomplish, you'd also have to guess where Main Isle is. The currents could carry you far away in the Iron Sea before you died."

"Do you know where Purgatory Main Isle is?"

"Not precisely. I do know that we've received hundreds of PMI local waivers for whales and kraken, so PMI must be near their battlezone."

"Can you introduce me to them?"

"They *live under the water*, Ralph." The skeleton tapped its finger against the void where its lips would have been. "Though the whales must come up to breathe, I suppose. That's what whales do, no?"

Ralph nodded.

"I'll see what I can do. Give me two days. That's about when you'll be dead from lack of water, anyway. Just sit tight."

"Come back soon," Ralph said encouragingly. But the skeleton was already gone.

# CHAPTER LI

The sun was setting and Ralph, doing his best to beat back dueling pangs of thirst and hunger, huddled in his web cocoon to wait for the skeleton's return. Once the night arrived, it was cool and pleasant, but he knew that, come morning, daylight would again beat into his skin. *What would it feel like*, he wondered, *to die of sunburn?*

But he only had to wonder for one night, since with dawn came the sound of something large slapping the water outside his vessel.

It was a whale breaching, smacking the surface in a tremendous spray. It threw itself into the air and came crashing back into the sea a few times before gliding over to Ralph's perilously tilting craft. Its head emerged from the water; even that head was already twice the size of his cocoon, and fitted with a sleek steel helmet that had been hammered on with scab-crusted tacks.

"Hello," Ralph said.

He expected a manly baritone, but the whale's voice was so high-pitched as to be almost inaudible. "You're Ralph?" it asked.

"Yes," Ralph said.

"I'm to take you four hundred fathoms below. As a favor to the narrator, to get you moving along. Are you ready?"

"Who's the narrator?"

"Come on, get on."

"I, what, hold on to your flipper?"

"Dorsal fin, please. Otherwise I can't steer."

The whale curled so more of its body was exposed. Ralph gingerly stepped from the cocoon to its back. He gripped the fin at the center and admired the whale's fine helmet, and the massive steel plates bolted to its flukes. "Are you a soldier?" Ralph asked.

The whale nodded, a spectacular shimmy that almost pitched Ralph into the sea. "Just got called up. Shipping back out to duty. You're ready?"

Ralph said yes, and the whale dove. Not unforeseeably, Ralph was thrown and left bobbing at the surface of the iron sea. The whale re-surfaced minutes later. "What happened?" it asked.

"I couldn't hold on. No chance."

"Oh," the whale said. "I should have thought of that." Its flippers sagged in discouragement.

"You've never had anyone ride you before?"

"Calves, sure. But no humans."

"Could you go slower?"

"Not if we want to get you four hundred fathoms deep. I'd never get up enough momentum. I have an idea, though. Get off for a second, would you?"

Ralph heaved himself back into his rocking cocoon and watched as the whale performed an elaborate dance, its armored head and tail glinting below the surface as it twirled and sang.

When it returned to the surface, it had two water sprites in tow. (To those who are unacquainted with water sprites: They are lovely and almost shapeless, like the mist from a hose spigot on a sunny day.)

They carried between them a length of shimmering cord, which the whale had them bind around Ralph's wrists and ankles. They giggled and slapped him as they did, their vaporous touches making Ralph shiver pleasantly. Then the whale opened its mouth, exposing long strips of baleen. Words were exchanged in some sea-language, then the sprites lifted Ralph out of the cocoon and positioned him against the baleen, right where the front teeth would have been. The whale's mouth was covered with grimy plankton, and smelled like a wharf on a hot day.

The whale asked if Ralph was ready and he nodded, though he wondered what it was, precisely, that he had declared himself ready for.

The whale dove. Ordinary flukes are powered by the strongest muscles in the animal kingdom — and magical flukes, well! Ralph found himself instantly pressed upon by thousands of gallons of water. It rolled his eyelids, shoved its way down his throat and filled his stomach and lungs. He was blasted by plankton, the more resourceful of which clutched his clothing as their peers were sucked into the whale's gullet.

They dove farther and farther, until all was black and cold. The rapid increase in pressure caused Ralph's eardrums to burst, which would have hurt terribly if he hadn't been distracted by the more pressing sensation of zooming to the bottom of the ocean.

By the time he was fifty leagues beneath the surface, Ralph had passed out. Which was good, since by two hundred leagues he was dead, and the one hundred fifty leagues in between would have been extremely disagreeable.

ALIVE!!!
(ideal)

Recently-Living
(not too nice, but
could be worse)

Soon-to-be-Dead
(most unpleasant)

TOTALLY
DEAD.
(avoid when at all possible)

# CHAPTER LII

Ralph first noticed that there was no color. But Purgatory wasn't black-and-white, either — it was full of luminous grays, grays like tweed, grays that hinted at thousands of colors latent somewhere within, grays flecked in colors like goldenrod and periwinkle, grays with dried flowers inside.

It was also, though thousands of leagues under the sea, blessedly dry.

The third thing Ralph noticed was a distinct lack of ghosts and zombies. The people who passed him looked like normal peasant folk, if understandably more preoccupied. He had materialized high in the branches of a deadwood tree, and as he worked to gain his bearings he watched the commoners pass in and out of their slate city. He was eager to get on with his search for Beatrice. First, though, he had to determine whether the people down here would try to kill him.

Wait — he was dead. Could he still be killed?

The idea of being dead made him anxious, and to divert himself he guessed what the hair color of the passing peasants would be, were it not gray. Identifying blonds was easy; distinguishing reds from browns was significantly more difficult.

He eavesdropped on their conversations, listening for Beatrice's name. They talked mainly of peasanty things, bread loaves and taxes and hounds.

Eventually Ralph started to hear one word repeated over and over — "clutch." It was a term that he had only ever known to be applied to secondhand cars, and he couldn't imagine how it could relate to a fantastic land. He rolled to hear better.

The conversationalists in question were a pair of washerwomen (both with hair that would probably be gray in any context, Ralph noted), lugging basketfuls of wet clothing toward the gate and resting every few paces. Their names, he very soon surmised, were Ada and Alda. "I heard," Ada said, "that Antonia has felt the Clutch."

"No! When?"

"This morning. She was passing programs out for services, and suddenly she went even whiter than she usually is. She tried to cover it up — you know Antonia — but we all knew what had happened."

Alda tsked. "I don't understand how people think they can hide it. You'd think, given all that's happened, that people wouldn't still try to keep secrets."

Ada grunted and gave her laundry basket a tug.

"Ada? You haven't felt it, have you?"

"No," Ada snapped. "Of course not."

They pulled their baskets in silence. They were drawing out of range — Ralph had to crawl to the edge of a branch to hear them. "How long has Antonia been with us?" Ada asked.

"No one remembers exactly. Aurelio tried to calculate it, after I told him she'd felt the Clutch. He thinks it was forty-one days or so."

Ada sighed mechanically, in the manner of people reading of morbid but far-off things. "Poor Antonia. Now a filthy undead."

Alda shook her head. "So sad."

"Let us lay our trust in Gid."

"Yes, let us lay our trust in Him."

They crested a hill and were gone.

Ralph descended from the tree. The sun seemed to be setting (it was tough to tell without color), and he imagined it would be prudent to be behind walls after nightfall.

The city reminded him of Durbanshire and Chessie's castle, in that the townsfolk would stare studiously at the ground, involve themselves in the stitching of their garments, anything to avoid meeting Ralph's outsider eyes. As he passed along the cobblestone streets he began to feel very much alone, to an extent he hadn't felt since that terrible year when he couldn't attend birthday parties and had been mercilessly teased about his paladin.

He began sneaking glances at himself to see what could be so off-putting about his appearance. There wasn't anything so odd about him, was there? Pants and a T-shirt, its red stained in rings with the dried salt of the sea. Hair greasy but fairly tamed, shoes soggy but with nice — then he realized it: He was in color.

He passed through the town as if he were a ship's prow, crowds of locals wordlessly falling to either side. He beat back his sudden sense of loneliness by focusing on memorizing the lay of the town, noting that he passed nothing but residences — no bars, no inns. And no Beatrice. As nightfall drew nearer, Ralph climbed a set of stone steps and wandered the city battlements, eventually perching on the edge and watching the gray sun draw back its light to reveal the moon.

During the earliest part of man's existence, he was in constant contact with the dead. Ceremonies, phantom voices, tombs, all provided a means to access those who were no longer alive. Those who were yet living —

Ralph was startled to hear the book's narration broadcast in his head.

— would speak to those who were already gone, and so knew what to expect upon their own deaths, learning that the stage between life and death was not short. Purgatory Main Isle was divided into two cities, that of the Recently-Living and that of the Soon-to-be-Dead. Half a being's time would be spent in the first city, and then he would feel the Clutch and pass to the second, only to drop into farther, even more gruesome, realms once that second period had passed.

"Excuse me," Ralph called to the invisible catwalks. "Hello?"

The citizens of the two cities used to mingle freely, the Recently-Living and the Soon-to-be-Dead sharing their slow declines. But the Soon-to-be-Dead (which is how they have chosen to call themselves now that "undead" has become so overdone) were stinky, and had correspondingly dismal outlooks on life. So, many ages ago, the mayor of the Recently-Living city decided that if he forbade the Soon-to-be-Dead from visiting the Recently-Living's city, their nastiness would stop making everyone even gloomier than they already were. So a decree was passed. Though he banned travel between the city-states, in the interests of diplomacy the Recently-Living mayor offered to send an emissary to the border of the two cities once every three years, if the Soon-to-be-Dead would do the same.

The Soon-to-be-Dead have never sent a single emissary. Every three years, one of the Recently-Living would travel to the same old rotting wooden table set up in the woods and wait until dawn for a ghostly emissary that never arrived.

So it has been for thousands of years.

Until now.

"Until now?" Ralph yelled up to the catwalks.

But the narrator pretended not to hear him.

Ralph cheekily repeated his question.

The narration shut off entirely. It couldn't reward such character pertness.

# CHAPTER LIII

"Hey!" Ralph yelled. "You come down here and tell me precisely what's going on!"

The city's night watchmen eyed Ralph suspiciously, for it's very difficult to carry off yelling at the night sky without looking shifty.

Ralph was frustrated. He felt that in some ways he might as well still have been bedridden in Regina's cottage, listening to a tale told on a stupid teddy bear. Clearly, he realized, the story transpiring around him was directed by forces much more powerful than he. But rather than give in to its currents, as any well-behaved character would do, he rankled.

Lucky for our despairing Ralph, the death count of this novel thus far was high, which meant a flood of fresh beings entering Purgatory. What with the hundreds of characters dispatched over the course of these three plots, one or two familiar faces were bound to have been randomly selected to appear in Purgatory Main Isle. And one of them came walking along right then.

Or, more accurately, flying.

Yes, it was Prestidigitator. Not the Daphne impersonation, but the real fairy, who had died back in the bunny blast and had been assigned to PMI before the mass death of the Snow Queen's Flood. She had been scouring the city of the Recently-Living for some time, hoping to find Ralph or Cecil, and her searching had gotten more and more frantic, since she had recently felt the Clutch and knew she would soon pass over to the Soon-to-be-Dead. Sure, hunting continually meant getting no sleep for a week — but there was plenty of time to sleep once she was totally dead, right?

You can imagine her delight to come upon Ralph. Granted, her glee was tempered when she saw Ralph crazily yelling at the sky, but it was immense nonetheless. She alighted on his shoulder and wrapped her daisy-pale fairy arms around his neck.

"Ralph!" she squeaked in joy. "You've died!"

Being reminded of his predicament didn't help Ralph's mood. But there's no overestimating the charm of Prestidigitator's button features. He embraced her.

Once he'd released her they exchanged whatever pleasantries they could think of while in Purgatory. "Have you . . . felt the Clutch yet?" she eventually asked, nervously nibbling on a wingtip.

"No, I don't think so," he said.

Prestidigitator gasped, the gust of which pulled her forward a few inches. "Oh! Of course you wouldn't — you're in *color!*"

Ralph peered at his clothing. "Yes, I suppose I am. Any idea what that's about?"

Prestidigitator shook her head, stunned.

Ralph then took a deep breath and recounted his recent adventures in search of Beatrice, culminating in his apparent death on the baleen of a whale, his arrival in Purgatory Main Isle, and hearing the narration broadcast in his head.

Prestidigitator was unimpressed, as fairies will be, at something as banal as a book narrating itself to one of its characters. But Purgatory politics had her fascinated. "So they send an emissary every few years, huh?"

"Every three years, yeah. If the jerk narrator is to be trusted."

A nearby tree fell on the city wall and nearly flattened Ralph, who sprang to his feet in alarm. At this point any true character should have been quaking in fear at the awesome power of the Book; but instead, as Ralph was a testy young geek, he sulked.

"Well," Prestidigitator said once she'd returned (she had been buffeted some fathoms away by the falling tree), "I'm going to guess — only a guess, mind you — that those three years will be up tonight."

"Why do you think that?"

"That's the way life works when you're a fairy. Stick with me."

"Do you know where the rotten table is?" Ralph asked.

Prestidigitator shivered. "Yes."

The trail to the border led through more territories than a trail rightfully should. At first it was a forest lane, then a rocky mountain path, then a gravel perimeter of a skating lake, then a crystal canyon bridge, then a rope bridge in a wood canopy, then an underground tunnel, all in only an hour of hiking. It was like the whole world had been compressed to the snow globe scale of Purgatory Main Isle. Ralph, awed into silence, held Prestidigitator's hand as they progressed.

The quality of the grayscale was changing, the darks sliding on a continuum from tweed to sepia to gunmetal to a set of flat tones, from the black-and-white of film to that of newsprint. By the time they reached the perimeter clearing, the only colors remaining were pure black and pure white with no shading in between, so that they looked to be traveling through a land of simple cutouts and low-tech photocopies.

There was no vegetation in the narrow clearing, just shadowed chalk. At one side of a rough-cut table, flipping the crumbling pages of a leather-bound book, was the Recently-Living emissary. He appeared to have died sometime in the nineteenth century; he wore upon his head a tall traveling hat, on which the velvet had frayed and stood out like a mist of fuzzy curls. His long coat was shapeless from a century of wear.

"Do we introduce ourselves?" Ralph wondered to Prestidigitator from where they were hidden behind a tree at the edge of the chilly glen. "Or is that forbidden? What do you think?"

Prestidigitator wrapped a wing around Ralph's mouth. For, across the clearing, a second figure had emerged.

The emissary coughed twice in shock, straightened his old coat, and squinted.

Through the crackling branches lurched an undead creature.

Conventional storytelling sets up a rather arbitrary distinction between the skeleton and the zombie. The story usually goes thusly: Zombies are lumbering, pallid creatures with a good amount of flesh dangling from them, while skeletons are rickety figures that have long been picked clean of muscles, organs, and sinew. Now, of course, the months post-death are actually a slow process of decomposition. Sure, you start out looking zombie-ish, but as chunks of flesh rot and fall away you wind up looking more and more like a skeleton. So it's foolish to say there's one group of zombies, here, and one group of skeletons, there, as foolish as saying everyone is either kind or mean, smart or dumb, feminine or masculine. This particular undead had a fair amount of muscle remaining around her spinal column and a big goopy piece of flesh on one knee, and had managed to retain a chunk of brain that dangled limply from one side of her fractured skull like a wet sock. When she spoke, she revealed one circular staircase of a tooth in her jaw. You can call her a skeleton or a zombie — I'll call her an undead and be done with it.

The Recently-Living emissary closed his book and made the sign of the cross as the undead woman shuffled toward the table. For a diplomat, he seemed entirely unprepared to encounter anyone. After removing his hat, he flicked his fingers through his hair (literally: one hair), placed the hat neatly on the table, stood up, held out his hand as if for a shake, thought better of it, sat down, and put his hat back on. Then he took the hat back off and held it over his nose, for the other emissary was very stinky.

The Soon-to-be-Dead emissary didn't sit at the table (the Recently-Living emissary thought this was to intimidate him, though little did he know that it was only because the undead find it very hard to regain a standing position without the benefit of cartilage), and when she spoke it was with a booming voice that emerged from the center of her carved-out chest. "Those you call undead have a demand. We have decided that the boundary between the lands of the Recently-Living and the Soon-to-be-Dead is unfair. The Recently-Living have too much lollipop and sunbeam, the Soon-to-be-Dead too much hangnail and gloom. We thereby insist that the boundary be redrawn."

The Recently-Living emissary worked hard to formulate a response as he watched one of the Soon-to-be-Dead's lips fall off. "Oh?" he said, gagging.

"We have thought long about how best to do this. You have no choice but to accept our plan."

"I say, that sounds most unfair." The Recently-Living emissary was about to continue, but was stilled by the undead emissary's angry expression, underscored by a sudden throbbing of her exposed brain.

"The Soon-to-be-Dead's plan is that this night, at the stroke of midnight, after the last rays of the white sun have disappeared, the Soon-to-be-Dead and the Recently-Living will send their fastest riders from the city gates. Where the two horsemen collide, the boundary will be."

The Recently-Living emissary found his voice. "This is a landgrab? And based on how *fast* we are? That's ridiculous." He paused, thinking for a moment. "I'm not even sure we have any horses."

The Soon-to-be-Dead emissary extracted a piece of parchment from between her rotting leg muscles. "The undead have written their demand for your superiors to peruse. At midnight, we will send our ghost queen, Annabelle, racing toward you."

The Recently-Living emissary pulled the damp paper from her hands. "You want me to bring this back to Lord Gid?"

"No," the undead emissary said. "We wish one of the three watching to bring it back." And with that, she cleanly sunk the remaining bones of a hand into the Now-Recently-Recently-Living emissary's stomach. His guts shivered out over her skeletal hand like so much cream. He twitched and slumped over the table as the undead emissary shuffled away.

"Ralph!" Prestidigitator squeaked once they were again alone. "What was all of that about?"

"I don't know," Ralph said, his stomach heaving. He stepped into the clearing. "But she said there were three of us."

He spun around. "Who's there?" he called.

There was a rustling in a thicket, and who should emerge but Beatrice, plain and lovely Beatrice.

# CHAPTER LIV

Beatrice stepped over the barren chalk ground and checked the pulse of the Now-Thoroughly-Dead-But-Recently-Living emissary.[1]

"Beatrice?" Ralph called. "Is that you?"

But she ignored him. Already she was tearing toward the Soon-to-be-Dead city.

Ralph sprinted to catch up with her. "Where are you going?"

"I won't be able to find the Soon-to-be-Dead city on my own," she panted. "Tailing the emissary is my only chance of seeing my mother again."

"Your mother is a zombie?" Ralph asked.

"She's not in the Recently-Living city. Either she's undead or she's gone entirely. And you heard the emissary say the name of the ghost queen was Annabelle. This is my chance to find out if it's her."

They reached a line of charcoal trees. "I have to run," she said. "The trail is getting cold."

---

[1] *n.b.*: What happens when someone who is already dead dies is actually quite complex, and not always the outcome one would expect. I recommend that those further interested consult *After the Afterlife: Under the Underworld* or works of similar scholarly merit.

"I'm coming with you," Ralph said firmly.

"I'd try to talk you out of it," Beatrice said, "but I'm terrified of doing this alone."

"Let's go."

"Someone needs to deliver the undead's parchment to the Recently-Living."

"Don't worry about that," Prestidigitator said. She had already flitted to the shoulders of the dead emissary and picked up the rank decree. She nodded dutifully in Ralph and Beatrice's direction, then zipped toward the Recently-Living city.

Beatrice and Ralph began their dash into the realm of the undead.

# CHAPTER LV

Shadows moved in the oily light, creeping closer with each step Ralph and Beatrice took. Some were shapes and some were figures, always growing and shrinking. They were everywhere Ralph and Beatrice looked, thronging the path and tangling in the breezes above.

As they chased the undead emissary, Ralph and Beatrice sprinted through territories similar to those Ralph had passed through to come to the clearing, only in washed-out shades and reversed order. By the time they reached the end, even the grayness had seeped out. The landscape was an overexposed white, as if etched in scrimshaw and left to bleach, and was even more thickly teeming with shadows. Ralph and Beatrice slipped between them, hands held tightly.

Finally the undead emissary slowed before a massive wall. The city of the Soon-to-be-Dead appeared to be identical to that of the Recently-Living — only at this side of Purgatory, the city had no discernible entrance. Ralph and Beatrice hid at the edge of the wood and watched the emissary run her bone hands over the seams of the white rock. Eventually she located a certain stone, jabbed her fingers around it as if to pluck it out, then dove through. The wall admitted her as easily as if she were a hologram.

"Do you think there are any guards?" Ralph whispered.

"I don't see any," Beatrice whispered back. "There might be, like, invisible guards, but we're probably okay."

They tried putting their fingers through various stones, with scuffed knuckles the sole result. Then Beatrice's hand slid through one of the rocks. "Found it," she said.

"Wait," Ralph said. "Let me go first."

"Are you kidding? They'll spot you right away."

Ralph looked down at himself. His many colors were all the more highlighted in the whitewashed world of the undead. "What's *up* with that?" he wondered.

"I don't know," Beatrice said. "No offense, but you're a total liability."

"Thanks," Ralph said glumly.

Beatrice took his hand. "I'm so glad to have you here. But I'm going first, and I won't claim you if you're spotted."

With that she disappeared into the stone. Ralph took a deep breath and leaped after.

He promptly bounced back, with a scratched forehead and ringing ears. He pressed a fingertip against the stone. It didn't give, not one bit.

Eventually Beatrice reappeared. "No luck?"

Ralph shook his head.

She poked him in the chest. "I'm starting to think you might not be dead at all, my friend. Hmm. I'm going to have to find a rope or something," she said. "You concentrate on staying inconspicuous. I'll be right back."

Ralph nodded as she disappeared. He didn't relish being alone with the shadows, but he hadn't much choice.

He crouched in a hollow at the base of a tree and kept his focus trained on the top of the fortress wall. The worst thing would be to miss the drop of the rope entirely.

The terror Ralph's surroundings brought out in him was fluttery and shallow, like that produced by a child's imagination. He remembered the sensation well from the camping trips he used to go on with his parents. The days were great fun — games of catch, practicing his xylophone, so many prospective rocks to add to his collection — until he had to go brush his teeth. During the nighttime walk to the campsite bathrooms, his flashlight would trace feeble circles of known things on the ground — decaying leaves, twig cairns, the reflections of rodent eyes — while the infinite darkness was left unknown. Even when camping years later he was unable to walk to the bathroom without eventually dashing headlong, hordes of imagined phantoms pursuing him. He would return to the tent breathless and hiding it.

He felt twinges of the same sensation now. But somehow this reincarnated fear was . . . not lessened, but more directed. Because now he didn't have to imagine the evil beings stalking the night — they were all quite evident. The shadows had become so numerous that they had coalesced into bigger shapes, forming ghoulish pyramids, great whips of their dead matter lashing the sky.

For now, they ignored Ralph entirely; this peculiar, brightly colored young man mattered nothing to them.

Finally he caught movement at the top of the wall, and saw something drop over. Doing his best (and failing) to blot the shadows from his mind, he stole across to the wall and examined it. It wasn't a typical rope — instead it was a stretch of bones, knotted together with tendons and entrails. He grasped the end and started to climb, and as he did, the rushing sound of the shadows ceased entirely. Glancing back, he saw that they had paused in their endless toils to stare at him.

Then they started throwing themselves at the rope.

Ralph squeezed his eyes shut and clutched the bones as the first shadows hit him. But he felt only a slight chill. He opened his eyes. The shadows were slashing out at him with their shadow hands, but they passed right through him.

Ralph gritted his chattering teeth and started climbing again. The larger femur and humerus bones made for easy going, but more often than not he was gripping intestine or tendon. Eventually he made it to the top and heaved himself over the side.

Beatrice was waiting for him on the battlement. She began to scramble down the wall to the city below, but Ralph laid a hand on her arm. "Where are we going?" he asked.

"To see my mother and my sister again," Beatrice said.

"Sister!"

Beatrice nodded.

"You mean Daphne?"

"No, my half sister Annabel. My mum's other daughter."

"How do we know where they are?" Ralph asked. "How do we know they're even here?"

"I wished it so," Beatrice said simply, and with a flash of her filmy gray gown she was over the side.

Ralph soundlessly dropped after her into the undead city.

# CHAPTER LVI

Once Ralph's eyes acclimated to the light, he realized that the place they landed in wasn't much of a city at all, only smoky bonfires about which the undead shambled in random motions.

There were all varieties: some only bone, others whole except for a torn-away ear or eye. Banshees congressed around the palisades. Zombie imps ripped flesh from passersby and pelted one another. Flitting throughout were a large number of winged fairy skeletons with Chihuahua skulls, undoubtedly an influx from Cecil's war.

"I'm going on the assumption that we mustn't let them see us," Beatrice said as they cowered in the shadow of the wall.

Ralph, having seen *Night of the Living Dead*, agreed. "What kind of monsters do you think your mother and sister are?" he asked, after pausing to debate whether the question was rude.

"I don't know," Beatrice said.

"Did they die happy?" Ralph ventured.

"I imagine not. Mum was in a hospital, and my sister . . . I imagine not."

"Maybe they're ghosts. That sounds right."

"I don't see anything that I'd call a proper ghost," Beatrice said.

If I hadn't acted now, Ralph and Beatrice might have wandered around for hours searching for ghosts. And, for reasons you will soon find out, my darling Beatrice didn't have hours of life to waste. So I simply had the ghost cave momentarily glow orange. In a black-and-white world, it was a splendid enough display that Ralph and Beatrice noticed it immediately.

"Did you see that?" Ralph asked.

"Yes," Beatrice breathed.

Ghosts move very much like smoke-lifted ashes, charred and weightless, rising slowly with glowing edges and then meandering back down to the ground. These particular phantasms circled a cavernous pit in the open ground of the undead capital.

"I guess we have to go into that cesspool," Ralph said cautiously (and, I might add, a trifle judgmentally). "What if we observe it for a while, and wait to sneak in until the ghosts fall asleep?"

"I'm pretty sure ghosts don't sleep, Ralph. And even if they did . . . you don't happen to know the time, do you?" Beatrice asked.

"The time?" The notion that something like time existed here hadn't occurred to him. His calculator watch had been lost long ago. But wedged in his jeans pocket, beneath his pet rock Jeremiah, was his cell phone. Surely it wasn't possible . . . but when he lifted it out he saw that somehow it had survived traveling to the bottom of the sea. He shook it, awed.

Gentle reader, I apologize for the ample evidence of my hand. The plot-meddling will stop as soon as my delightful Beatrice gets herself back on track, I promise.

Ralph had once spent an entire week researching cell networks, and chose his carrier well: his cell phone had automatically set itself to the Purgatory Main Isle time zone. "It's five P.M.," Ralph reported.

"We don't have time to spare, then," Beatrice said. "I felt the Clutch ten and a half days ago, which means . . . well, it means we have only a little time before I turn into an undead."

Ralph squeezed Beatrice's hand. "How long exactly?"

"Until midnight."

They skirted the city wall, trying to avoid the gazes of the plentiful undead. After Ralph almost knocked over an especially bony specimen, they discovered that the more skeletal an undead is, the more blind it is. They used this to their advantage, ducking behind skeletons as they passed.

But skeletons provide very poor coverage. Even with their best efforts, Ralph and Beatrice were eventually spotted by the vampires who, it turns out, have excellent vision. Not to mention their fine skills of echolocation, which no amount of ducking behind skeletons, however skillfully executed, can circumvent.

An alarm cry went up while Ralph and Beatrice were still a good forty paces from the ghost cave. They backed against a wall as the undead began swarming toward them. Then, realizing the futility of cowering, Ralph led Beatrice in a sprint away from the wall and through a rapidly narrowing corridor of the foul creatures.

They stomped on the first few juvenile zombies they came to, and then kicked their way through a pack of skeletal dogs. In the process Ralph found one of their skulls in his hand, which he pitched like a softball, obliterating a rickety knight. By then the vampires had flown close. Right as they streaked through the white sky toward them, Ralph and Beatrice reached the lip of the ghost pit.

Phantoms floated up from the chasm and howled in their rush to pray to the moon.

Ralph and Beatrice clutched each other and threw themselves in.

# CHAPTER LVII

After the first wrenching second, the only sensation Ralph felt was the rush of humid wind against him; free fall became more freedom than falling. He and Beatrice plummeted in each other's arms, her thin hair lashing his face. He had no sense of the closeness of the walls, how far they had to go, or how many ghosts they whizzed past. They simply fell, their only thought wonderment at exactly when they would splatter. It wasn't the most urgent sensation, actually; splattering, after all, was nothing more than an unpredictable way to finally become like everyone else here.

The gusts from below thickened until they approximated hot panting. Ralph and Beatrice slowed before the fetid headwind. Once they reached idling speed, Ralph called to Beatrice, "You don't have a flashlight, do you?"

"No!" she shouted. "But what about your phone?"

Though it would provide only pathetic illumination, Ralph slid his cell phone out of his pocket, opened it . . .

. . . and closed it immediately.

Around them had flashed ghosts in a syrupy concentration. Legs and waists, twisted and transparent, supporting the remnants of mawlike chests and bloodied brows.

Beatrice and Ralph slowed more and more in the updraft, finally alighting on flesh-soft ground, the hum of spirits whizzing by as quiet and constant as the blood coursing in their ears.

Ralph wondered which direction to step. But before he needed to decide, a candle glow began approaching from far away. Its flickering illumination cast hardly enough light to reveal any gory details of what it passed. They couldn't see a wrist or a hand holding it, only the small flame passing through the dark. After witnessing hordes of undead, it was this simple, quiet impossibility that finally caused Ralph to move into full-blown panic.

He scrambled headlong in the opposite direction for only a second before he struck a stone wall. Running his hand along it, he found it curved in every direction. There was a crevice it might be possible to hide in, if only he could wedge his leg inside . . . but as he attempted to, he became aware that Beatrice was not beside him.

"Beatrice," he cried, "come on! We have to hide!"

But she didn't respond. Ralph hesitated at the edge of his crevice, then reached in the blind dark until he found her again, standing still in the center of the chamber, outlined in the candlelight.

"You don't have to come with me," Beatrice murmured.

Ralph took a deep breath and squeezed Beatrice's hand. He might have been scared, but he didn't want to be alone.

The candle came closer and closer.

They peered at it. The candle lingered before them for a few seconds while Ralph beat back the urge to close his eyes. When the small flame slowly withdrew the way it came, Ralph and Beatrice followed.


At first they seemed to be passing through a wide negative space, since the candlelight fell on nothing but a slackening concentration of spirits. But eventually the glow revealed roots and mossy rock overhangs. The light began to shine on other similar candle glows, one lined up after another at precise intervals. When Ralph's and Beatrice's footsteps began to strike smooth stones, it became apparent they were ascending a ramp.

Eventually the candle led them into a wedge-shaped chamber fully lit by chandeliers. Though it was shaped like the interior of a galleon, the walls were made of rock; if it was a ship, it was a ship without an exterior. The room swayed and tilted fractionally, as if pitched by small waves in the mass of stone below. Lining the walls of the hold were invisible servants also holding feeble candles, each phantom only evident as a disturbance in the candlesmoke.

In the center of the chamber, reclining on a mass of pillows, were two women. One was older but persistently holding onto youth, firm muscles evident beneath dry wrinkles, her legs tucked beneath her in advantageous position. The other was the young creature the older bore the memory of: features beautiful and regular enough to pass through the mind with traceless electricity, her expression cool but hinting at peals of glee within.

Beatrice bowed her head. "Mother."

"Come here," the older woman said.

Beatrice lifted her face — Ralph saw her jaw tremble — and approached her mother. When the woman placed her arms around her, Beatrice heaved a sob, though she didn't return the embrace.

The woman said, "Oh my Beatrice. You've come to me."

The younger woman rose from the cushions, smiled at Ralph, and held out her limp hand. "I'm Annabel," she said.

Ralph took her hand and wondered what to do with it. He had a guide-book on talking to girls back in his New Jersey bedroom, but he couldn't remember if it ever described a situation like this. "Hey, Annabel. I'm Ralph."

Beatrice's mother broke off from her daughter and looked at Ralph. "And who have you brought with you, Beatrice?"

"This is Ralph, Mum."

"Hello, Ralph. I'm Annabelle, Beatrice's mother."

"Two Annabelles!" Ralph said, dropping Annabel's hand. Then he added, "Very pleased to meet you."

"I know," Annabelle said, throwing herself back on the cushions. "The spellings are different, but you can't know that. It's impossibly confusing, I'll admit. I wanted my first daughter to have my name. Your main child has to suffer for all your crazy whims. Isn't that right, Annabel?"

Annabel flounced to the pillows, flung her hands around her mother's neck, and kissed her on the cheek, staring at Ralph the whole time. "That's right, Mum."

"Hi, Annabel," Beatrice said. "It's been a long time since I've seen you."

"Oh, I know!" Annabel said gaily. "I was what, six? I grew up *so much* between then and dying."

"You've been on my mind so much. I wish I could have seen you, but Father . . ."

"Yes, yes, yes, your dad wouldn't let you see us. Well, it's my fault for having the first wife for my mum!" Annabel broke out into laughter, in which she was soon joined by her mother. Their eyes gleamed.

Ralph's throat was dry. This was all too weird.

Beatrice spoke slowly: "I feel like in some ways you never left us. Either of you. Gert won't let him talk about it, but I feel like you're always on Father's mind."

"Why, Beatrice!" Annabelle said. "You've only just met up with us, after years apart. Last time you saw me, I was in a coffin! Do you have to be so serious? Let's have some *fun*."

"Some fun?" Beatrice asked solemnly.

"Ralph," Annabelle said, resolutely chipper. "Tell us about yourself."

Seeing Beatrice's sad bewilderment, Ralph did his best to steer the conversation into safer territory while she sorted through her feelings. He told them about his high school, his favorite teachers, then barreled into the children's three wishes, how it felt being the last survivor of the Snow Queen's Flood, the stench of baleen.

"So you're not even supposed to be here!" interrupted Annabel, taking Ralph's arm in her palm. "No wonder you're still bright!"

"But you're colorless," Annabelle said to Beatrice. "Does that mean you've died, my child? Have you come to stay with us?"

Beatrice nodded.

"Why did you choose to come to Purgatory forever?" Ralph asked Beatrice.

"I was tired of stuff. Lots of stuff. Like being so overlooked."

"Beatrice," Annabelle said. "You have a beautiful soul."

Beatrice wrinkled her nose. "I'm shy, Mum, that's what you mean, I'm shy."

"What's that saying, 'silence is the greatest wisdom'?"

"That was totally Gandhi," Annabel offered.

"Mum," said Beatrice. "Poetlike and beautiful is admired, poetlike and plain is ignored. No one gives a lick for what I think. I wish . . . I used to wish all the time that I could escape Gert and Dad and run to your flat, to live with you and Annabel. But I didn't know where you lived. And when I finally got Dad to tell me, you were already dead, both of you."

"Oh my God," Annabel said, a hand over her mouth. "So you bumped yourself off? You really *are* intense! *We're* not even that serious, and we're *ghosts.*"

"Come here," Annabelle said. Before she had even drawn Beatrice to her bosom, they both had begun to sob.

Annabel rolled her eyes and turned flirtatiously to Ralph. "They're going to be wallowing for a while. Do you want me to give you a tour? There's some really fun stuff around here."

"No thanks," Ralph said. "I'd rather stick around Beatrice, if that's okay."

"Sure, whatever," Annabel said.

Ralph positioned himself at one end of the stone galleon, as far as he could get from any of the invisible servants. He watched Beatrice murmur to her mother, her mother rock her in return. Annabel hovered nearby, biting her nails and pretending not to watch.

Beatrice had chosen to come to the Underworld; Ralph knew it wasn't really his place to talk her into finding a way to leave. And even if he did try, how could he undo her *death*? At the same time, he was certain no good could come of Beatrice fixating on the loss of her mother and sister. She could spend an eternity down here, first crying over her Annabel and Annabelle, later coming to mourn Cecil and Daphne and everything she had lost in her old life.

"How did you wind up here?" Ralph asked Annabel.

"Me? Oh, it's silly, really. Misadministered tetanus shot."

"You're kidding."

"Nope, it's true!"

"And your mom?"

"She was in a coma. And she got in that coma the same way Beatrice got here. She chose to."

"Oh," Ralph said. He rested his head in his hands.

Then something occurred to him. He darted to his feet and pulled out his cell phone.

"Oh my God," Annabel said. "Phones have gotten so *cool*. Can I see?"

He flipped it open and checked the time. 11:30 — only half an hour until Beatrice permanently slipped over to the undead.

He jostled Beatrice, who was murmuring lost words into her mother's ear. "Beatrice," he said. "You only have half an hour left."

She peered at him blearily. "So? This is where I want to be."

"I'm sorry," Annabelle said to Ralph, "but this really doesn't involve you. My daughter is staying here, with me."

Ralph felt a tug on his arm and saw Annabel beside him, fluttering her long lashes. "You could join us," she said. "It's simple enough to do."

Yikes.

"How do you know there's only half an hour left?" Annabelle asked.

"It's nearly midnight," Beatrice said dreamily to her mother.

"Nearly midnight!" exclaimed Annabelle. "The boundary race is at midnight!"

"So?" Beatrice asked.

"I am the queen, so I am the undead rider," said the ghostly Annabelle.

"I'll come with you," Beatrice said.

"As you wish, my love. You" — she pointed to Ralph — "have no choice but to follow. Unless you want to stay here with the phantoms."

Annabel sealed the door to the stone galleon. "To the surface!" she cried. Ralph watched the candles rearrange themselves as the invisible servants took their positions around the ship. The vessel began to ascend through the solid rock.

# CHAPTER LVIII

It is difficult to gauge one's progress in a ship that has neither deck nor portals. Ralph presumed they were heading upward only because the ship pitched back, strongly enough to knock him to the floor. The rock walls of the vessel moved and slid, accelerating until they became a flowing mass of stone streaming around the open space. A slight breeze sifted the close air of the hold, and as the ship jerked and tossed through various densities of rock, its four occupants made good use of the cushion pile in its center.

Eventually the stone began to lighten in color. Ralph was able to see, in the wall's cross-section, roots and small creatures that had made their homes in the soil. At one point a disoriented undead mole dropped into the hold and was promptly hurled back out by one of the invisible servants. As the gravel turned to silt, and the silt to sandy soil, the ship came to the surface outside the Soon-to-be-Dead city. As it had only been a void in the rock, once it arrived in the open air there was nothing left of the stone galleon but a pile of cushions in the middle of the ashen grass.

Annabelle rose to her feet and snapped imperiously. Suddenly she was clad in a jet-black gown, a crown nestled in her large hair, a regal version of her previous self. "Horse!" she commanded.

An undead engineer emerged from within the walls of the Soon-to-be-Dead city, coaxing a horse skeleton clad in battle armor. "The metal plates will slow it down," Annabelle said. "Remove them."

The engineer — a tall and awkwardly-composed skeleton who wore a monocle over one eye socket — pressed his finger bones to his skull in dismay. The armor had taken weeks to prepare: It was filigreed and etched with meticulously rendered scenes culled from undead cultural history. But at Annabelle's command the invisible servants set to work removing the metal-work masterpieces from the horse. It whinnied, a hollow wheeze.

Annabelle threw herself over its back.

"Mother," Beatrice said. "Could you call me a horse, too, so I can ride behind you?"

Annabelle nodded. She snapped her fingers and the engineer called forward another ornamented undead horse. Beatrice mounted it and looked at Ralph. "Coming?"

Ralph got on behind her.

"Annabel?" Beatrice asked.

Annabel shook her head, bit her lip, and gave a perky wave good-bye.

"The time!" Annabelle demanded. "The boundary race must commence at precisely twelve!"

Ralph pulled out his phone and checked. "11:59, no . . . midnight!"

Annabelle cried out, and the horses sped off toward the land of the Recently-Living.

Training undead horses is immensely difficult. When irritated they tend to maul their grooms, for one thing. But that's not even the worst of it.

The cornerstone of breaking in a living horse is food — sugar cubes, carrots, the like — and undead horses simply can't eat. It's comical when they try, as the food promptly slips between their ribs and lands on the ground. So the task of the Soon-to-be-Dead trainers — engineering a horse faster than any the Recently-Living could produce — was tricky. For one thing, skeletal horses tend to shed chunks of flesh when they gallop. Even cantering results in a catastrophic loss of cartilage. At about thirty miles per hour, skeletal horses' skulls lob off, ending the whole process right there. More zombielike horses don't fare much better. Despite its many striking qualities, rotting flesh is not aerodynamic. And as for their gait — a shuffling gallop is pleasing to neither rider nor spectator.

For these reasons and more, the undead engineers developed an almost-cyborg horse, an alloy of titanium and bone that galloped but lacked such horsely amenities as a tail and personality. The Soon-to-be-Dead creation was also, Ralph quickly noticed, severely lacking in comforts. The slap of his butt on its alloy rump was more rodeo than derby.

Annabelle's horse shot off as befitted a titanium-bone bullet, but Ralph and Beatrice's horse, weighed down in battle armor and carrying two passengers, struck off at half-pace. They easily tracked the scrambled evidence of Annabelle's passing — torn branches, ripped thickets — as they cantered through the underworld. Shadows ceased their bustling to watch them as they proceeded to the middle territory.

As they traveled, Ralph watched Beatrice closely, to see if anything changed when she became fully undead. But, so far at least, she seemed the same.

When they reached the clearing, they found no one there. "Look," Beatrice said, pointing at the far side. Ralph followed her finger and saw more sundered evidence of Annabelle's passage.

"Wow," he said, "she's rocking it. Shout-out to the undead."

They trotted by the rotten table and followed Annabelle's course. Even the most muddled tracker could follow the ice crystals the undead horse drooled in a steaming path through the underbrush. Once they had returned to the more colorful grays, it wasn't long before they reached the fortifications of the Recently-Living city.

Annabelle had dismounted from her horse and was standing breathless next to the slate wall, both hands touching the surface, as if it were home base in a high-stakes game of tag.

"What happened? Where's the other rider?" Ralph asked her, shuddering. Annabelle was far more ghostly now, a luminous horror in the true midnight of the Recently-Living land.

"He did not ride in time!" Annabelle cried out. Or, more accurately, wailed out, as proper ghosts do. "Lord Gid has failed! Let this be my final revenge." She raised her voice even higher. "Let it be known that all open land is now in the hands of the Soon-to-be-Dead! Stay in your pathetic city, Recently-Living; you will never again roam freely."

Somewhere from within the city: "What was that?"

From farther: "Dunno. Some ghost, I think."

"What's she ruckusing about?"

". . . think they've conquered all the land, or somesuch."

"Whatever."

Annabelle let out a bloodcurdling banshee scream.

To which, from a long distance, came a responding shout that was unmistakably Gideon's.

Annabelle, who had been too occupied with her own screeching to hear properly, whirled around. "What was that?"

"It was Father," Beatrice said softly.

"Giddy? What did he say?"

"I don't know. He yelled. He didn't say anything."

"It was a shout. A victory shout, from the sounds of it," Ralph offered cautiously. "What is your *dad* doing here?"

Beatrice shrugged.

"Don't be ridiculous," Annabelle said. "I won. What in the world would he have to be bloody victorious about?"

"Might there be more than one way to get to the Soon-to-be-Dead city?" Ralph suggested.

And it was true. After leaving the city of the Recently-Living, Gideon had passed along a forest lane, then a rocky mountain path, then a gravel perimeter to a skating lake, then a crystal canyon bridge, then *under* the rope bridge in a wood canopy, then through an underground tunnel. They had missed each other entirely.

"This is simply ridiculous. I've won," said Annabelle.

"But you can see that maybe Father could make the argument that *he's* won," Beatrice said politely.

Annabelle snarled at Beatrice and made as if to zap her, which was an extraordinarily alarming sight for a serious-minded girl who may or may not be fully undead and who was just reintroduced to her dead mother. She burst out in tears.

"Oh, I wasn't really going to strike you," Annabelle said crossly. "This is so frustrating, that's all. I'm beside myself." She seemed to calm down, then suddenly turned extraordinarily bright and screeched at such decibels that she knocked over Ralph, the crying Beatrice, and a nest of dead magpies, who rose squawking into the air. "Where are you, Gideon?" Annabelle called.

Gideon yelled something back from far away but, since he didn't share Annabelle's supernatural screeching abilities, whatever he said was unintelligible. Annabelle, Beatrice, and Ralph stared at each other, waiting for one of them to translate. When none of them did, Ralph spoke: "Do you think your dad still has his phone?"

Beatrice shrugged. Ralph pulled out his own phone and waited while it dialed — he was low on battery, and hadn't brought his charger. Even in Purgatory, Gideon must have screened his call, because he went to voicemail. Ralph left a message.

Gideon soon called back. "Ralph? What a surprise!"

Ralph put a hand over his free ear and smiled awkwardly into the phone. "Yes, well, I'm here with your first wife, and your daughter . . . well, their dead incarnations, anyway, and we were supposed to meet up with you and determine the boundaries between the Recently-Living and the Soon-to-be-Dead cities. But I guess we missed you."

"What was that last bit? You cut out."

"We missed you!"

"Oh, that's sweet. Well, I guess we'll have to swap places and try it all over again."

"Why are you here, anyway?"

"I'm sorry? I don't follow."

Ralph sighed, then spent a minute clarifying the proper route with Gideon and finished by hurriedly saying, "I got a beep for low battery. Listen, why don't we do the run from opposite sides, instead of switching back? We'll sort everything out when we meet up."

"Okay, that sounds fine . . . but a little addled, actually. Wouldn't I be racing for the wrong city?"

Ralph's voice went nasal as he determined the best solution to the problem. "We'll swap it. Whatever you gain for the undead will actually be mirror-imaged."

"I'll take your word for it."

"I'll be the judge. I'm not even dead, I don't think, so I'm impartial."

"Alrighty. Here I go!"

"No! Wait! Give me a head start, so I can get to the clearing first. What time do you have?"

"Wow, it's late! One fifty-four."

"Okay, we're synchronized. Take off at two."

"Got it."

"I'm going now."

"Could I talk to Annabelle with whatever battery's left?"

"Sure, you've got a minute or two," Ralph said, then offered the phone to Annabelle.

Eyes wide, she reached for it — and it dropped right through her ghostly fingers. "Hold on, Gideon," Ralph called as he propped the phone on an outcropping of the building stones. "Here you go."

Annabelle floated over and began to whisper into it.

"Let's leave them some privacy," Ralph said to Beatrice. She stared longingly at her ghost-mother, then nodded and joined Ralph on the back of the second horse. They sped back to the neutral clearing, arranged themselves on the rotten table, and waited in silence.

"How does all this feel?" Ralph finally asked. "Meeting your ghost-mother and sister and everything?" He glanced at his watch. "And being undead for almost two hours?" He scrutinized her. "You don't look that different."

Beatrice stared sullenly at the ground.

"Anything you want to talk about? All your body parts staying together?" Ralph tried.

Beatrice shook her head. Ralph put his hand around her shoulder. "We don't have to say anything, then," he said.

They heard a pair of shouts as Annabelle and Gideon took off.

"I've decided that I don't want to be down here anymore," Beatrice said. "I don't want to lose chunks of flesh or become a ghost."

"We'll find a way out," Ralph promised.

Which is something he shouldn't have done. Did he have the first clue as to the powerful forces binding the dead to Main Isle Purgatory? Did he have any idea how to quit a land that has no exit? Did he have the right to end a wish, instead of ceding to the far superior capabilities of a presiding member of the Royal Narratological Guild? No, of course not. He was just a kid who thought his own stitches were tighter than the fabric of the rest of the world, that he could stretch and tear where he liked and knit his own reality. Well, sorry, Ralph, it's not going to work this time. There are forces more impressive than you. You think you can be the one to save lovely, pained Beatrice, that this makes you the luckiest man in the world . . . and though it does, it's not as though she would pay you attention in any other situation. She's a rare, complex creature, no flash but all substance, someone too special for you. And you think, Ralph, you think you can make a promise and win her over — well, I'm not going to let you do that to her.

The ground shifted so that Ralph fell off the rotten table and landed hard on his immature face.

"What's happening?" Beatrice asked, worriedly pressing her hand to her chest.

At which point, to quiet her anxiety, the ground beneath them ceased shaking.

"I have no idea," Ralph said, staring stupidly about.

The skies rumbled, clouds appeared, and soon great gray drops of rain began to fall. The first bead struck Beatrice on the nose and ran serenely to the tip, hanging for a moment before splashing onto the soft rise of her breast. Then more and more drops fell, until Ralph and Beatrice were soaked through. They held each other close beneath the chill rain.

Which is when your narrator needs a moment to collect himself.

# CHAPTER LIX

The hero has to be the mover of his own story.

The hero has to be the mover of his own story.

The hero has to be the mover of his own story.

I lost control for a moment, and I humbly request forgiveness.

Let's see. Some exciting events were occurring, if I remember correctly. Oh yes. Our delightful teenagers were, naturally enough, agitated by the recent quaking of Purgatory (my fault, sorry) and the seeming apocalypse and all that, and exclaimed to each other about it for what would be an exhaustingly long time to read about. Let's cut through and rejoin them as they detect the distant patter of bone-titanium alloy hooves.

"Mum?" Beatrice exclaimed, leaping to her feet and nearly slipping in the mud. Ralph caught hold of her (yes, gallantly) and they stood holding each other as the staccato galloping got louder. "I knew Annabelle's horse would be faster!" she said.

But Ralph didn't respond, because he had detected the less controlled hoofbeats of a Recently-Living horse. Branches shook at the tops of trees; undead birds flew into the air. Though he sounded farther off, Gideon was racing at breakneck speed.

"Let's get out of the way," Ralph suggested as Annabelle's horse rocketed into the clearing. Bathed in scorching white flames, her hair whipping in a froth of exhilaration, the ghost rider shrieked in victory.

She had gone no more than a dozen feet past the rotten table, however, when Gideon's horse roared into the clearing. His steed skidded in the mud and, in a flurry of long limbs, came to a muddy crash at Annabelle's feet. Gideon managed to convert his fall into a shoddy dismount, and bowed politely once he had regained his footing.

As soon as he had arrived, a dull roar rose from the Soon-to-be-Dead city. All the undead howling at once: terrible.

"I have won," Annabelle said from her perch. To punctuate her words, her metal horse dropped a line of steaming crystal drool.

"By three meters," Gideon said, walking the length to the table. "And I got turned around and wound up doing the crystal canyon bridge twice. Not that I'm asking you to bend the rules for me, but I wanted to point that out."

"Yes, Giddy, you've always found ways to make even my most minor victories hollow."

"Come on, this is about more than us, no?" Gideon said, gesturing at the distant cities.

"Yes," said Annabelle, turning translucent and then returning to a blaze, which Ralph thought a very effective way to emphasize a point. "But it is no coincidence that we are the riders, no?"

"I'm quite sure I don't follow," Gideon said.

"Your daughter might," Annabelle said.

They turned to Beatrice, who until now had been focusing on the conversation with a rapt loss of self-consciousness, the way one might read a love letter in solitude.

"Beatrice?" Gideon said. He dropped his crop and went to her side. "Honey?"

"Hullo, Father," Beatrice said quietly.

"Why are you here?" he asked, suddenly choking. "Are you . . . ?"

Beatrice nodded. "And you are . . . ?"

Gideon nodded.

They held each other for a moment. Then Gideon heaved a sigh of irritation. "That was really brainless of you, Beatrice. You needn't have died for a long time."

"I thought I might belong here," Beatrice said.

"Yes, yes, I get it," Gideon snapped.

"She does belong here," Annabelle said.

"No," Gideon said. "I'm rather certain she doesn't."

"She can stay with me and her half sister," Annabelle said.

"Annabel's undead, too?"

Annabelle nodded.

A hollowed ram's horn trumpeted in the distance. The treetops in the direction of the Soon-to-be-Dead city began to shake.

"What is that about?" Gideon asked.

"My countrymen have a right to come celebrate," Annabelle sniffed.

"You've gained *three meters!* Okay, Beatrice, we can't let the undead find me or Ralph here. You have to decide quickly: Do you prefer being closer to dead or closer to alive?"

"Don't make me choose between you and my mother. It's not fair."

"Oh, it's not like that, honey," Annabelle said.

"I want my real mother back," Beatrice said.

"You never even knew her. Gert is your mother," Gideon said.

"It doesn't feel that way," Beatrice said.

"How dare you!" Annabelle shrieked at Gideon. Her voice sounded like multiple voices . . . and, Ralph realized, it was. For the younger Annabel had appeared behind her mother and was echoing her words. And her rage was directed, not at Gideon, but at her mother. "I've been a *perfect daughter*. And here you go, mooning over this lame girl. She's not even pretty."

At which point Beatrice — sad, poetic Beatrice — tackled her ghostly sister. The two went down in a shimmering tumble.

Now, this may seem unexpected. *Beatrice!* you exclaim, *Beatrice in a fistfight?* But Beatrice had always known that the dead Annabel occupied a special early place in her father's heart, and was jealous. Annabel was the original A who left Beatrice and her siblings B, C, and D. Being named Beatrice was like living on the fourteenth floor of a building without a thirteenth. She surprised herself with the depth of the rage that bubbled out onto Annabel. As for how Beatrice could tackle a formless ghost — well, when you're angry enough, you can tackle anything.

Ralph watched the two young women roll in the mud, and although the bulk of his thoughts were on Beatrice's well-being, a fair number of them were on the scene's similarity to one he had seen weeks before on late-night cable.

"Ooh! Giddy, make them stop!" screeched Annabelle. When she tried to pull them apart, she was only able to pull back Annabel, which gave Beatrice ample opportunity to slug her ghostly sister in the gut.

For his part, Gideon was only able to restrain Beatrice. And so Ralph found himself the central figure of quite a scene: angry Beatrice restrained by Gideon, angry Annabel restrained by Annabelle, and swarms of ghouls emerging at the edge of the clearing.

And that was, of course, before the zombie pheasants descended.

They came in vast numbers — seventeen hundred, in fact. Emerged from perches within the trees, from the gray skies, from the ground itself, ripping wet holes in the soil and themselves, dropping plumage and carnage in equal amounts. Their wing-beats alone would have been deafening, but the squawking! The quaking of each gun-shot rib cage!

Gideon, who had once spent a birthday weekend hunting these very same seventeen hundred pheasants, didn't stand much of a chance. Pheasant beaks are feeble — but at seventeen hundred strong! Pheasant scratches are minor — but at seventeen hundred strong! Pheasant carrying power is limited — but at sixteen-hundred-ninety-eight strong! (Gideon had by now managed to crush two beneath his boots.) In no time, Gideon was pecked, gashed, and lifted into the sky. The last any of them saw of him was a pheasant-covered silhouette diminishing into the distant corners of Purgatory Main Isle.

By the time Gideon was gone, by the time Ralph had taken Beatrice into his arms, the clearing was quite clogged with ravenous ghouls.

"Get back!" Ralph cried, making a sloppy sign of the cross as the foul creatures shuffled over the pheasant-churned soil.

"You're not, like, a priest," Annabel said, giggling. "That's not going to work."

"Mum!" Beatrice said. "Make them stay away from us."

Annabelle spoke magical words, but only a few of the monsters stopped their advance. The rest were only a few feet away, and shambling ever nearer.

"They can't cross the new boundary, right?" Ralph asked as Beatrice bent over, retching at their stench. "All we have to do is get back over to the side of the Recently-Living."

But even as he spoke, the circle of undead closed tight around them. Beatrice and Ralph didn't have much distance to go to escape, but they would nonetheless need to battle their way across scores of ghouls and ghasts, vampires and banshees. The tight halo of Annabelle's light kept the monsters at bay, but even so they were inching forward into the glow.

"Mother!" Beatrice cried. "What do we do?"

"I don't know, my child," she said. "I've clearly made a big mistake."

"A mistake?" Beatrice asked, dodging the ragged paw of a zombie wolf.

"I called in the pheasants," Annabelle said. "But I didn't think this many other undead would follow."

"You . . ." Beatrice said. "You killed my father."

"Now, be reasonable — you know I didn't. This is a wish. Everything here's part of your mental state. *You* killed your father."

"I did not! You did."

"You say po-tay-to, I say po-tah-to."

Ralph grabbed a fairy skull and swung the still-attached spinal column like a whip, keeping a trio of lusty banshees at bay.

Annabelle spoke again. "Fine, yes, Beatrice, I had a bone to pick with Gideon. So to speak. My daughter would have had better medical attention after her tetanus incident if I wasn't a working mum abandoned in a dingy flat by her wealthy lover. And the sadness I felt after Annabel's death led me to wish my own. His —"

"So what are these undead after?" Ralph asked urgently.

"Well, you, of course," Annabelle said, blinking at Ralph as a skeletal flying snake passed through her glimmering rib cage and streaked toward his throat. "You're still in color," she explained as Beatrice ripped the winged serpent from the air. "That makes them very upset. The undead are adamant about enforcing their traditions. And you're a massive break from the norm."

"That should be impossible, right? That's Ralph's alive in Purgatory?" Beatrice panted.

"Well, yes," Annabelle conceded. "I suppose so."

The snake's vertebrae popped as Beatrice crushed it. The sound was unexpected, a kitchen sound, and it disoriented Ralph. He wondered: Could it be that he hadn't died, that the whale had gotten him there by some means other than his death? Or that the narrator's giving him a special accommodation to come here could have rendered him somehow immortal? It made him think of how the others had arrived — if dying above brought you here, could it be that being killed here . . . resulted in life?

"I can see in your eyes that you understand it," young Annabel whispered, her face suddenly at his elbow. "Severe trauma in the realm of the dead leads to *life!*"

Ralph thought about Annabel's words. The first chill hands of the ghouls had locked onto his thighs, and he could feel his flesh beginning to pull beneath their nails: it was definitely worth a shot.

"I have the power to un-kill?" he asked.

"Yes!" screeched Annabel. "Yes, you do!"

Ralph looked at Beatrice, who was locking with a rotting harpy, pushing against her beating wings. He couldn't bring himself to try it out on her. "Annabel," he said. "I'm sorry for this. Maybe."

He grabbed a cutlass from a skeletal buccaneer and ran her through.

She turned a more ghostly gray and fell back, clutching her belly and staring at Ralph in shock.

# CHAPTER LX

Now, Ralph's reasoning wasn't all that loopy. Or, let's be honest; it absolutely was. But admit it: You thought it was going to work. You're used to rewards coming to those who act spur-of-the-moment on an irrational conclusion based on patchy evidence in a high-stakes climax. That this suggestion was supplied by a ghostly young woman who had already revealed herself to be an enemy of Beatrice should have factored into Ralph's thinking, yes, but that's just another in a long list of demerits for our sorry hero.

After he stabbed her, Ralph thought he was watching Annabel disappear. In truth, the pretty young ghostess was only astonished. Ghosts turn ghostlier grays when shocked, seeming to vanish before quickly returning to their normal color, like a cigar struck by a gust of wind. Therefore, to Ralph's delight, his theory appeared to have worked. The older Annabelle, astonished to see her daughter so coldly run through, grayed as well. But did Ralph notice that, and realize the disheartening implication? Nope.

"Beatrice!" he cried. "I can undo all of this! I can send you back home."

Beatrice seemed about to shake her head, until an undead chorus teacher yanked her hair back, exposing her long, pale neck. The nurse's horrid mouth opened wide, her slack lips revealing row upon row of eggshell teeth.

"Yes, please do," Beatrice croaked.

Ralph raised the cutlass above her throat. She gazed at him pleadingly. "Are you sure about this?" he asked.

The nurse's yellow teeth puckered her fair skin. "Hurry!" Beatrice pleaded.

Ralph brought the blade down and traced a deep red line along Beatrice's neck. The undead screeched in rage when, after a few shattering seconds, Beatrice's lifeblood had bled itself out onto the ground. Ralph held the cutlass blade out to Annabelle, who was screeching in fury over the assault of her daughters. She was more than happy to do her part.

Soon Ralph was dead next to Beatrice. The ravenous undead, with Beatrice's enraged mother at their head, consumed their united flesh.

Except for the toes. The undead don't like the taste of toes.

# BOOK V:
# THE PRIVATE LIVES
# OF NARRATORS

# CHAPTER LXI

It seems a fitting end for our presumptuous hero.

*Can I muck about in other people's stories because I happened to have been present while a royal spell was being cast? Can I worship computers and binary code above all other things, yet lumber into a tale made of wonder? Can I dupe the loveliest poetess ever to exist? Can I disrupt an otherwise structurally perfect triad of parallel negotiating-parental-boundaries tales?*

We know Ralph's answer to all of these questions, and we spit on him for it. That middling domestic shorthair of a boy.

And, to make it all worse, a tinny voice protests from somewhere that "I demand a new narrator!"

Where from, you might ask? Cease such wonderings. Reader, unite with me, and take no more interest in Ralph.

"New narrator, please!"

Reader, you're not doing your work.

"Hello? Anybody there?"

Let's sing a song, shall we? I'll try to take care of this in the meantime.

"Ouch, hey!"

*Frère Jacques, frère Jacques, dormez-vous? Dormez-vous?*

"How about a light in here? Please!"

Blast.

# CHAPTER LXII

While you were turning these pages, I took a moment to clear my head, as I hope you did as well. Before we continue, let it be noted for the record: When I tried to stop Ralph's tale, it was for his own good.

In summary: When we last saw them, Ralph and Beatrice were dead. You'll remember that Ralph had been slain by Annabelle, who was grieving over her daughter, who wasn't dead-dead at all, and popped up shortly after, hungry for pork chops.

Now, Annabel's theory that you can un-kill was false, a jealous ploy to do away with her sister. But she and Ralph both were unaware of an equally persistent theory, one that actually turns out to be true. Narrative discontinuity is the most powerful tool at a rebellious character's disposal — in sheer point of fact, it's the only tool at a rebellious character's disposal. And since Ralph killed Beatrice, which was unforeseeable by anyone (including me), he's right in the middle of it.

From the *Seminar in Advanced Topics in Storytelling* syllabus:

> Week II. *Dealing with the Unruly Character.*
>
> In the Monday and Wednesday sessions we will examine the strategies characters have historically employed to circumvent

what they varyingly consider narrator despotism, loopholes, or deus ex machina. Readings (*=required):

From *Literary Hypotheticals, a Workbook*:

pp. 102–110, "The Playwright's Roar: The Bear Blocking the Capulet Crypt." *

p. 181 inset, "Scheherazade's 89th Night: Laryngitis." *

pp. 210–212, "Fellowship Only?: Frodo and Sam and the Small-Press Tolkien."

pp. 190–204, "What Hansel's Shrink Said" *

From the *Story Troubleshooting* workbook:

Appendix C: Rips in Narrative Integrity *

Appendix D: Subduing a Freed Character

So, yes, Ralph's unwitting deployment of Advanced Narrative Discontinuity Theory generated difficulties for your already beleaguered narrator. Nothing too grave, mind you, but a story's rails must be set before the train takes off, so to speak, and Ralph's unexpected killing of Beatrice was a significant derailment. I'll need another moment to sort things through and make all of this tie back into a coherent story, that's all. If you'll excuse me, I'll think things through out loud until I can come up with a plan.

Our petulant young hero — an immature little boy, really — came awake at the very moment the Underworld fragmented. Even in the night sky there are stray filaments of starlight; even behind your closed eyelids penetrate a few hardy rays, but when Ralph opened his eyes, he found true nothingness. The loss of the Underworld was, like all true calamities, soon begun and finished, living much longer in memory. In the replay, Ralph felt the ground fall away, not down but away, so the emptiness was sudden and narrow, closing on his chest like lips on a finger.

What was on his mind? Was he terrified to have ripped the fabric of the universe? Was he overawed to have burst the careful majesty of Beatrice's story, a rupture produced by the slash of a cutlass?

Of course not. He stood suspended in the emptiness and waited for something to happen. So very book-character of him. He was disoriented, naturally, but he scanned about as if there were rays of light to fill his eyes, called out as if there were anyone to hear him.

In the meantime, I'm sitting at my desk in the catwalks, scribbling as I flip pages beneath my reading light, and trying to figure out how to salvage my story, now that Beatrice's wish has unexpectedly terminated, and I've no more spare employees or a single pence left in the discretionary budget.


Ralph's first clue that he hadn't perished entirely was that he was *standing* in the absolute nothingness. For surely one cannot stand without something to stand on?

As a light clicked on far above — a reading lamp bulb — he could make out more and more of his surroundings.

He found that he was in a storytelling attic of sorts. The floor was made of clear, hard nothing. There were also clear hard nothing tables, barrels, and benches, all of them cluttered with sets and figurines. Many of his favorite characters from childhood were there, along with others that he didn't recognize. Swordsmen, pregnant doctors, ancient infants, monks and bards and bookshop clerks. And then there were settings — magnificent dioramas of mountain slopes, laboratories, spaceships, living rooms (God, how very many living rooms). When he peered at them, he saw that the attention to detail was astounding; except for their small size, there was no telling the sets from reality. Within them were miniature pianos that emitted sweeping scores of their own accord, tennis rackets that volleyed fluorescent pinheads, miniature suns hot to the touch, and able to be shrouded in any number of different clouds — some rainy and dark, some puffy and white — that were kept hanging on a nearby rack when not in use.

Ralph picked up a figurine — an elderly woman carrying a cigarette holder and a shiny black pocketbook — and dropped it into what appeared to be a South American cantina. She sprang to life as soon as she entered, finding a tenable reason to be there (she clumsily commented aloud that her twelve-stop flight to surprise her philandering businessman husband in New Zealand had a layover in Bogotá). He watched as she sat at the bar to order a drink and made breezy comments to the blinking bartender. When Ralph put his head close to the miniature set, the little diorama looked like all the universe. At full swing, this area could have thousands of quests going on at one time.

"Hello?" Ralph called to the elderly woman. But because *she* was a *well-behaved* character, she wouldn't allow herself to hear anything outside of her own story.

So he moved on.

After wandering for an hour, it became clear that this cold hard nothing space was infinite, or at least extraordinarily large. He found any number of sullen young women, but none of them was quite the sullen young woman he was looking for.

His plan, once he located Beatrice, was to find a way out, to return to his own home and his own parents and his own boring life. But there was no diorama for his real world, no figurines of his own parents.

Ralph figured there had to be some clever way to get out of the attic. But, he was coming to realize, that was the hardest thing about being in a story; he didn't really have any choices.

"Hello?" he called up to me. "Could you throw me a line, buddy?"

Of course I didn't answer.

What happened next? I guess Ralph really had to go, because he peed behind a chemist's laboratory set piece. He hadn't found a bathroom anywhere in the Underworld, so he must have been holding it for quite a while.

What else? He rummaged around for food, with no luck — it was all too small, crunchy, and inorganic; he once brought a miniature horse to his lips, but got afraid he'd choke on a hoof. So instead he sat and got depressed for a while.

It had been a long time since he'd eaten anything; he couldn't remember the last time, actually, though he was too anxious to actually feel hungry. He sat in the dim light of the empty stage and waited.

For what?

Anything, he supposed.

Ralph heard a slight creaking in the attic, looked over, and thought he spied a ghostly figure hovering far away.

"Beatrice?" Ralph called.

He heard her rush toward him, then a crash and a curse as she slammed into Oz on her way over.

"Hold on. I'll come to you," said Ralph, whose eyes had better adjusted to the near-darkness. He took Beatrice's hand, and she crushed herself against him.

"Ralph, Ralph, Ralph," she said.

"What is it?" he said, suddenly convinced he was about to be eaten.

"I was sure you were gone forever. Like Chessie's son." Her face wet the crook of his arm.

"It's okay, I'm here. Shh."

"Thank God." A pause. "Um, where *is* here?"

"Hmm," Ralph said, wondering how to answer. He sounded, for the first time in his life, a bit like his father. "How did you get here? Maybe that will tell us."

"Well, I think your killing me —"

"Oh my God, that's right. Yipes. Are you okay?"

"Yes, fine. I think your killing me finished my quest, in a weird way. I passed out and woke up in my everyday world, the way it's supposed to go. Only, traditionally, you're supposed to wake up with everything totally back to normal, so much so that you're not even sure your wish actually happened. But I was still gray. And I could walk through things. And the castle was still in the clouds. Gert is super-cranky about that, by the way."

"She's going to kill me."

"Maybe. Who cares? Anyway, since I'm still a ghost, I was the only one of the family able to get down to the ground. Cecil wanted to climb but Mother and Father wouldn't let him. They wouldn't let me, either, for that matter, but I ignored them, threw myself out the basement, and glided down. It was amazing — the vale was crawling with Royal Narratological Guild people in their pajamas yapping on cell phones, trying to figure out what to do. All I had to do, though, was catch the right gusts of wind, and I totally avoided them.

"I headed for London instead, because I wanted to chase down Chessie. I found her holed up in bed in her Kensington flat, with the door triple-barred and a couple of armed men standing guard. She was probably freaked out that the Royal Narratological Guild was going to come after her for botching another wish. Which they probably were, come to think of it. In any case, I floated right in. She ran farther upstairs and slammed the door closed. I passed through that door, too, of course, and finally cornered her in her bathroom. She was hysterical.

"At first I'd wanted to . . . well, to thank her, actually. For giving me the opportunity to see my mother again. And to complain that I didn't have more time to chat properly with her. I wasn't sure if I was going to bring up my ghostliness, because even now I'm still kind of digging it, and don't want anyone to take it away. When I opened my mouth all that came out were questions about you. She'd been the one to grant the wishes, and I figured it was her responsibility to find a way to get you back.

"But she didn't know how to fix anything. All she could say was that she was sure the Royal Narratological Guild wouldn't allow you to rot away inside the 'cold hard nothing storytelling attic.' She pretended to be carefree, but she felt terrible about it, Ralph, I could tell. I spent most of the night consoling *her*. Come morning, she had a bodyguard get us eggs and bacon and she downed a mimosa while we ate brunch on her big puffy bed. That's when she came up with the idea."

"What idea?" Ralph asked.

# CHAPTER LXIII

Like anyone else, a narrator needs a home. It's been our guild's proudest feat, to tell stories so confidently that no one questions our means. How did anyone hear the secrets the evil regent muttered as he hid in the wardrobe? Who was there to describe the heroine's final swim in the lake? A narrator, of course — but we need some place wherein to direct and observe.

Generally, we lie in catwalks above the action, at little wooden desks with single lightbulbs and a few reams of paper on which to write down everything. Anything that needs to happen storywise, we need merely imagine and it appears. So we spend our lives envisioning stories and watching them play out; our hands never stop scribbling. We make sure that nothing in the wish is tall enough to reach us, so as to prevent any awkward character-narrator interactions.

But before you read what comes next and place your judgment on me, I want you to realize one thing: You've been expecting me to devise some means to foil these hellions, but all the while I've been scribbling away with this quill. There! Those five letters, *q-u-i-l-l*, cost me time, as did this sentence to house them. Try to imagine what should happen next, even as you're busy reading these words. None too easy, no? I haven't been in this business for centuries like Maarten Sumperson, and don't have an infinite number of other stories to fall back on — I need some lead time to stay ahead of the action.

Here I sit at my desk, writing these words, now staring down at Ralph and Beatrice and finding myself powerless to imagine anything plausible to stop them.

They cross between the sets until they get to the sector containing the Japanese sci-fi props, passing a dozen gecko-sized Godzillas before coming to Mothra. After shivering in delight to be in the presence of such an icon of geekiness, Ralph plucks the miniature giant insect from her Infant Island and loops a length of chain (which they earlier procured from a mining set) about her midsection. Then, like a bridesmaid with a wedding dove, he tosses Mothra into the air.

As clichés go, the moth to the flame is a classic, and I'm embarrassed not to have been a few steps ahead of those two young upstarts. The hand-sized Mothra zooms straight for my exposed lightbulb. Her godlike powers of flight lift Ralph and Beatrice, who have chained themselves behind her, my feeble bulb illuminating the whites of their eyes as they zoom toward me.

# CHAPTER LXIV

As you can imagine, appearing in one's own scene taxes one's mental resources tremendously, which is why you'll forgive me if these words come at a dribble. Even as I write this paragraph they've said so many things, too many to transcribe.

I cannot say a word — all my thoughts are frittered by my shame and trained on the writing task at hand. Taking advantage of my struggle, Ralph steals behind my desk and reads over the current page:

> *are frittered by my shame and trained on the writing task at hand. Taking advantage of my struggle, Ralph steals behind my desk and reads over the current page*

"Stop," Beatrice says softly. "Please. Put the pen down."

But I can't stop. That is the first commandment of them all.

Once, before I found my current employment, back when I was nothing more than a child living with his mother, I remember traveling home from school a day early because my boarding school mates had been being as uncivil to me as ever. My mother was away, probably off in the States filming a television spot. I remember opening a kitchen cupboard and withdrawing a box of chips and seeing a chef on the front holding a box of chips, on which box was pictured a chef holding a box of chips, on which was pictured a chef holding a box. I fell into that last box, closed the cupboard, and had to order pizza for dinner.

In Ralph I see the same bedazzlement at the reading of himself within himself. It is a thrill that we all turn to in our selfish moments, the vanity of thinking about ourselves thinking about ourselves. But it's a thrill that can easily turn to paralysis and despair, so I try to shield him from my futile scribbles by turning my body. My quill is slick with horror at the predicament I've gotten myself in, facing the prospect of getting lost within the infinity of my own pages, spending eternity trapped in this one moment.

"Stop it right now!" Ralph says, and reaches toward the quill. He almost pries it from my fingers before I can write this.

"You little worm!" I say. "If you don't climb back down, I'll — I don't know." I'm distracted by the heavy clink of Mothra's chain as she hurls herself again and again against the exposed lightbulb. The fact is, I do know exactly what I'll do, if only I can find the mental space to do it. But I can't muster the concentration to make the right words come out.

"You can't railroad us like this," Ralph bellows. "We're real people, not puppets!"

"Maurice," Beatrice says, laying a hand on my shoulder. "It *is* Maurice, isn't it?"

"You know him?" Ralph sputters. "And I did *not* just 'sputter'!"

"Maurice," Beatrice continues, "are you here against your will? Have they made you a slave?"

"You can't change what I've become," I say.

"There must be some way," Beatrice says. "Tell us you want us to save you, and we'll find a way."

"You think I have the best job ever," I say to Ralph. "That I sit up here like a little god and cheerfully make everything the way I want it to be. But this *is* my life, this is *all of it*. No one alongside me, no friend or mother. No special person to love. No one, even, to wave up at me once in a while and acknowledge that they care that I exist. My life is my job, my job is my life. And your pathetic geek version of it, your precious job at MonoMyth, will get you the chance to make your stories and still have your own life outside of them. I'd give anything, anything . . .'"

"We'll get you out," Beatrice says.

"No! I wouldn't trade this away. I just miss my old life. You've caught me in a weak moment, seeing the two of you together. My composure will come back, I'm sure."

"It's okay not to be in control," Beatrice says.

"I hear the sob story," Ralph says coldly, jostling my quill when my word choice irks him, "but you made Chessie try to kill me. Multiple times."

"Of course I did," I spit. "Narrating the Battersby wishes was my one chance to be near my mother again. I had to pull so many strings to get assigned this job. I've looked forward for years to the chance to sit up here and be near her, to breathe the same air as her. And you came along and monopolized my own mother, ruined my stories even as you took her attention away from them, from me. So *yes*, I tried to kill you. You deserved it."

"I don't notice you trying to kill me anymore," Ralph sniffs.

"No," I say tiredly. "I've quite given up."

"Why don't you tell him exactly who you are?" Beatrice says, in her guileless way I love so, asking the questions others hold in their fists.

I want to answer her question.

But ask for more than is given and you will receive the kind of answer that leaves only hunger; turn a final page to find the next one blank and behind that blank page only tiresome closing remarks, a library barcode, and a dingy slipcover.

I stop writing and so vanish from view, as do the book, the lamp, the storytelling attic, these last words.

**NARRATOLOGICAL GUILD NOTE:**
Having identified the preceding chapter as the last in which the narrator is at all reliable, we have stricken the remainder from the record and instead resorted to the transcripts of the emergency meeting of the Royal Narratological Guild's Technical Review Board, the pertinent elements of which are herewith inserted.

# ROYAL NARRATOLOGICAL GUILD
# TECHNICAL REVIEW BOARD

## SUMMER SESSION EMERGENCY ADDITIONAL MEETING

Atrium Suites
Buckingham Palace, Annex #-3
Buckingham Palace Road
London, SWIA IAA

## RNGTRB MEMBERS PRESENT

Dame Melinda Chevally, CHAIR *

Ms. Gladys Norwich *

Mr. Aldis Haines *

Mrs. Clotilde Micklethwait *

Mr. Maarten Sumperson *

## SENIOR PROFESSIONAL STAFF

Edwina Baum (assistant)

Imogen Baum (assistant)

Rhody Baum (assistant)

Colossus of Parnassus (transcriber)

Lord Feverel of Alsatia (security)

Helicon III (annotator)

## ATTENDEES

Duchess Chessimyn of Cheshire, Wish-Granter

Maurice of Cheshire, Narrator *

Mary and Steve ██████, Parents of Subject

Ralph ██████, Subject

Beatrice Battersby, Witness

Gertrude and Gideon Battersby, Parents of Witness

(* denotes a certified member of the RNG)

Some names/details blackened to protect identities

CCC

# PROCEEDINGS

**CHEVALLY:** Good morning. On behalf of the Royal Narratological Guild's Technical Review Board, I'd like to welcome all of you back to the Summer Session, for our special additional meeting. I trust you were all notified in a prompt manner.

Tradition, of course, calls for any meeting with new attendees to begin with introductions. In order to set an expedient tone, I'd like to go first and model a suitable response. My name is Dame Melinda Chevally, and I am the chair of the Technical Review Board. My professional life has become that of a consultant, as I have transitioned to an administrative role after the Twenty-first Century Storytelling Diminution.

I would now ask the other members of the guild to raise their hands as I introduce them.

[OMITTED PORTION]

Is the Duchess Chessie of Cheshire present?

**C. OF CHESHIRE:** Yes, Madame.

**CHEVALLY:** I'll remind you to answer the Board's questions as precisely as possible, and cede any and all decision-making to an institution that does, after all, have centuries of experience in such affairs. Understanding that we are adjudicating the grave matter of your narrator's removal from service, the Board would like you to tell us what you remember of your conversation with Miss Beatrice Battersby, after she appeared in your bathroom in ghost form.

**C. of CHESHIRE:** I'd be happy to, Melinda, not that you've given me a terrific amount of choice in the matter. I tried to calm her. I told her I was sure the Guild wouldn't let Ralph rot in the storytelling attic, no matter what happened to his story. And yes, I let her know the reason why I never received a wish of my own as a child.

**CHEVALLY:** Would you care to elaborate?

**C. of CHESHIRE:** My sisters, sitting right there and there —

**GERTRUDE BATTERSBY:** Hello.

**MARY ▮▮▮▮▮:** Hi, everyone.

**C. of CHESHIRE:** How to say it . . . they had a much more secure place in my family. Mary was my mother's handmaid, practical-minded, an adult from the time she was a child. Gert was the beauty, an imperial firstborn. I was somewhere in the middle, and . . . let's say I spent a lot of time away from the house, out with friends. The summer when our parents decided it was time to grant us all wishes I had been especially poorly behaved. I was running around with a soldier's son, and my parents hated him. They were sure — and they were right — that if I got a wish, I would wish to marry him. So they simply didn't grant me any wish at all. You have to understand the time period — wishes were THE THING, and not getting one . . . ooh! I've always felt that I'm missing that . . . invisible badge, and I've never been a real part of the royal circles since. So it's become a sort of fixation for me, as you can understand. I think everyone who is eligible should get a wish. It's our birthright.

**CHEVALLY:** Do you recall what your sisters wished for?

**C. of CHESHIRE:** Oh dear. Let's see. Gert wished to be the belle of the ball, something like that. She's like a grown-up version of her daughter Daphne. She's what children like that become.

**GERTRUDE BATTERSBY:** I wished to be loved. That's all. And for the record I officially don't appreciate the tone my sister just took.

**CHEVALLY:** And Mary?

**C. of CHESHIRE:** I . . . bloody hell, I honestly don't remember.

**MARY ▮▮▮▮▮▮▮▮:** I wished for peace. I thought it would be some bigger peace, like an end to a war somewhere, but my quest ended up showing me how to be satisfied with boredom. It's not the most dramatic thing. My own sister can't even remember what I wished for. But I'm very content.

**CHEVALLY:** So we can assume that your own lack of a wish led you to want to give one to Daphne, Cecil, and Beatrice?

**C. of CHESHIRE:** Yes, that's exactly it.

**SUMPERSON:** I hate to play the cynic, but it's hard to overlook the fact that Chessie had a more selfish reason, as well.

**CHEVALLY:** Do continue.

**SUMPERSON:** Well, we can't forget the Kelling Provision in Article 4.

**CHEVALLY:** Would you be so good as to reeducate the Board?

**SUMPERSON:** We haven't had an occasion to use it for years, so the Board's ignorance is excusable. But it states that a royal who grows to adulthood without having been granted a wish can still have that wish granted, if and only if she grants three wishes to her family members. It was originally devised as an emergency stopgap measure to provide a rapid resurgence in guild usage, were the ritual of wish-granting ever to decline to dangerously low levels.

**CHEVALLY:** So you're implying that Chessie granted wishes to the Battersby children in order to have a wish of her own granted?

**SUMPERSON:** Yes. And to receive her royalties once the wish was transcribed into story and sold.

**CHEVALLY:** Please respond, Duchess.

**C. of CHESHIRE:** I didn't do it for the money.

**MARY ▮▮▮▮▮▮:** Let me bring her a tissue, please.

**C. of CHESHIRE:** Thank you. [Blows nose] I make plenty of money already, thank you. But yes, I did it for the wish. I wanted my own wish granted.

**MARY** ███████: Before we go any further, I'd like to declare that I think any motivation, even the most self-interested, is acceptable if it means a wish gets granted.

**RALPH** ███████: What? Since when?

**MARY** ███████: Since I saw the new Ralph.

**CHEVALLY:** We have noted your opinion, Mary, but the Board cannot overlook the rule that self-serving wish-granting is forbidden.

**C. of CHESHIRE:** I'm sorry. I'm so sorry.

**MARY** ███████: It's okay, Chessie. Personally I think all wish-granting is self-serving. That's just the way it is; it doesn't make it any less important.

**SUMPERSON:** Enough! What transpired here has been a debacle, the most poorly executed series of wishes in centuries. Commenced with no prep time, handled by a narrator who hadn't the experience necessary to enact them. Need I list the grievances? There was a Choose Your Own Adventure section. Mentions of "poo." An evident libidinal attraction by the narrator for at least one of the Misses Battersby, possibly both. And need I add that Maurice took one of our guild's most revered tales, my own *Snow Queen*, and cut out the first three-quarters? I had to override him and insert a special storytelling bear to keep Ralph on course. The offenses are innumerable — there is no debating that his immediate disbarment is the only possible resolution.

**CHEVALLY:** No one here doubts that this has been a grave embarrassment for the Guild.

**C. of CHESHIRE:** Might I try to explain myself further?

**CHEVALLY:** That sounds like a smashing idea.

**C. of CHESHIRE:** I want to set this straight: My wish wasn't that selfish at all. I granted the Battersby wishes in order to get my son back. I hereby wish for my son to return to me.

**MARY ▮▮▮▮▮▮▮▮:** (quickly) And I grant your wish.

**RALPH ▮▮▮▮▮▮▮▮:** Mom!

**SUMPERSON:** What? A wish-granting within a Board meeting? This is preposterous. I demand we adjourn immediately. And none of this sentimental rubbish she's trotting out alters the fact that the Duchess of Cheshire, who has proven a craven businesswoman, stands to make thousands of pounds sterling off the sales of these wish stories.

**MARY ▮▮▮▮▮▮▮▮:** Sir, I was granting my sister's wish only symbolically. It's a redundant wish, for she's already had her son returned.

**C. of CHESHIRE:** I'm sorry? What was that?

**MARY ▮▮▮▮▮▮▮▮:** Would you consider calling him to the stand, Dame Chevally?

CCCVI

**CHEVALLY:** I suppose it is time. Lord Feverel, please bring in Master Maurice of Cheshire.

**C. of CHESHIRE:** !

**M. of CHESHIRE:** Hi, Mum.

**C. of CHESHIRE:** !

**CHEVALLY:** If the young master will remove himself from his mother's embrace.

**C. of CHESHIRE:** But . . . how are you alive?

**CHEVALLY:** Transcriber, let the record reflect that the narrator mentioned previously throughout this transcript is properly named Maurice of Cheshire, son of Duchess Chessimyn of Cheshire.

**C. of PARNASSUS:** Noted.

**C. of CHESHIRE:** Oh. Oh my, of course.

**MICKLETHWAIT:** What did your son wish for?

**C. of CHESHIRE:** Infinity. To be infinite. I almost didn't grant it, it was so abstract . . . and now I see he got it.

**M. of CHESHIRE:** I would have done anything to tell you, Mum. But you know guild rules: Once you become a narrator, no communicating to non-narrators.

**SUMPERSON:** A rule you recently broke, I might add.

**C. of CHESHIRE:** You're alive. You're alive . . . forever!

**M. of CHESHIRE:** They were going to give the Battersby wishes to Maarty Sumperson to narrate, but I insisted. I begged J. J. Mucklebackit to duck out of performing, so that you would have to step in. It was my only chance to be near you again.

**SUMPERSON:** None of this changes the fact that you are no longer an accredited narrator. I'm sorry, the rules are very clear.

**M. of CHESHIRE:** Dame Chair, is there no appeal?

**CHEVALLY:** I'm afraid not. Once you've lost control of a story and are unable to steer it back on course, you lose your license. Our charter is very clear on the matter.

**M. of CHESHIRE:** Well, I guess that's it, then.

**RALPH ███████:** Doesn't Chessie still get her wish?

**CHEVALLY:** No, sadly. She made it already. Even though it was redundant, it still counts.

**RALPH** ███████████: Well . . . I haven't received my wish yet.

**CHEVALLY:** I'm sorry?

**RALPH** ███████████: Chessie said I could have a wish after all of the Battersby children got theirs. We never got around to it before I wound up in the attic.

**B. BATTERSBY:** Ralph, don't. Your wish should be for you.

**M. of CHESHIRE:** What are you saying? That you'll wish for me to be reinstated as a narrator?

**RALPH** ███████████: You tried. You struck just the wrong tone on every occasion, and messed up tons of it, but you tried.

**M. of CHESHIRE:** You'd do that? For me?

**RALPH** ███████████: I wish for Maurice to finish his job and publish all of this adventure, not just the wishes themselves but my time in New Jersey before, and even this meeting. And maybe he'd consider granting me the opportunity to use it for —

**MARY** ███████████: Okay. I do solemnly grant —

**SUMPERSON:** Someone stop her!

**M. of CHESHIRE:** I'll miss you, Mother.

**C. of CHESHIRE:** I love you.

**MARY** ██████████: I do solemnly grant thee thy wish, dreaming, in accordance with the fine tradition of Royal wish-granting, that you find thy greatest desire, and in so doing come to know thyself.

[Whereupon, the meeting was frantically concluded]

NOTE: Rights to the preceding have recently been reserved by MonoMyth Gaming, LLC. Please forward any legal concerns to their offices.